# RESCUE ME

## VM RHEAULT

# CHAPTER ONE

*Lily*

I sit in the corner with a glass of red wine, facing the entire room. The moment I sat down, I noted every exit, and unwillingly, my eyes dart to the door every time a patron enters the elegant bar attached to the hotel. I never used to be this way, but that's what a few years of violence will do to you, I suppose. I'm getting better, but I'll need time before I can go back to the way I used to be. The way I used to be before I knew what an angry man's fist felt like smashing against my body.

The bar is soothing, all cherrywood and white tablecloths. Fern fronds tickle my cheek, and the room is filled with the dark green leaves. They remind me of my mother's penchant for plants, though she never could keep them alive for very long.

I brush my hair away from my face and rub my eyes. I should go up and go to bed. I need to find a job, and with the help of an employment agency, I have a few interviews lined up for this week. This is my fresh start, and I don't want to blow it. I like it here, and I don't want to leave.

"You look as tired as I feel."

I stiffen, and I berate myself. How could I let someone sneak up on me? I must be more tired than I thought.

A man holding a beer bottle stands next to my table, his grey suit rumpled, a hand shoved into the pocket of his dress slacks. His jaw is covered with whiskers, and the dreary look in his eyes is something I can relate to. I haven't felt hope in a long time.

"Can I sit?" he asks, gesturing to the empty bench of the banquette.

If I let him sit next to me, I won't be able to escape.

Escape what? Keaton's gone.

Lifting a shoulder, I say, "Sure," and scoot over a little in invitation.

"I'm Sam—"

"I know who you are."

He sinks onto the bench, leans back, and closes his eyes, the beer bottle still clutched in one hand like a lifeline. I can relate to that too, but I haven't let alcohol become a crutch. It would be too easy to dive into a bottle and not come out again.

I sip my wine.

Samuel Sharpe, entrepreneur and billionaire extraordinaire. I know who he is now, but I hadn't before moving to Carthage, Minnesota, the city where my mother grew up. I've been here a week, trying to breathe, trying to find some semblance of normalcy that disappeared when I married, but in that week, there hasn't been a day that's gone by where Sam Sharpe hasn't come up in some way, somehow. Even the hotel I'm staying at until I can find a place to live, and this bar, belong to him.

He pulls from his beer, his hand wrapped loosely around the glass, and lowers the sweating bottle onto the table. Cracking his eyes open, he gives me a brief glance before closing them again, his body melting into the padded bench.

I know what it's like to need space but not want to be alone. He could have sat at the bar and chatted with the bartender, or any woman sitting alone hoping for an invitation upstairs would have gladly kept him company. But those two choices would have cost him, and he chose me, a limp dishrag of a woman because he knew I'm just as worn down as he is.

It's not a compliment by any means, and I don't take it as one. To look gutted, and to be recognized for it, that's no compliment.

The kinship, the . . . maybe not camaraderie, but he saw something familiar in me, and if I, in my broken state, can give him something, then I'll take that as my compliment.

It's rare to have nothing but something to give at the same time. When you're at rock bottom and you still have something someone needs, it can be that very thing that lifts you up.

His dark blond hair shines under the yellowish-orange glow of the dim lights, but his skin has a sickly pallor. His tie is loose around his neck, the top button of his dress shirt undone. A long day at work, maybe.

Billionaire.

It's not a completely foreign idea. I grew up in New York state, and the concept of that kind of money isn't as far away as it could have been had I grown up in rural Iowa or some such. Before Sam Sharpe sat next to me, if someone had asked me what my chances were that I'd meet one, I'd have said slim to none.

Right time, right place, or, judging by the lines creasing his forehead, wrong time, wrong place. He's hurting.

He tilts his head at me, his eyes still closed. "Were you meeting someone? Am I interrupting something?"

"No."

He nods. "If you want me to go, just tell me."

"You're fine."

"Thanks."

The bartender meets my gaze, asking if we want another round. Sam's bottle is too dark for me to see how much he has left, and I shouldn't have another, but my glass is almost empty and I don't want to leave.

I nod, and the bartender fills our drink orders and carries them to the table himself. The bar isn't busy, in fact, the waitress who served me disappeared a while ago and never came back. I exchange a fifty for the drinks. "Keep it."

"You didn't have to do that," Sam says, lifting the bottle to his mouth. He drains it in three smooth swallows, his Adam's apple bobbing in his throat.

"I know." I finish my glass and push it to the edge of the table near Sam's empty bottle. I catch the faint scent of his cologne, and I drag a breath into my lungs. Clean, with a hint of citrus maybe, so unlike Keaton's heavy, musky scent. He was like that, Keaton. Heavy. Heavy with gloom, heavy with rules, heavy with entitlement. So heavy he broke me.

"Are you staying at the hotel?" he asks, opening his eyes and looking at me, treating me to the intensity of his stare. He may be tired and rundown, but his eyes, God. A piercing blue, and sharp, like his name. No matter how tired he would ever be, he wouldn't miss anything. Suddenly, I know out of anyone in this city, I would be safest with him.

"No. I was meeting a girlfriend, but she canceled," I lie.

"Lucky for me," he says.

The bell rings over the door, and automatically, I look to see who's coming or going. Two women enter the bar, laughing, and the bartender waves.

I turn my attention back to Sam. "Why?"

"You seem to know what I need."

"Another beer?"

"Peace," he says, resting his head against the wall and wrapping his hand around the full bottle.

"Unfortunately, I have that in short supply."

"Shame."

"But I'll give you what I can."

His eyes are narrow slits. "What if I want more?"

"You can't take what's not there," I say.

He rubs the pad of his thumb over my knuckles, his skin cool from the bottle, and I force myself not to yank my hand out of his grasp. He's not going to hurt me. Not all men are like Keaton, who would just as soon bash you in the face as smile at you. I don't know much about Sam Sharpe, but I believe my woman's intuition when it says I can trust him. At least, trust him with my body. My heart, well, that's a different matter. Sam's weariness, I bet that's brought a lot of women to their knees. The hurt, the looks, the money.

I'm not looking for something like that. I need another man like a fish needs a bicycle, as one of my mother's favorite sayings goes. No, I'm good. I don't need Sam's pain. I have plenty of my own.

I keep my hand where it is and sip my wine. It's getting late, and I should go soon. It's going to be a long week of job hunting. I have a bit of a cushion—I was smart enough to do that for myself—and I won't have to accept the first thing that's offered to me, but I'll breathe easier when I have a paycheck coming in and I can pay my bills without using my savings.

Sam releases my hand to lift his beer bottle to his mouth.

I finish my wine, and when the alcohol hits me, I'm a little too woozy for my taste. My tolerance is nothing, and the two glasses of the delicate red were enough to put a fizz in my blood that's not unpleasant, but dangerous, nonetheless.

I'm reaching for my purse, words of goodbye on the tip of my tongue, when he says, his voice rough with panic, "Go upstairs with me."

# CHAPTER TWO

*Sam*

It's difficult to explain to someone who's never been there what low feels like. I mean, not low, like you're having a bad day and a good night's sleep will make it go away. I mean, *low*. Nothing in the world will fix it, and maybe you don't want to fix it because you've made a place for yourself there. You're comfortable there. It was a painful drop, but now that you're there, why try to change it?

The redhead at the table, sitting alone and sipping a glass of wine, when I saw her, I knew she'd understand. How low she'd fallen was written all over her beautiful face, and to say I felt a connection would be a gross understatement.

I welcomed it as much as I feared it. She was as low as I am, but she had the power to lift me up, and I don't want to be lifted up.

I sat anyway, and her presence did something to me. Something I reveled in. Something I despised. She made me feel how

I felt when I first met my wife. Like she knew me, before I'd said one word.

She let me sit, let me drink my beer in silence, ordered another without me having to ask. Something so small, so simple, the right key fitting into the right lock.

Just like that, my guard came down and shattered into a million pieces at her feet. She could have asked anything of me, and I would have given it to her.

Yet she said nothing, sipped her wine, lost in whatever world had pushed her so low.

My heartbeat sped up when she reached for her purse. I couldn't lose her, not yet. I felt something when I held her hand, something I hadn't felt in years, something I didn't think I'd find again. She straightened on the bench, the strap of her purse in her hand, the wineglass empty, and desperately, so desperately, I said, "Go upstairs with me."

She freezes, slowly turns toward me, and I tense. This could go either way. She knows who I am and she could trip all over herself to crawl into bed with me, hoping for cash, hoping for jewelry, hoping for more, or she could slap me and tell me to fuck off for treating her like an upscale whore.

There are dark shadows under her eyes, smudges indicating lack of sleep, but also, ever so slightly, the remnants of a bruise along the top of one of her elegant cheekbones. Her nose is just the right size for her face, her lips a delicate coral pink. Her skin is an alabaster decorated with freckles the color of copper, and I drink her in as I wait for her answer. She's classically beautiful, and it wouldn't surprise me if somewhere in her family tree she has a hint of noble blood. Aristocracy dating back generations.

I reach out to trace the bruise under her eye, and she

blanches, leaning away before stopping herself. She's not used to a kind touch, and if I ever meet the son of a bitch who marked her face, I'll make him pay.

"All right," she finally says, her voice low with a hint of a tremble.

"All right," I echo, dumbfounded she agreed. My cock isn't quite so confused, and he hardens eagerly, already wanting to break the dry spell borne of sadness and loss.

I slide out of the banquette and help her from the bench. Her left hand is bare, in fact, she doesn't wear any jewelry, and she's dressed in a cream sheath and nude heels. Her height surprises me, the top of her head reaching my mouth. Her shoes give her an extra inch, but even without them, she's taller than any woman I've ever dated.

Our fingers linked, I usher her through the door that connects the bar to the hotel. The bartender watches and tries to catch her eye to check in, see that she's okay or offer her an out if she needs one. I don't pause long enough to let them share a look. I can't let her change her mind.

It was Samantha's idea that I keep a suite reserved at the hotel. I'd scoffed, gotten angry at her, actually, for suggesting such a sordid thing, but after the fury wore off, I changed my mind. I would never invite someone to my penthouse, and one day the grief would wear off and I'd want to find a woman, find a connection. My grief isn't gone, but this woman, she does something to me, and I want to explore it.

We ride the elevator up to the fortieth floor. Tension bounces around the box as we wait, and she stands rigidly next to me, her eyes staring straight ahead. When the doors glide open, she steps forward, but I hold out my arm, blocking her exit. "You can say no."

I offer out of courtesy, out of politeness, but inside, I'm quaking. I need her. I need this, and if she decides she doesn't want it . . . I thought I'd fallen as low as I could, but that might not be accurate after all.

"Sam," she says, my name like honey oozing out of her mouth, dripping hot down my skin, "I already said yes."

I jerk my head in acknowledgement, too scared to say more. I have her consent and that's all I need.

We step out of the elevator, and silently, we walk down the hallway to a corner suite, our arms brushing. I keep the keycard in my wallet and I tap it against the sensor. The lock clicks open, the sound too loud in the quiet. It's nothing fancy, a simple two-room suite that has a small fridge, microwave, Keurig, and mini bar. She wanders around the sitting room and pauses at the window, pushing the curtains back to peer across the city.

"Do you bring many women here?" she asks as I open the mini bar and pour us both a glass of whiskey.

"I've never used this room before." It's the truth, and when she meets my eyes in the dark, only the city lights in which to see my face, she knows it. I prepare for the next question, "Why do you have it?" but it doesn't come. The woman from downstairs is still here, the peace I found with her present in the way she holds herself, in the way she gracefully accepts the glass and lifts it to her lips.

Silence.

Her silence and the comfort she carries with her shroud me in a cocoon, and I grip it close to me as I swallow the whiskey in my glass.

She does the same and places her glass next to mine on the desk, mine smudged by my fingerprints, hers with a trace of coral lipstick.

Gently, I tug her purse from her grasp and set it near our glasses, the small rectangle with the thin strap looking right, like it belongs.

Lights streak across her face, setting her eyes ablaze, as if I'd added fire to our whiskey. She hasn't been touched kindly, and I keep that in mind as I reach for her. A flicker of fear is there and then gone, and she doesn't back away when I cup her cheek in my hand. Her skin is soft, the line of her jaw, fragile. A tremble runs through her body, but despite it, she steps closer and rests her hands on my shoulders.

I try to read her face. It seems like this would be the time for words, to ask if she's sure or to promise I won't hurt her, but they would be too loud, too sharp, in the softness of the suite, so I don't say anything. She tilts her head and rises onto her toes, bringing us eye to eye. I meet her the rest of the way and seal my lips over hers.

A low whine vibrates from the back of her throat, and it matches the tearing of my heart. I haven't kissed another woman since my wife, and it pains me to feel the pleasure of this woman's lips. The tenderness, the wisps of her breath as she pants against my skin. I need more, and I lick at her, asking her to let me in. She does, and I push my tongue into her mouth, tasting her. Whiskey, fear, need. It's all there as I take what I want, tangling my fingers in her hair, pulling her closer. She does the same, and our bodies fit together like a puzzle piece finding its mate.

I should know her name. It would be right to say her name, but I didn't ask and now it's too late.

She works at the knot in my tie, her fingers yanking at the silk. I capture her wrists and say, "Easy."

"I'm sorry." She drops her hands.

"There's nothing to be sorry for. It's nice, to be wanted, don't you think?"

Fear flickers in her eyes and I slowly start to put together what she's afraid of. An abusive boyfriend, an ex-husband, perhaps, someone who wanted her too much. Jealousy that turned into hatred. I can watch the story play across her face, where it isn't nice to be wanted, to be valued and treasured, because it turns into something that's not so nice.

"I won't hurt you." The words are less than nothing, but I say them anyway.

"I believe that or I wouldn't be here."

"Good."

I lift her hands to the knot at my throat, and this time she unknots the silk with a steady hand. She lets it hang around my neck and starts on the buttons of my shirt. I blow out a breath. I can't help but remember the last time my wife undressed me, and my heart aches. It feels wrong to be here now, yet it doesn't, as if Tabitha were telling me it's okay to move on without her.

I'd done my best, and as she gripped my hand, she told me it was enough.

Those words are what kept me from falling apart.

She brushes her fingers over my chest. The memories haven't affected my cock and he stands to attention, her touch teasing, alluding to what's next, and it begs.

I skim my fingers over the zipper at the back of her dress. "Can I?"

"Yes." She toes off her pumps and stands barefoot.

The zipper is made of plastic, but it glides down the teeth without catching. I run it between her shoulder blades, down her spine, to her lower back where it stops just above her ass. She isn't waif thin like I expected, and her breasts are lush, held up with a cream lace bra.

She pushes the dress down to the floor, revealing a flat stomach but slight pooch right above her pelvic bone that melds into the wide hips that give her an hourglass figure. My mother would say that means she's built for birthing, not a romantic thought as she stands in front of me in matching panties, waiting for me to . . . judge her, perhaps compliment her, but words dry in my mouth. I don't know if she has any children, don't know anything about this woman except she gave me permission to use her, to keep her with me for just a little bit longer.

"I'm not young anymore," she murmurs, blushing.

I scoff. "Trust me, neither am I."

Trailing her fingers lightly over my ribs and abs she says, "You're doing okay."

I trace my finger along her collarbone to the hollow between her breasts. "And so are you."

She smiles, the neon lights catching her face, and I know she's treating me to a rare occurrence. Someone stole them, thieved them, and now the remainders are hidden in a secret hoard. She won't give them freely, and I'm honored to be a recipient of something so scarce.

I tip my head back as she steps out of her dress and nudges it to the side with her toe. "It's been a long time since I've done something like this," I admit. I have a beautiful woman standing in front of me dressed in nothing but a lace bra and matching panties, and I don't know what to do with her.

In the adjacent bedroom, the king bed beckons, the bedspread smoothed, four pillows plumped at the headboard. I know I should be getting her from here to there, but my finesse dried up with my age and I have no idea how to make the transition from floor to bed.

"Would it be okay if I . . .?" She steps closer and reaches for my belt buckle.

I blow out a sigh and hope she can't hear the relief. "That would work."

She unbuckles my belt and as she does, her hands graze my cock. I jerk in surprise and from a guilt I don't want to acknowledge. My wife would be happy for me, but it's little consolation when I'm standing with a nameless woman I've known less than an hour.

"You're not as rusty as you think." She cups my cock through the thin material of my boxer briefs and I surge into her hand.

"Some things you don't forget."

"And some things you don't, no matter how much you want to."

"Yeah." There are plenty of things I'll never be able to erase from my memories, and I *don't* want to. I can't let them slip away as if they never existed. I may need to move on, but I'll drag the past with me for as long as I can.

She pushes my pants down my legs, gracefully crouching at my feet, placing her eye to eye with my cock. I don't want a blowjob, and I grasp her upper arm before she gets any ideas. "Let's go to bed."

Her eyes widen, and I loosen my grip. "I'm sorry. I just didn't want, you know."

"Oh." She gently pulls away and pads over the plush carpet and through the archway that connects the rooms, her panties hugging the sweet curve of her ass. "You don't have to, you know, either. For me. Sex is fine."

I nod tersely. I hadn't gotten that far, going down on her. My wife loved oral sex, and she let me go at her whenever I wanted, which was often because it was a safe way for her to enjoy making love. I can still taste her, when I'm missing her so much, when her touch resembles nothing but ghosts. I can still hear her moan, and I'm thankful this woman understood me enough to give me the out.

She stands on one side of the bed, I stand on the other, and we finish undressing. She's tucked into the shadows and it's not bright enough to see her breasts as she unhooks her bra and drops it to the floor or the patch of hair between her legs when she rids herself of her panties. She can see me more clearly, the lights coming in through the window highlighting my body, and she stills when I take off my briefs and my cock springs free. I've never thought myself bigger or better than any other man, and my wife was satisfied. That's all that mattered to me.

"Okay?" I ask, pulling the bedspread and top sheet down the mattress. She might not be scared of me with our clothes on, but I don't want her to think I'll hurt her in bed, either.

"Yes. You're fine."

She does the same on her side of the bed, and naked, we slip between the sheets at the same time.

I should have closed the curtains. I would have been better at this in the dark.

Now the glow accentuates her face, but instead of having second thoughts, I cuddle her to me and cover her mouth with mine as she fits against me and wraps her arms around my neck.

We settle onto the pillows, and while I kiss her, I explore the line of her waist, the swell of her hip, and her long, slim thigh. She widens her legs, and I brush my fingers over the dusting of hair.

She exhales, her breath jagged, and wraps her hand around my cock.

I hiss, her touch setting my nerves on fire.

She moves her mouth from my lips to my jaw, her nose grazing my cheek, and rests her leg over my hip. We're lined up perfectly, and the tip of my cock nudges her slit. "Do I need a condom?" I want in, my cock wants in, but I ask before this goes any further. I could get her pregnant, and then what? She knows who I am, but I have no idea who this beautiful woman is. I should be thinking birth control, NDAs, paternity tests, and eighteen years of child support, but there's nothing but burying myself deep inside her and letting her drown my sorrows.

"No."

I believe her, for no other reason than I simply do, and without another word, I let her guide my cock inside her. The tip breeches her tight opening and I moan.

With a hand to her ass, my fingers sinking into her skin, I push her down and she consumes me in wet, scorching-hot heat. I hold her still and we pause for a moment. I want to give her a second to get used to me inside her, and I need the time to find control. It's been so long, and I don't want to go off like a geyser before she has a chance to enjoy it. For all I know, this could be her first positive sexual experience in some time, and I want it good for her too.

That reminds me to ask. "You doing okay?"

She lifts her head and nips at my bottom lip. Playful. "I'm doing okay. You?"

I cup one of her breasts in my hand and the weight is comfortable in my palm. Her nipple is already hard, and I squeeze gently. I know it affects her because her muscles hug my cock in response and I shudder. "Yeah, I'm good."

When I feel like I'm not going to explode, I roll her onto her back and settle between her legs. We were lying in an awkward position and I easily could have hauled her on top of me and let her have the lead, but I'm old-fashioned and missionary is my favorite way to have sex. "You are so beautiful," I say, brushing a strand of hair off her cheek.

She turns her head. "You already have me in bed, there's no need for that," she says to the wall.

I want her to look at me, and I pull out and push back in as far as I can go with one slow, but forceful, motion. She gasps, and startled, her eyes meet mine. "I wouldn't say it if it wasn't true. I don't know what kind of asshole you've had in your life up until now, but he didn't deserve you, and I hope, since you're here with me, it means you've told him to go to hell."

"Why?"

"Why what?" I frown.

"Why am I here with you?"

I could tell her a lot of things, but I decide to tell her the truth. "When I'm with you, I forget, and that's hard for me because as much as I want to forget, I need to remember."

"Sam." Her voice is dreams and wishes, promises not spoken. Promises not hers to make nor mine to hear.

Tenderly, I begin to move. I may not know this woman's name, but this isn't a quick fuck for me. I can't call it making love. It's not. I made love to my wife, but not this woman, not tonight. There needs to be a word for it. Intimacy. We're being intimate, sharing bits of each other we may not have shared with anyone else, and it humbles me she trusted me enough to give part of herself to me.

I withdraw and hold myself above her, wanting enough space to reach for her clit. She mews when I touch her there, and she skims her hands over my chest, her fingernails raking over my nipples.

"I want you to come," I say, circling the slippery nub, feeling it grow under my touch.

"Sam. No—"

"I want you to come." I rub harder, faster.

She trembles and starts to sweat. The musky scent of her arousal hangs in the air, catching my nose. Nature takes over, and I move as I slick my fingers over her clit, needing my release as much as I need to give her hers.

"Sam." She sobs my name, tilting her hips, her muscles grasping at my cock. Her body quakes, the orgasm rolling through her. After several moments she relaxes, her watery cry echoing through the room.

"I wanted it good for you, baby," I whisper, kissing the tears off her cheeks.

Slowly, I start to move again, back and forth, in and out. She's so wet my thrusts are smooth and unhindered.

I wanted to hold off longer, but two and a half years of abstinence are working against me and I come. My cock shoots inside her for what feels like forever, and finally, depleted, worn down to the bone, I drop onto her, lifeless.

I'm so tired, and I think she can feel it. She holds me despite how hot the room suddenly turned and how stifling the air is. Sweat saturates my skin and I stink of a long day at work and more than a little regret. None of that bothers her as she hugs me and whispers, "Shh, shh," into my ear.

My cock shrinks now that he's had his fun, and reluctantly, I roll off her, my dick sliding out in a gush. I don't want to get up and clean off, and I drop my head onto a pillow.

She wiggles onto her side and lays her head on my shoulder. I wrap my arm around her and press a kiss to the top of her head.

This used to be my favorite part. We'd lie and talk until well past midnight, making plans for the next day, as well as years and years into the future. Trips, what I'd be doing with the company. I've never sat down and ticked off what we managed to accomplish. I don't think I could bear crossing out the items we were never able to do.

A bucket list.

A wish list.

We had time to do a lot, but not all, and I lost heart to do the rest.

She plays with the smattering of hair on my chest. "Do you want me to go?"

I weigh her question, weigh my answer. "No." I would feel

lonelier alone than if she stayed. I tighten my hold. I want her here.

"Okay."

She drifts, and I watch the lights streak across the walls. Carthage is always busy. If New York is the city that never sleeps, Carthage is the city that never naps. I prefer the city on a smaller scale, Samantha saying she'd rather be a big fish in a little pond, and I've never disagreed. But lately, I've been restless, looking for change. I never thought I'd find it with a sad redhead at a bar.

I fall asleep with my face buried in her curls, her body wrapped around mine. Our musk permeates the air, but I don't find it disgusting. We didn't make love, but it was more than just sex.

The rising sun lightening the room rouses me from my sleep, and without opening my eyes, I reach for her. I know before my hand finds her cool pillow that she's gone.

I draw in a shaky breath and try to convince myself it's for the best. I'm not ready for a relationship, especially nothing as complicated as what I would have had with her. The bruise on her cheek, the way she would flinch when I wanted to touch her. The tears at my unexpected generosity, getting her off before I came. It all points to something I can't deal with, and I should be glad she left.

It was a huge step, me asking her to come up here, baring myself in more ways than one. It was a necessary step toward moving on with a life I wasn't sure was worth living without my wife.

Propping myself onto an elbow, I stare at the orange wall, the sunrise replacing the neon lights.

I miss her already.

I didn't ask her name.

"You look unwell. Are you feeling all right?"

I look up from my desk, tapping my pen against the surface. Samantha steps into my office, her suit crisp, her blonde hair pinned into a twist at the back of her head.

It's been a week since I asked my mystery woman to go up to my room, and I can't get her out of my head. Her red hair, her freckles. The scent of her skin and the tears on her cheeks. I've thought about nothing else since I woke up alone. I went back to the bar, hoping to see her again, but nothing. I asked the bartender if he knew her name. He remembered me, remembered me inviting her to my room, but she paid in cash, he said, and he, too, never asked for her name.

I've been surly, out of sorts. I don't know where she came from or where she went. Carthage isn't New York but looking for a lone woman in a city this size is like looking for a needle in a haystack. Impossible.

I've lost her.

Leaning back in my chair, I say, "I used the room."

Samantha steps farther into my office, her heels silent on the carpet. Sammie is my father's brother's daughter, and there's no one I would trust more with my business or my secrets. She was Tabby's best friend, and life had been good. Life had been very, very good.

She studies me, leaning a hip against the edge of my desk, her arms crossed over her chest. You'd think her cold and calculating if you met her like this, but I know the other side of her, the denim shorts, tank tops, and ponytails side of her, the get-her-hands-dirty-with-her-two-sons side of her. I appreciate both sides and give her credit for being able to turn one side off and the other one on when the situation calls for it. I was a lucky man to have two women balance me. Now I'm down to one, and Sammie's all I have left.

Her eyes warm with compassion and understanding. "I'm happy for you, Sam. I really am. Are you going to see her again?"

"I can't." I purse my lips and turn away. I've done nothing but beat myself up for my stupidness and have done nothing but try to find a remedy.

She sucks in a breath. "Tabby would want—"

"That's not why!" I snap, throwing my pen across the room. It clatters against the TV and lands on the floor where a confused cleaning person will find it and wonder what it's doing there.

Samantha takes my temper in stride. "Then why?"

"Because I was a fucking idiot and didn't get her name. I have no way of finding her."

"Where did you meet her? Did you ask there?"

I glare. "Don't you think I would have tried that? Any of it? All of it? I met her at the bar attached to the hotel, and I asked the bartender. He remembered her but didn't know her name. I asked the front desk at the hotel, but they had no fucking idea who I was talking about. She was waiting for a friend who canceled on her. That's it. That's all I know besides the fact I fucked up."

"What was she like?" Samantha asks, her voice low.

"God, Sammie, she was," I say, huffing a laugh, "she was perfect. Came up to my chin, and we fit together, you know? We fit. She was quiet, let me think. She wasn't . . . She wasn't used to kindness. There was something beaten down about her, and I guess that's why I felt close to her. She was soft, and her kisses were . . . pure. Innocent. No, not innocent. Unselfish, maybe. She wasn't asking for anything. At first, I thought it was for the best. I'm not ready. I'm not—" I say firmly when she opens her mouth to object— "but I didn't think I'd feel like this after she left. I didn't think I'd go out of my mind looking for her."

Sammie kneels in front of me, holds one of my hands in hers. "Maybe it was meant to be. She came into your life to help you step forward. You did, and now her part in your life is over. You took an important step, and I'm happy for you. These past two years have been hard, watching you suffer has been hard on all of us, and I wish I could thank her for showing you there's more to life than grief."

I squeeze her hand, grateful I have someone like her in my life. I don't know what I would have done without her the past two years. I heave to my feet and she rises from her haunches. "I need to forget about it. She's gone. It's been a week, and I've done all I can do." I lean against a window, the city of Carthage displayed before me. Any man in my position would feel like he has everything he could ever want. I used to think that with enough money I could buy happiness, and I have, to an extent. I can travel wherever, whenever I want, I can point to a building and buy it. But I'll never be able to buy what I found in that redhead's arms as she held me, our unfortunate lives binding us together in pain and heartache.

"She knew you, didn't she? Knew who you are, I mean. Do you think she would want to find you?"

I pause, surprised. She *did* know who I am and finding me would be easy for her—if she wanted to, and clearly, she doesn't. I lift a shoulder. "She knew, and I guess it's telling she hasn't contacted me. I don't know the signs well, but I think she was just out of an abusive relationship. Maybe she was using me like I was using her. To move forward, to step in a direction that scared her, but was necessary. I said I'm not ready, but I don't think she was, either. When I woke up and she was gone, I was almost glad. I didn't want that on my plate, not after the few years I've had, but then sometimes I think, well, maybe it would have been worth it, to take it on, for what we could've had together. It's a moot point, and I've tried to push it out of my mind."

A corner of her mouth lifts up. "I won't badger you about it. All I'll say is, I'm glad you were able to connect with someone. You're healing, and that means a lot to me."

I don't feel like I'm healing. Not now. When I was nestled between her legs, my cock buried inside her, I felt something. A spark of something, but that's dead now, and I'm back to where I was before I fell asleep with her cuddled next to me.

"What do we have going on today?" I ask, changing the subject.

"HR is going through applications and conducting interviews to replace Honey, and once the applicants pass the second interview, they'll send them up here to talk to you. After the last temp debacle, we want to stop problems before they start."

The temporary PA the agency sent over to replace Honey, my PA who went on maternity leave and decided not to come back, was as soft and as kind as a roll of barbed wire. We clashed on so many levels she didn't last until lunchtime. I never want to deal with someone like that again, and I told Samantha I wanted approval of my next assistant. If I'm going to work with her, or him, I want to like them.

"Okay, good. Anything else?"

"A meeting with Allessandra Biggotti and her handlers. She's in it up to her eyeballs again," she says, shaking her head, a worried frown creasing her forehead.

Allessandra, the country's highest paid popstar, and the country's most notorious partier, finds trouble every second of every day. Unfortunately, her damage control fills my bank account, and they'll pay. SharperImage is the world's leading

PR firm. We can talk anyone out of trouble, any time, and they put up with our homebase in Carthage because we get the job done. I've swept a sheikh's rape charges under the rug, turned mafia bad boys into angels, and twisted the president of the United States's infidelities into something positive for our country.

"Ever wonder how I can scratch anyone off a shitlist, but I can't seem to figure it out for myself?" I mumble, picking up my iPad off my desk. We'll need to figure out a plan before Allessandra and her handlers arrive. They'll want to know what magic spell we can cast now, and it won't matter they aren't here to fill us in. Whatever shit she's stepped in will be front-page news.

"You haven't done so bad," she says, looking at me over her shoulder and holding my office door open for me.

"Because of you."

In a rare display of affection reserved for her boys and husband, she turns and hugs me, her cheek pressed to my tie. "I'd do anything for you, you know that."

"And I appreciate it more than I can ever say."

# CHAPTER THREE

*Lily*

After I managed to slip out of bed without waking him, and dressing just enough that if I ran into someone in the hallway I wouldn't embarrass myself, I took the elevator down to the thirtieth floor where my own room is located. It's not as fancy as the suite Sam has on reserve, but it's a comfortable and surprisingly affordable place to lay low while I look for a job.

My thighs were sticky with his semen, and my skin smelled like him, masculine and hot. He was good to me, something I'd conditioned myself not to expect, and his tenderness was more than I let myself hope for.

I can't explain exactly why I didn't spend the night, only that I'd rather leave on my own than him tell me in the morning that a night of sex was as far as he was willing to go, or worse yet, that it had been a mistake. I know misery when I see it, and all I wanted was to comfort him in some small way, nothing more. I felt I had, and when the night gave way to the first glimmer of dawn, I left.

I still wouldn't stay despite the lingering feeling of him inside me, his lips pressed against mine.

He told me I'm beautiful, and a tiny corner of my heart believed him.

A week has gone by since that night, and I've avoided him. Well, I didn't want to risk the off chance he would look for me, and I've never been back to the bar and I don't loiter in the hotel's lobby. I thought I saw him once, talking to the front desk agent, but it could have been any blond man wearing a suit asking about a room. I didn't want to tempt Fate, and I used the side door from then on.

Once I find a job, I can look for an apartment and I'll never have to worry about running into him in the city. We're in completely different economic and social classes, and my neighborhood won't be his.

I've been working with an employment agency, looking for a temp-to hire position. In the week since I shared a bed with Samuel Sharpe, I've taken test after test at the agency and worked a handful of hours at a handful of companies. It's not so much they can't place me, but I need to earn a certain amount of money because I refuse to live in a hovel. I'm skilled, and once the director at the agency understood I had something between my ears, she started to guide me toward more lucrative, and difficult, positions.

Today I sit in one of the agency's conference rooms waiting for a list of interview appointments. On the bright side, the week that has gone by gave the parting bruise Keaton gifted me time to fade, and I've checked in with a friend in New York a couple of times. It appears he's accepted the divorce as well as he's going to, and he's let me go. I can find a position with a decent company, build a new life, and maybe, at some point, I'll start dating. Miraculously, Keaton hasn't scared me off men for the rest of my life, and it would be nice if I could find someone to keep the evening hours from feeling so desolate.

But not with Sam. Not with him.

He's desolation in the flesh and I can't handle that.

"Here, Miss Fowler," Dottie Mueller says, handing me a piece of paper.

I've been working with Dottie since I decided to use a professional agency, mainly because the top tier positions won't consider outside resumés. I understand, and it's how I'd gotten my last position as an assistant to the CEO of a large chain of retail stores in the city where Keaton and I lived. In that position, I was granted a steep clothing discount and because of that, I can dress for the position I need to have. This placement agency has access to all the top companies, and now that I've proven my worth, the list I'm holding should garner me a good position with a boss who will respect me and not treat me like a whore or a barista.

"Thank you," I say, folding it in two and shoving it into my purse. I'm dressed for a round of interviews in a black sheath dress, slim neon pink belt, and matching pink heels. I want to look professional, but like someone who can roll with the punches. I mean, figuratively. I twisted my hair into a bun at the back of my head and kept a light hand with the makeup.

"Do us proud," she says before turning her attention to a younger woman sitting next to me. I don't know what her qualifications are, but they must be on par with mine to have made it as far as I have.

I'll do this agency proud. I have no choice. If the company that hires me decides I won't work out and fires me, the agency will have to return the finder's fee. I don't need that black mark in my file.

I'm at the mercy of city transportation, but today I'll treat myself to cab rides across the city. I stand on the sidewalk and pull the paper out of my purse. I have an interview at Sharper-Image at ten, and it's nine-thirty now. Dottie wasted half an hour while I waited for her to print me the list of interviews.

I know SharperImage. It's the company Sam owns, a PR firm that has put him at the top and made him his billions. He represents everyone from the richest popstar to prime ministers to sports athletes who can't keep their dicks in their pants. The information at the bottom of the listing indicates the position is for their director of human resources. I do have that particular skill set, but it wasn't quite what I was looking for. Still, in a company the size of SharperImage, I doubt I would ever cross paths with Samuel Sharpe, and cautiously, I decide to at least go to the interview. The estimated pay isn't exactly what I was hoping for, but I could negotiate and see what happens. I don't know who's conducting the interview if they need an HR direc-tor, but that could put me in a good position to bargain.

I hail a taxi, my hot pink purse hanging from my shoulder. I like the pink. Someone once told me with my red hair I look ugly in pink, and ever since, I've worn the color in defiance.

Sam said I was beautiful, lying on top of me, his fingers twisted in my hair, gazing down at me like I just saved his life.

I hope, wherever he ends up, that he'll be okay.

The taxi lets me out in front of their building set off the street by concrete steps almost as long as the entire block. The revolving doors make me grin. I can't help it. I've always loved them, and when I was a child, my mother would let me twirl around and around, it didn't matter who I upset. She'd stand and laugh as I pushed that door, skirts flying, until I got dizzy.

I don't give in to the impulse to do so now, walking through security like the adult I am, cringing inside, scanning the lobby for Sam, wanting to see him but wanting to avoid it just as much. I shouldn't be here. I should call Dottie on the burner phone I purchased when I arrived in Carthage and tell her I need to turn down the interview at SharperImage, but I need the agency's help and I don't want to come across as flighty and undependable.

A security guard guides me through the metal detector while my purse chugs through the x-ray that will scan my belongings. I don't have much besides my wallet, a tube of hot pink lipstick that matches my purse, belt, and shoes, and a folder full of printed resumés because we can't always trust technology. The agency supplies them electronically, but I've saved my own ass a time or two and it has endeared me to the person I've helped.

I flinch a little as the guard's hand encircles my upper arm, but I try not to let it show. It was Keaton's favorite way of forcing me to look at him, his fingers digging into my skin to the bone.

He releases me to let me pass, and I do so without incident. I'm not wearing jewelry, and the buckle on my belt must not be something the machine is looking for.

A different security guard hands me my purse, and I thank him with a nod and a smile.

The lobby is full of people, some standing in line at a coffee kiosk, the rich aroma floating through the cavernous room floored with grey and cream marble. On my way out, maybe I'll treat myself to a cup. I try not to drink too much caffeine as it can fuel my anxiety. I don't have panic attacks often, but since I left Keaton, I'm constantly looking over my shoulder and only my friend's insistence that he's still in New York lets me relax.

"How can I help you?" a security guard asks as I approach the bank of elevators.

"I need human resources for SharperImage," I say, trying to

scan the black and white board hanging on the wall between two lifts. There are so many floors and so many departments that there's no way I can find what I'm looking for before he can assist me.

"Twenty-fifth floor," he says, pushing the Up button for me with a gloved hand.

"Thank you."

"Job interview?"

"Actually, yes," I say, meeting his eyes. I'm too jittery to hold a conversation, my senses on alert for Sam, but this may be my place of work and you never get a second chance to make a first impression.

"Knock 'em dead," he says, grinning. He holds the elevator doors open and I step inside.

"Thank you."

Others shuffle in with me, and since I'm nearest the panel, everyone tells me what floor they need. I push their choices along with mine and when I'm done, most of the buttons are lit up.

The ride is long enough I'm nervous by the time I reach the twenty-fifth floor. I'm qualified to do the job, and there's no reason why they wouldn't hire me unless I ask for too much money or someone with more experience edges me out. That can happen. I also don't have all the certificates I could earn because HR isn't what gets me out of bed in the morning.

I step off the elevator alone, and I push through the glass doors to the human resources office. The receptionist is a bubbly brunette chattering on the phone, and I stand in front of her desk. She glances my way and holds up a finger, but before she can end the call and greet me, a woman wearing a severely cut skirt and blazer combination marches from around the corner and looks me up and down.

"Are you Lily Fowler?" she asks, standing an inch away from me.

"Yes. I'm here for the—"

"You've been escalated," she says, opening one of the glass doors. "Samantha Sharpe's assistant just had a baby, and you're needed on the executive floor more than down here."

*Oh, no. No, no.* There's no way I can work on the executive floor. "I would really prefer—"

"Do you want a job or not?" she asks, pushing me through the doorway and back into the hallway. I don't like her hands on me and I step aside.

"Not that badly." I knew it wasn't a good idea to accept an interview at SharperImage.

She sighs like I'm inconveniencing her. Maybe I am. Maybe she'll get fired if she doesn't fill Samantha Sharpe's assistant opening. That shouldn't be my problem, but stress pulls at her eyes and I feel sorry for her.

"You're from a temp agency, right? A week, tops. I'll put a note in your file that it's not a permanent position."

"But what if—"

"Go. Now. She needed someone an hour ago."

She lets the door close with a bump, and through the glass, I watch her march away, the receptionist giving her a side-eye.

No introduction, nothing. I shouldn't trust that woman. I should leave right now, but they have my name and if I don't show up on the executive floor, she'll call Dottie and the list of jobs I have in my purse will disappear in a puff of smoke.

I can tell Samantha . . . what? What can I tell her? I don't know who she is. Sam's sister? Wife? No, I don't think he would have slept with me if he was married, but Samantha Sharpe is something to Sam, and this is a complication I do not need.

"Fuck." The expletive slips out of my mouth earning me an amused look from a woman waiting for the elevator. "Sorry, bad day."

She smiles in sympathy. "Mondays are like that. What floor?"

I sigh. "All the way up."

"You don't sound happy about it," she says as the doors slide open.

"There are other places I'd rather be."

"Oh, I don't know about that. Maybe you'll see Sam Sharpe. He's walking eye candy. My husband says he's the only reason I love my job, and well, a girl can't lie, can she?"

"And rich," I say drolly, watching the floors click by.

"Never hurts. I hope your day is better."

"Thanks."

We stop and the doors open revealing a tasteful lobby done in blacks and greys, black leather loveseats, coffee tables littered with magazines, and plants in large planters sitting on the floor. SharperImage is written in white script letters above the receptionist's head, and she speaks confidently into a headset. The woman I shared the elevator with disappears down a hallway and I'm left alone near an ottoman wishing like mad I could leave.

I approach the receptionist, and she pauses answering the phone just long enough for me to say, "I'm Samantha Sharpe's temporary assistant, Lily Fowler." Potential. I should have added that. The receptionist looks confused, her eyebrows knitted together as she pushes a button and says into her headset, "Ms. Sharpe, I have your new assistant waiting in the lobby. Lily Fowler."

She listens for a moment and turns to me. "Ms. Sharpe says to have a seat and she'll be with you in a moment."

"Thank you."

"I love your purse," she says before going back to answering and transferring phone calls.

I'm too nervous to sit, and I pace the lobby instead, my arms folded in front of me. If Sam steps out of an office somewhere and sees me. God. Well, it wouldn't be the worst thing that could happen, but I don't know if I hurt him when I left or if he was relieved when he woke up alone. I don't want to know. Either scenario has the power to hurt me, and it's better if I avoid it completely.

*I should go,* I think for the thousandth time, but I need the agency's help finding a job. I'll meet Samantha Sharpe, do the interview. No one would hire me, even for a temp job, without some kind of interview, and I can say I don't feel I'm a good match and leave as quickly as I can and still save face. My next interview is at one. I can find a quiet place to have lunch, regroup, and start over as if this disastrous morning never happened.

"Miss Fowler?"

I turn toward the voice. A slim blonde woman dressed in a cream suit walks toward me, her hair the same shade as Sam's twisted and pinned at the back of her head. She holds out her hand, and I grasp it, her handshake firm and confident.

"Yes, thank you. I was downstairs at HR. The placement agency sent me to interview for the director's position and I was told, rather sharply, that your assistant just had a baby and I was to fill in." I want to add that this whole thing has been a terrible mistake, but she doesn't give me the chance, never releasing my hand and towing me down a hallway and past several cubbies where people are talking into headsets or typing frantically at their keyboards.

"That was probably Cindy. She's a bit overwhelmed as we

*do* need a new HR director, but she must have skimmed your resumé and thought you a better fit up here. You didn't have your heart set on HR, did you?" she asks, looking at me, her head tilted upward. Wearing my heels, I'm taller than she is by at least half a foot.

"Well, no," I admit. "I find there's too much human in the resources part of things."

Samantha laughs. "It is a different way of seeing people, and it's not for everyone. Still, I think you'd do well. You have something about you. Empathy, maybe."

I slow my stride. I was about to pass her, and I don't know where we're going. "Being an underdog makes it easy to relate to another."

She stops outside an office door, SAMANTHA SHARPE etched into a name plaque. At a desk two feet away sits a woman talking on the phone, and she has all the markings of a PA. I don't know what's going on here, but I'm liking it less and less. I need to leave.

Samantha looks me up and down. She's pretty, her features petite, her eyebrows elegantly arched over blue eyes that are similar in shape and color to Sam's. "Somehow I don't think things get you down for long. At any rate, Cindy had it wrong, which is just another testament to how messy our HR department is right now. I'd be better off sending you back down there—you seem to know how to get things done—but it's not my assistant who had the baby. It's Sam's, and he's in desperate need of someone who can help him."

"Ms. Sharpe, I can't—"

I don't speak quickly enough and she opens the door, pulling me along with her. I don't have time to balk or jerk away (what is it with people in this company touching me?) before I'm standing in Sam's office, Samantha by my side.

"Sam, your first interviewee is here. I think she'll be perfect."

He's sitting at his desk, his head bowed over a piece of paper, a hand shoved into his hair.

I freeze and wait for him to lift his head. He does, in slow motion, while my heart slams against my ribs.

Sam meets my gaze and he looks no better than he did when we met at the bar. Shadows rest under his eyes, his jaw covered in stubble though it isn't even eleven o'clock. His suit is rumpled, like he dressed off his floor, and he needs a haircut.

His lips part, and I think of them on mine, firm yet soft, wanting, needing, yet unwilling to take. I've never met a man who needed so much but was afraid to ask for so little.

"What's her name?" he asks in a voice that turns my legs to jelly.

"Lily Fowler." Samantha looks between us, the air suddenly thick with tension.

Sam rises from his chair and rounds his desk.

I'm rooted to the floor. The building could be on fire, and I would have no choice but to stay. It's impossible to move, weighed down under Sam's scrutiny. He stops in front of me and raises a hand to my face.

I flinch, always, but he doesn't stop. He skims the backs of his fingers over my cheek.

"Sam!" Samantha snaps, not understanding that he and I have a history that has nothing to do with assistants who have given birth, or HR departments that need a director, or PR firms. We have a history as tenuous, but as strong, as a spider's web. I haven't forgotten how he felt inside me, and his smoldering eyes tell me the same.

He's thought about me, and that alone is enough to bring me to my knees.

"Why did you go?" he asks.

Why did I go? *Why did I go?* Because it was a one night stand? Because he's a billionaire and I'm a nobody trying to find a better life after a shitty marriage? Because he looked so damaged and I'm so fucking torn down how could I have even *thought* I had anything more than my body to give him?

"Did you want me to stay?" I counter. I don't know what made him as shredded as he is. He never volunteered the information, and I sure as hell didn't ask.

He opens his mouth to, I don't know. What could he possibly say?

Samantha steps back. "Sam. Is she . . .? Is she the one you've been looking for?"

Sam rubs his thumb over my lips. It's instinct to want to lick at him, taste his skin. That's not exactly how I wanted to make my first, well, second, impression with Samuel Sharpe. By licking him during our interview. I've done plenty of that already.

He drops his hand and his eyes ice over. "Get her out of here."

"Sam—" Samantha tries again.

"What did I say?" he barks. "For once, fucking do what I ask."

I back out of his office, using the door to the hallway, not the adjoining door Samantha used. The heel of my pump snags on the carpet. I stumble against the wall, my head hitting a picture's frame, and the sharp corner scrapes my temple.

"I'm sorry, Miss Fowler," Samantha says, closing the door behind her. "We normally don't treat potential—"

"Forget it. I knew when I saw this interview was on my list I should have avoided coming here. I had to do what the agency asked because I couldn't afford to skip it and have someone complain."

I look around, lost. All I want is to find an elevator and get out of here like Sam said.

"We could still use an HR director," Samantha says, leading me down the hallway. I have my bearings after we round a corner, and I head for the elevator as quickly as I can. Samantha trots in her heels to keep up with me.

I give her an incredulous look over my shoulder. "Do you think Sam wants me here?"

She grabs my arm as I jab at the elevator's Down button. Again, more touching, and I set my jaw.

"I think he wants you here more than he's wanted anything since his wife passed away."

The fight oozes out of me. "Is that what happened?"

"Yeah. Two years ago."

"He must have loved her very much if he's still grieving."

"She was his everything."

I nod. That explains so much, and my heart hurts for the man still in love with his dead wife. The elevator doors glide open. "If you could call the agency and tell them we weren't a good fit, I would appreciate it. I have other interviews slated for today."

"Of course. I'm sorry, Miss Fowler. I hope this doesn't cast SharperImage in a bad light."

"No. What happened between me and Sam . . . I shouldn't have come. Goodbye."

I step into the elevator, and Samantha keeps eye contact with me until the doors close.

The coffee kiosk is still doing a brisk business, and I wait in line and order a large decaf café mocha. I need the sugar, but I can do without the caffeine. Outside, I sit on a ledge with flowers and little tree-like plants growing at my back and watch the pedestrians walk by, talking on their phones or trying to sidestep others while they scroll. It's a beautiful fall day, the leaves of the trees lining the streets turning yellow and orange. The air holds a hint of winter, just a slight hint of the cold weather to come.

As I sit, awareness gradually slithers over my skin, light and faint at first, and then it grows heavier as the minutes tick by. I look back to the SharperImage building, but Sam isn't there. I sweep the sidewalks, searching for anyone who's looking at me, but I don't see anyone suspicious. I'm paranoid Keaton followed me from New York, but the divorce is finalized. Obeying the court order, he wasn't present when I removed my clothing and personal items from the house we shared—a house he kept.

I didn't care and still don't. That house was never a home. He could sell it for a million dollars over the asking price and I wouldn't want a single penny. I don't want anything that has to do with him.

The way Sam caressed my cheek. He might have been angry I left that night, but he forgave me, for a second, at least, in his relief at having found me. Maybe it *had* been him at the reservation desk looking for me. Well, whatever made him happy I stepped into his office didn't last. If what Samantha said is true, I don't think Sam's ready for a new relationship, just like I'm not ready for anything serious. I'm still walking in Keaton's shadow, and Sam sleeps with his wife's ghost.

No, it's better he kicked me out of his office, and I'm not going to pretend otherwise.

I throw my cup away, too full of coffee and adrenaline to want lunch. I'll take a taxi to my next interview. I can use the time to freshen up and familiarize myself with the building. A bank's CEO needs a new executive assistant. I need a little boring in my life, and the position is just what I need. Stable, predictable. And the CEO is a woman. Perfect.

Standing at the curb and lifting my hand, I'm about to hail

a taxi when someone grabs my wrist. Rage explodes behind my eyes in a red haze and bursts through my body. I am so tired of people touching me. I twirl, ready to give the asshole who thinks he has the right to handle me a good tongue-lashing, but I pop like a pierced balloon. Sam is there, so much pain and desperation in his eyes.

"Come back inside. Take the position and have dinner with me tonight."

# CHAPTER FOUR

*Sam*

"What the fuck was that?" Samantha asks, rounding on me. "Go after her."

I hunch over my desk, the thrill and disbelief the woman I'd been searching for had been standing in my office not ten seconds before still ping-ponging around in my heart. She was here, standing right here, and I touched her face, just like I'd done so many times in my dreams.

The shock of it, the utter wickedness of wanting another woman so soon after my wife's death, slammed into me so hard there wasn't anything I could do but distance myself as far and as fast as I could. I wanted to touch her, remind myself how lush and ripe her lips were. If Samantha wouldn't have been with her, I would have kissed her, and the way she looked at me, she would have let me.

Thank God Samantha was here.

Lily. Her name is Lily. As beautiful as she is.

"I can't."

It was only after she left and my head cleared that I realized what I'd done. Her soft brown eyes, the freckles covering her skin. The way she said my name. Grief of a different sort shot me down.

Loss.

How many ways is there to lose someone?

"Why? You're obviously attracted to her. She wasn't in your office for a second before you had to touch her. She's the one? The one you slept with?"

"Yeah."

"It's no wonder you picked her up. She's gorgeous."

"It's more than that. I felt like she understood me. I can't explain it. I just know I can't. Tabby's parents—"

"Can fucking go to hell," Samantha says, her voice cracking like a whip through my office. "They can't expect you to stay single forever, mourn forever. What you do now is none of their business."

"I'm their son-in-law."

"Used to be. *Used to be.*"

I lean back in my chair. I still talk to Tabby's parents regularly. Samantha's made it no secret she thinks it's not good for me. I don't know what's right or what's wrong anymore.

"Go after her, Sam. See where it leads."

Her suggestion sounds so innocent. Turn on a side road, see where it leads. Follow your heart, see where it leads. I slide out one of my desk drawers, and from the bottom, pull out a picture of Tabby and me standing downstairs in the lobby. I don't keep it on my desk, just like I don't wear my wedding ring anymore.

She was so quiet, so fragile, but she'd been up for anything, anytime. Spontaneous road trips, middle-of-the-night ice cream runs. Even before her cancer diagnosis, she lived every day like it was her last, but she'd somehow know when I was tired. She'd curl up in my lap on the recliner and we'd nap the day away, her head on my shoulder, my arm around her. I'd wake up with my legs numb, my feet asleep, but there's no place else I would rather have been.

"Go after her."

I meet her eyes. Her husband is still living, healthy, a foreman on a construction crew across the city, building new homes. Her children are adorable little demons. She has everything, has never known what it's like to lose something. A piece of your heart. A piece of your soul.

And to meet someone who has the potential to give them back to you? What are the odds?

Who is she to urge me to do something that could hurt? Layer the hurt on top of what I've already lived through?

But what if, by some extreme miracle, there *is* something there, something that could deepen, heal my hurt? And in return, I could heal hers? She left not only because I ordered her to, but because she was also looking out for her own welfare. I can't forget that. An abusive ex. Her bruise healed, but the way she flinched when I touched her cheek, she has a long way to go before she could accept anything I want to give her.

"She's already gone."

Samantha steps farther into the room and shoves her hands on her hips. "Sam, you didn't build this company up by being a coward, and I remember how you met Tabby. You weren't a coward then, either. You've always taken whatever you want. What is it about this woman that scares you?" She tilts her head. "Because she does scare you, doesn't she?"

I fall back on the same excuse I always use. "I'm not ready."

"That doesn't mean you can't go after her and take it slow. Get to know her. You may realize she's not the one after all, but, Sam. What if she is? You're going to waste a chance and throw it away?"

I rub my hands over my face.

Neon lights flashing over her skin.

The way she let me roll her onto her back and take her.

Her complete awe when I made her come before I found my own release.

Her body wrapped around mine when we were done.

My face in her hair as I fell asleep.

How often I think about that night. How that simple night has turned into dreams and nightmares, mixing together until I can't tell one from the other. Is Lily my heaven or will she send me to hell?

I bolt from my chair and out the door, catching a glimpse of Samantha's face revealing a little approval and a lot of relief.

The elevator moves so slowly, and I sag against the wall as I descend, my stomach pitching. I sat for too long, and she'll be gone. As I rush through the lobby, dodge security, and push through the revolving doors, I try to console myself with the fact I have more than I did the first time she disappeared.

I skid to a stunned stop when I see her at the curb. She's still here. Maybe she went to the bathroom, or she ran into someone she knew and spoke for a few minutes. Whatever the reason, I thank Christ, and I rush to the sidewalk before a taxi can stop.

Her wrist is slender and delicate in my grip, and she stiffens in anger until she turns around and sees me standing behind her.

"Come back inside. Take the position and have dinner with me tonight."

"Why?"

I devour her face, the emotions fluttering over her features.

"Because I'm afraid of the man I'll turn into if you don't."

She searches my eyes. She knows I'm not any better off than when I picked her up in the bar.

"Samantha told me about your wife."

Of course she did. She can't keep a secret to save her life. I found that out one year when I bought Tabby a new car and on Christmas morning it wasn't a surprise. I was so angry I didn't talk to Sammie for weeks. It didn't cure her penchant for talk. Or for meddling.

I move my hand from her wrist and lace her fingers with mine. "There are things I want to know about you, too. Like why you don't like being touched. Like why you flinch every time I put my hand near your face. Like why you need a job and you're using a placement agency. I want to know who you are . . . Lily." I say her name, the syllables sounding right and sweet on my tongue.

She looks over her shoulder and down the sidewalk. It's lunch hour and the streets are full of people on their breaks running errands or finding a quick bite to eat. I should, too. My appetite has been nonexistent since Tabby passed away. I look forward to sharing meals with Lily, and I want to start today, right now.

Stepping away from the curb, she pulls her hand away, and I back up too, giving her the room she seems to need.

"I'll take the position. Your assistant, right?" she asks.

I nod.

"And . . . dinner?"

"Just to talk. I don't want you to think that because of how we met, I'll expect things."

A corner of her mouth lifts up. With another quick glance down the sidewalk, she says, "Okay. I accept the job, and—" she swallows— "dinner."

The relief that bolts through me threatens to send me onto my ass. "Thank you."

She pauses on the sidewalk, her red hair blending in with the autumn hue of the trees. "I'm sorry about your wife."

I hold out my hand, and after looking at it, debating, tentatively, she reaches out to take it.

"So am I."

Samantha's waiting for us by the elevator, and her face lights with a smile when I step out with Lily.

Lily stops and stares at the tile. "This is a bit awkward."

Glancing between Lily and me, Samantha says, "Let me call your employment agency. I'll tell them it's for a three-month temp-to-hire and if you feel like you truly aren't a good fit, you have a way out, okay?"

Lily lifts her head. "You haven't called them yet?"

"I was waiting, just in case."

"Thank you. That's kind."

"I hope you like working here, Miss Fowler," Samantha says, all business now to set Lily at ease.

"I hope so, too."

It's difficult to let Lily go when I only just found her again, but Samantha walks her down to HR to start the new-hire paperwork and settle her in. I sit in my office, Allessandra Biggotti's file in front of me. I should find some stable ground, do some work. Samantha's been tolerant because she loved Tabby almost as much as I did, but that won't keep the company running and Allessandra's going to need all my brains in the game if she's going to get out of this with her reputation intact.

Before I do that, I call Shiloh, Samantha's PA, and ask her to make reservations at my favorite restaurant. "Tell them to reserve the rooftop for eight o'clock."

It isn't a frequent request. Tabby hated it when I threw my

weight and money around, but for some reason I don't think Lily will mind, and she'll appreciate the privacy.

I stare out the window, a finger pressed to my lips, noting my slip-up. I can't keep comparing them. Already they're miles from each other in terms of looks and temperament. If I constantly search for bits of Tabby in Lily, I'll be disappointed, and it's not fair to Lily if I do that to her. If I pursue this—and I'm still not sure this is something I can do despite Samantha's encouragement and my own despair at having lost Lily once already—I'll have to be okay with the fact that they are two very different women. Tabby is gone, and Fate has given me a second chance.

I don't want to ruin it being an obtuse, insensitive jackass.

I take the picture of us out of my drawer. She would want this. I believe that. It's not something I'm saying to console myself and to feel better about sleeping with Lily and chasing her down like a desperate dog. Tabby cared about my happiness—always checking in, making sure I was okay—just as I cared for hers. I want to believe that these past two years would have made her angry, wasting my time mourning something that can't be undone, but I knew my wife well. She would deny it, but she would . . . not like it, but I think it would have given her a small amount of satisfaction I hadn't let her go quickly or easily. But, she would say, the novelty of my pain wearing thin, it's time to get on with it. That was her favorite phrase when she knew I was procrastinating.

Time to get on with it.

If only it was that easy.

Knowing Lily is here, I have a difficult time concentrating on the tasks at hand. All I can think about is dinner tonight, spending time with her, getting to know her, and the numbers on the clock turn at an excruciatingly unhurried speed. Allessandra's plight does nothing for me. She's a troublemaker, constantly on the verge of self-destruction, and what I'll do for her will only stall the inevitable: an overdose in a hotel bathroom while everyone fights over blame and money.

I'm working on ways to spin her latest breakdown when Lily raps lightly on my doorjamb. I left my office door open all afternoon and catching glimpses of her walking down the hallway or working with Shiloh helped me breathe easier. Lily isn't a figment of my imagination, a vision borne of wanting something so terribly my mind created her from nothing. She's here, at least for the next three months, while we figure out where this is going to go. Where it *can* go.

"Samantha says I'm free to leave. Do you stay past five?" she asks, leaning against the doorjamb, her bright pink purse hanging from the crook of her elbow.

"I never used to," I say honestly. Tabby never put up with it. After she passed away, work was all I had left and it would be a common occurrence for me to stay at the office until the cleaning crew arrived, the whir of the vacuums interrupting my scant concentration until I was forced to leave.

Lily understands and gives me an almost imperceptible nod. "Are we still meeting for dinner?"

"Dinner, yes. Meeting, no. I'll pick you up. I made reservations for eight. Where are you staying?" I push away from my desk and stand next to her at the door. Having her close, but not *close*, is a torture all on its own, and I raise my hand, slowly, taking care she understands my intentions, before caressing her cheek. She still flinches, and a slight shudder runs through her body.

She licks her lips, and her skin glistens with the thin coating of saliva. "At the Regency."

"The hotel you and I . . .?"

"Yes. I was waiting to look for an apartment until I found a job."

I can hear that story later. "Then I'll wait for you in the lobby say, seven forty-five? Will you have enough time to dress?"

"Yes, that's fine. I'll see you then."

She turns to go.

"Lily."

She meets my eyes and the thing that attracted me before as we sat in the bar's banquette in silence hits me in full force once again. I don't need to explain, don't need to say pretty words. She knows exactly what I'm thinking, what I'm feeling, and she gives me the time to just *be*. Even if that time is ten seconds standing in the middle of the hallway. I can't put into words the consolation that gives me. How soothing it is to be accepted for not only who I am, but what I am and the bits and pieces of the pain that hold me together even as they destroy me.

When she turns to go this time, I let her, my eyes following her elegant figure until she turns the corner toward the elevators.

Samantha joins me a few minutes later as I gather paperwork to bring home. It's a Monday, and I can't keep Lily at dinner too late. I may have time after I drop her off to do an hour or two of work.

"She's very smart," Samantha says, leaning a hip against my desk. "She has a lot of common sense and can think outside the box. If she had any experience in PR, she could do my job."

"Then she'll fit in?" I hadn't considered the risk of mixing business with pleasure. If she couldn't do her job and we had to let her go, I'm not sure how our budding relationship would have fared. It's best I don't have to find out.

"She will. She's exactly what we need and Shiloh likes her and offered to train her."

"Good."

"Any word on Allessandra?" she asks.

"Besides the fact she's fucked? No. Her handlers will be here Wednesday to work out a game plan. At this point, she doesn't need PR, she needs therapy and parents who give a shit about her."

"Well, I doubt she'll get one without the other. Sometimes I'm glad my boys don't have any real talent."

"They're young yet," I say, thinking of my nephews. "You could have a top NFL pick on your hands."

Samantha huffs a laugh. "Not if Clint has anything to say about it. Shiloh says you and Lily are going to dinner tonight."

"We are. The rooftop at Sargento's."

She opens her mouth to say something, then stops.

"What?" I can never not listen to what she has to say. She's always been dead-on with advice. If it hadn't been for her, I would have let Lily go this morning and I'm not sure what kind of state I'd be in right now if that had happened.

"That was yours and Tabby's favorite restaurant."

"Yes, it was. So?"

"So . . . never mind. I hope you have a lovely time. You deserve it, and she's darling."

"No. Tell me what you were going to say, but be quick about it. I need to go home and shower and change."

"I just think—" She sighs. "Carthage is a big city, and I just think it might be better if you tried new places. Do you want Tabby's presence hanging over you and Lily everywhere you go because you can't try new things? Find a new favorite restaurant. Please don't be mad."

Stuffing the paperwork into my briefcase, I say, "I'm not mad. You're right. Lily deserves more than feeling like she's second best. It's too late to do anything about it now, but you're right. There are other places we can go, places we can explore together. Tabby and I were married for over fifteen years. I'm going to need time to realize there are different ways to do things."

Samantha squeezes my arm. "That's why I didn't want to say anything. I don't want you to think I'm going to bust your balls every time we talk."

I pull a face to make her laugh. I don't like it when our relationship is strained. "I would never think that."

"Good. I better get going myself. I have to pick the boys up. The after-school program said if I'm late one more time they'll start charging me. Good luck, Sam. I'm happy for you."

I tell her the truth. "Couldn't have done it without you."

She lifts an eyebrow. "Somehow, I think you would have. I just gave you an extra push. Goodnight."

"Goodnight."

My car is waiting downstairs, and Archer, my driver, errand runner, private investigator when I need one, and occasional bodyguard, navigates the rush hour traffic. Fall is in the air and sitting on the rooftop at Sargento's will be pleasant. I wish Samantha wouldn't have said anything. I don't know if the thought would have ever crossed my mind, or maybe it would have, eventually. When taking Lily to all the places Tabby and I enjoyed would have made me feel like a third wheel along with Lily's broken spirit and Tabby's ghost.

On the other hand, Lily and I may not click, and thinking of future dates could be pointless. While what we've found in the few moments we've stolen together have been nothing short of phenomenal—for me, at least—there's no guarantee it will be enough to sustain a viable relationship, and at this point, I'm not sure it's what I want. I could be in over my head.

All I know is that since Lily stepped into my office this morning for her job interview, I feel like I've woken from a coma. Things are clear, but I'm confused. I don't understand what's happening, yet everyone is telling me it's going to be okay.

"Sir?" Archer prompts me.

I catch his eyes in the review mirror.

"You were going home?" he asks.

We're double parked outside my building. "Right. Thank you. I'll need the limo tonight at seven-thirty."

"Yes, sir."

I still live in the penthouse Tabby and I bought to celebrate when my earnings from SharperImage topped fifty million. That was a long time ago, and I haven't considered moving or selling. I'll never be able to invite Lily up here. I could never bring another woman into the haven Tabby and I created together, the place where we said our final goodbyes.

I shower and change. Sargento's is a trendy Italian place, and I dress in a clean suit and loose tie. I can still feel Tabby brushing my suit jacket of invisible lint, straightening my tie, smoothing her fingers over my shirt. She'd say she wanted me to look my best, but we both knew she just wanted her hands on me, and I had no complaints.

I didn't realize this would be so hard. Swallowing a lump in my throat, I run my fingers through my hair, something else Tabby would do, saying I looked sexy. I don't want to look sexy, and I comb it instead, like I would for work.

Maybe I can't do this.

Picturing Lily leaning against my doorjamb at the office pushes me forward. I want to see her.

"Wait here," I tell the limo driver when he stops at the curb in front of the Regency.

"Yes, sir."

Lily's waiting in the lobby, sitting on the arm of a loveseat. She's beautiful wearing a dark green dress, her hair loose around her shoulders, but she looks tense, her eyes lighting on every person in agitation, stiffening when a young couple walks too close to her to reach the front desk. She's scared.

"Lily," I say, approaching her. "Did something happen?"

She rises from the armrest, black sandals glittering on her feet, and smiles sheepishly. "Do I look nervous?"

"A little."

"It's been a while since I've been on a date," she says, accepting my offer to help her outside and wrapping her arms around mine.

"There's no one who could understand that more than me." The hotel's doorman opens the glass door for us, and we step onto the sidewalk and into the fall evening. A few crunchy leaves skitter across the concrete in the breeze, and the sun is hiding behind a building, casting a warm orange glow over the city.

She stumbles as we approach the limo, the driver waiting near the passenger door, his hands clasped behind his back, his feet spread. She hesitates before she slides into the back, and I follow. Leaning into the bench, I watch her look around. I bet there's nothing she doesn't miss.

"I've . . . never ridden in one of these before," she admits when she notices me staring at her.

"Too much?" If it is, I won't order a limo again. I want her comfortable around me and I don't mind driving myself places.

"No. Well, no. I suppose you're used to it." Her hands fidget in her lap.

"It was a slow progression. Now it's something I take for granted."

She looks out the window at the light evening traffic. "Isn't it funny what we get used to? What becomes commonplace?"

"Then there are some things you may never get used to," I say, thinking of Tabby's absence and the hole she left behind. I took her for granted, thinking we would die old together.

Lily turns away from the window and blinks. "Yes, I suppose there are some things that are so unsettling you may never get used to the fact that they're going to be part of your life forever."

I don't know if she's talking about my life or hers. Gently, I hold her hand. "I'm more than your employer, Lily. If what we're doing doesn't work out, I will always be your friend. If you need anything, tell me, and I'll do whatever I can to give it to you."

"Some things can't be bought."

"The best things can't be bought," I correct her.

She rests her head on my shoulder. I kiss the top of her head and we ride the rest of the way in silence.

A crowd of reporters stands on the sidewalk in front of the building that houses Sargento's hoping to dig up a nugget of gossip, and Samantha's warning rings in my ears. I should never have brought Lily here.

She, too, balks when the limo idles at the curb and the driver steps from behind the wheel to help us out. Photographers take our picture, and reporters and the gossip bloggers shout questions at me. "Mr. Sharpe! Who's your date tonight?" "Sam! Look this way! Are you finally over your wife's death?" "Sam! What's your date's name? Does she know about your wife?"

The limo driver shields us the best he can, the photographers holding their cameras and phones above their heads trying for a clear shot of Lily and me entering the building. Lily cowers into my back, hiding her face.

"Fuck, I am so sorry," I mutter, needing a few moments to

regroup in the quiet lobby. "It's been a while since I've had to put up with that. They don't care when all I do is work."

"The attention is a little overwhelming," Lily says, smoothing her hair with shaking hands.

"It's one of those things I've gotten used to," I say, punching the Up button at the elevator bank. Sargento's is located on the top floor. They have inside dining, and, of course, the rooftop seating.

The doors glide open, and we step inside, faint piped-in music playing a melody I don't recognize.

"Do you like it?" she asks.

I select the button for the restaurant's floor. "I don't want to be as famous as my clients. Nothing good comes from that kind of fame."

The elevator doors open to the entry way of the restaurant, and the head chef and owner greets me by name. "Sam, welcome back. I was so sorry to hear about Tabitha. My deepest condolences."

I haven't been back since Tabby's death, and I glance quickly at Lily. Her face is a smooth, emotionless mask. "Thank you, Riccardo. This is Lily. Miss Fowler."

Riccardo reaches for her hand and squeezes. "It's very nice to meet you."

"Thank you. It's nice to meet you, too."

"Please, allow me to escort you to the roof."

This is already more awkward than it should be, and I wave him off. "Don't let us keep you. I know the way."

He frowns. "Are you sure? It's no trouble."

I tilt my head at Lily, hoping he gets the message. "I'll see to it."

"As you wish," he says, nodding. "I'll send a server up momentarily to take your drink order."

"Thank you."

I tug on Lily's hand, grateful to leave Riccardo behind.

"Tabitha? That was your wife's name? Did you come here often?" Lily asks as I help her up a wide staircase that leads to the rooftop dining area.

I open the door for her, and she sucks in a breath.

Twinkle lights hang from wires strung over the roof and all the tables have been removed but for ours that sits near the edge allowing us a breathtaking view of the city. A mild breeze blows, and it ruffles the leaves of the plants and the trees that decorate the space. Pigeons coo from their hideouts, and later, one or two might be brave enough to join us and beg for food. There isn't any music up here, which is what I like best. It's quiet except for the traffic noises that carry to us and the sound of a jet flying by on occasion. When Tabby and I ate here, we felt like the only two people in the world.

I let go of Lily's hand, and she wanders around, the lights turning her hair to fire. Her dress's hem swishes around her knees, her heels click against the floor, and she slowly turns in a circle, her head tipped up in wonder.

"We came here more than any other place."

"I can't blame you."

A server appears dressed in black, and I help Lily into her chair. She sets her purse on the floor next to her feet.

"What would you like? A glass of wine?" I ask. The table is set with elegant china, and there isn't a menu. Riccardo trusts me to order for both of us.

"That sounds nice."

I order a bottle of white. When the server comes back, I plan on ordering a platter of lobster fettuccini and it will be a perfect complement.

I lean back in my chair and inhale. The air smells cleaner up here, and I grip the edge of the table when a sudden rush of wooziness hits me. There's so much to process. This past week,

I thought I'd lost Lily forever, and when I found her, I sent her away. That she's here, sitting across from me and gazing across the city, fills me with emotions I can only guess. Guilt and fear. Joy. Apprehension. And something I haven't felt in so long I'm not sure if I'm fooling myself. Hope. I've been mourning for years, and I never once thought that could change.

Lily sits quietly, letting me acclimate. She can feel the chaos and lets me have time to get it under control.

The server interrupts with the wine, and after I sample it and approve, she pours for both of us. I order mushrooms stuffed with crab and cheese as an appetizer, the fettuccini, and chocolate cake for dessert. Riccardo will be disappointed I didn't order the tiramisu, but that was a particular favorite of Tabby's and I'm already pressing my luck, mixing memories like a college kid mixes his booze, hoping he doesn't throw up.

Lily holds her wineglass to her chest, just under her chin. She tilts her head, and the little candles on the table turn her brown eyes into burnt umber. "Can I ask you a question?"

I gulp my wine. "We wouldn't be able to have much of a conversation if I say no."

She smiles. They ravage me, every time. Vague, as if she can't fully unleash one for fear of punishment. "Are you really a billionaire?"

I clear my throat and hold my hand up flat, tilting it back and forth. "On a good day, perhaps I can hit the billion-dollar mark. I donate a lot of money, and I invest—stocks, property, art. If you're asking if I could pull a billion dollars out of my bank accounts, then no. I'm not that liquid. Why?"

"I'm just curious. I've never met someone that rich before. My life was very . . . simple, I suppose you could say. I worked, did the grocery shopping. Our— My house had a large back-yard with lots of trees, and I spent a lot of time there. It was quiet."

"Where was this?" I'm glad she started talking about herself first, before I could ask a question she didn't want to answer. I noticed her slip. She lived with someone. An ex of some sort. A simple roommate wouldn't put so much pain in her eyes.

"In a city a few hours outside of New York."

The server chooses that moment to bring our appetizer to the table. I want to curse her but I'm hungry, and for the first time in a long while, I'm going to enjoy my meal. The mushrooms are still sizzling in their dish, and my stomach rumbles. "May I?" I ask, holding the serving spoon and gesturing to her plate.

"Yes, thank you."

"How did you end up in Minnesota?" I add two mushrooms to her small plate.

She lays the white cloth napkin in her lap and picks up her fork. "My mother grew up here. She's said she had a happy childhood, if a childhood can be happy, and I thought I would take a chance."

There's a lot to unpack there, and I wait for her to finish a mushroom and sip her wine before I ask my next question. "You didn't have a happy childhood?"

"It wasn't anything my parents did or didn't do. I was taller than most of my classmates, gangly, and with freckles, I didn't have many friends. I didn't grow into myself until high school, but by then the bullies had gotten their licks in and my self-esteem was never the same."

"Are you and your parents close?"

She shakes her head and stares at her plate. "We had a falling out a few years ago. We haven't spoken in a long time."

"I'm sorry to hear that."

"Life gives, life takes."

I set my fork down and cover her hand with mine. "Lily."

She lifts a shoulder, pulls her hand away, and rests it in her lap under the table. "It's okay. I knew the choices I was making and they knew the choices they were. Now we live with the consequences."

"Do you miss them?"

"More than I thought I would."

The server must have been watching us, and the second we finish our mushrooms, she's clearing our plates. It's only a moment later Riccardo serves the steaming platter of pasta and lobster and a basket of garlic rolls himself. "Are you enjoying your evening?" he asks, folding the heat pads he used to carry the platter to the table.

"This is gorgeous," Lily says, gesturing to the entire rooftop.

"Thank you. You're seeing it at its best. It's usually a little more crowded."

She shoots me a look. "I wouldn't have minded."

"I would have. I wanted you to myself."

"And I'm interrupting," Riccardo says. "Don't leave without saying goodbye."

"We won't."

We're left alone, and I let Lily serve herself.

"Wait. You're not allergic to shellfish, are you? There's lobster in there."

She pauses, the serving spoon and fork poised above the platter. "No, but thank you for thinking of it. I would have said something when you ordered."

"You're welcome. Oh," I say, stiffening, "the rolls probably have gluten in them."

"Sam. I'm not allergic or sensitive to anything. I don't have a high tolerance for alcohol, but that's all. I'm fine, really. Thank you."

I nod. There's so much more I want to ask her, but she's been open with me and I don't want to push her further than she wants to go. I want to know who she was living with in

New York. I want to know why she and her parents had a falling out. The move here and why she's living out of a hotel answered some of my questions but not all. I want to guzzle her down like a thirsty man on a hot day, but I show restraint and let her eat in silence.

The pasta dish is delicious, the sauce a buttery, garlicky, heaven. The crusted rolls are flaky and light, and I think this is the most I've eaten since Tabby passed away. I haven't wanted to eat, haven't wanted to do much of anything, too consumed with living without her to do any living without her.

The sun sets while we eat, and only the delicate pinks and purples are left streaking the sky. The first stars come out, the brightest one I'm told not even a star at all, but a satellite, or Pluto. I forget which. The breeze blows at Lily's hair, and I want to tuck the strands behind her ear. I resist, letting her have the space she's given me. I'm not the only one dealing with loss.

"You and your wife came here often?" Lily asks when our dinner dishes and wineglasses are cleared. The server said she would be back with our cake and coffee, and there's a quiet lull as we wait to be interrupted one last time.

"We had a few favorites, here and there." I don't like talking about the life I had with Tabby. I don't want Lily to think I'm going to compare everything we do. I already had that talk with myself and thanks to Samantha, I understand eating at Sargento's was a mistake.

"Would you mind, if you have time, showing me around the city?" she asks. "I don't know anyone here and it would be nice to have someone to . . ." She trails off, her cheeks a faint pink in the tealights. She wants to spend more time with me, and I send up a quiet prayer of thanks.

"I would love to. Thank you for asking."

"Thank you for saying yes."

She meets my eyes and that feeling comes back, the one

where she knows everything I'm thinking, every emotion clanking around my heart. It's the acceptance, the quiet support I crave, and it's here now, weaving around us and binding me to her.

Every second I spend with her, I fall in love a little more, but months later, when I look back on this moment, that's not what I would have called it.

I would have called it the first signs of trouble, but I still wouldn't have stopped it.

# CHAPTER FIVE



The server sets our dessert plate in the middle of the table, two silver spoons flanking the enormous piece of chocolate cake. The wedge is topped with dollops of whipped cream and sprinkled with chocolate flakes. The coffee smells delicious and just what I need to clear my head after two glasses of wine and pasta so decadent I don't think I need to eat for the next few days.

I can understand why this was Sam and Tabitha's favorite place, and if I hadn't seen the apprehension on Sam's face when Riccardo mentioned his wife when we first arrived, I wouldn't have minded coming back. Riccardo obviously missed his friend.

Friends, true friends, are a foreign concept to me. I don't have any childhood friends, no outcasts bound together by playground or gym class humiliation and embarrassment. The people I met in college are long gone. The few I'd managed to make before I met Keaton dried up when I married him, and he cut me off from everyone and everything but my job. And then he'd made it clear he was letting me work because we needed the money. He wanted me barefoot and pregnant, literally chained to the kitchen stove if he could have gotten away with it, but luckily that hadn't worked out for him.

"How is Samantha related to you?" I ask, choosing a spoon and dipping it into the mountain of whipped cream.

"She's my cousin. Our fathers are brothers. They were the ones who founded SharperImage and once they got it off the ground, they handed it over to us. They run a marketing firm in Carthage now, a few hours, a few clients. Marketing isn't too far off from PR, and it suits them."

"You look a lot alike."

Sam smiles, and his eyes crinkle at the corners. It gives him a boyish look that I bet hasn't graced his face since his wife passed away. "We should. Our fathers are identical twins, and her two boys are fraternal twins. She has two older brothers, but they're singletons. We have a large family."

"You're an only child?"

"I am, but I grew up with Samantha and her brothers. I didn't feel like I was an only child."

"You don't have any children? You and Tabitha?"

"No, we didn't have kids. She was sick, and her doctor didn't advise us trying. It would have taken too much of a toll on her health. It's better, I think. I'm not cut out to be a single dad. You?"

The fettuccine rolls in my stomach thinking about having children with Keaton. It would have been a nightmare. I wouldn't have been able to leave without them, and he never would have let us all go. "No. My ex-husband was . . . domineering, and I didn't want the added stress of taking care of a child."

"Do you want kids?" he asks, looking down at the plate of

cake and scooping up a spoonful of frosting. I don't know why the question feels like a test, but all I can do is answer honestly and hope what he hears doesn't put him off.

"I'm getting a little old for it. I'll be thirty-nine in November and I don't know if it's something I want to bother with. I think I'd rather try to find happiness on my own than worry about meeting someone and hoping we click in enough time for me to get pregnant and avoid complications. I'm healthy, but sometimes I feel my age."

It's not that I've never thought about children, it's that I never thought I'd be in a position to have them.

"It's what scared me, when Tabby died. That I would grow old alone."

It's not the time to be glib, but it would be easy to joke. "Sam, you're kind, handsome, and rich. I don't think, once you're ready to move on, that you would have any trouble finding someone to share your life with."

"Possibly. You're divorced then?"

I nod. We haven't gotten to my whys and whens and I'm reluctant to reach that part of our conversation. Maybe not tonight, but at some point, unless I break this off, he's going to want to know. He deserves to know why I flinch every time he wants to touch my face.

"Do you think about remarrying?"

Between us, the dessert is slowly disappearing, but the last bite I took turns to mud in my mouth and I set my spoon aside and pick up my coffee cup instead. I force down the gooey cake with a large gulp of the rich coffee. I stand from the table and walk to the edge of the rooftop, bringing my cup with me.

The city's lights begin to blink on, and I can feel the energy as the city wakes for the night. Carthage is bigger than the city I fled, and I was pleased, hoping the size would help keep me hidden. Then I accept a date with a sometimes-billionaire and my face, or the back of my head, is going to be splashed every-where tomorrow. I should have invited him up to my room. At least room service would have been private.

Sam follows me, pushing his chest into my side, crowding me. It's his nature, to touch, and though I want to cringe away, I don't. He doesn't mean any harm, but my heart still flutters in agitation and a sheen of nervous perspiration mists my skin.

"Lily?" His voice is low, gravely, mixed with a hint of concern.

"I'm sorry. I just, you know. I'm tired of belonging to some-one." That's what Keaton always said. I belonged to him, that he owned me, and there wasn't anything I could do without his permission. There's that saying that birds are happiest in cages because they know they're safe, but I wasn't happy, and I wasn't safe, in the cage Keaton kept me in.

"What if," he whispers, dragging his hand over my hair, "he wants to belong to you?"

I resist the urge to push him away. We've been intimate, as intimate as two people can possibly be. He doesn't think he has a right to touch me, I can feel his hesitancy, but it puts us on familiar ground that shouldn't be familiar to people who just met.

"I'm not ready to accept that kind of responsibility."

He drops his hand. "How long have you been divorced?"

"We've been separated for a little while, but the divorce didn't go through until two weeks ago."

He steps back. "That's not long."

"No, it's not. Sam, when we met at the bar, I was lost, broken. I know you saw the bruise on my face. You made some of that go away, sitting with me. You reminded me that I don't have to be alone if I don't want to be, and when you asked me to go to your room, I felt the consequences for saying no would be far greater than saying yes. I wanted to be with you, but I didn't think you'd find me."

"You didn't want to be found."

I lean against the rail and look out over the city. "I must have, on some level, or I never would have went to that interview. I would have stayed as far away from your building as I possibly could."

Sam rests an elbow on the rail and crosses his ankles. He looks like a model, the breeze ruffling his hair, his cheeks and jaw clean-shaven. A new look since the past couple of times I've seen him he looked haggard and scruffy.

"I get it," he finally says.

"You do?" I thought he'd push me.

"Why do you think I kicked you out of my office this morning? I'm not any more ready for this than you are. I didn't know when I sat with you in the bar I would feel such a connection. I know you felt it too, and I know it's why you left in the middle of the night. It frightened you. As long as I don't frighten you, we might have a chance. I don't completely understand what you're running from, Lily, but I will never hurt you."

I sip my coffee, cooling now. "Then what should we do?"

He nudges me so I'm facing him and presses his body close to mine. Again, in my heels, we line up just right, and he wraps his arms around me. I'm beginning to learn that Sam is a romantic, that his wife's death hasn't switched off that part of him. Lucky for me because Keaton hadn't been anywhere near romantic, and I need it if I'm going to make any progress in a relationship with another man.

Touching the tip of his nose to mine, he says, "Let me show you around Carthage. I want to spend time with you. I feel like I've known you for a million years but know nothing about you."

His face is half an inch away from mine, and tilting my head, I brush my lips over his.

A sigh shudders through him, and he pulls me close as I wrap my arms around his neck and lace my fingers through his hair. His kisses are soft, yet firm, warm, asking for nothing but giving everything. I lick at his lips, asking him to deepen the kiss, and with a hand to the back of my head, he does.

Desire pools in my belly, and my panties dampen. I didn't want to be attracted to him. It would have made things easier if I wasn't, but the connection is there, stronger than ever. I can let Keaton steal this from me, too, or I can fight him off. I didn't escape New York to live afraid. I didn't escape to live alone. My mother warned me he would suffocate me, and he did.

But I'm not dead yet.

Sam lifts his head but doesn't let me go.

I rest my cheek against his shoulder and say, "Do you feel strange, meeting how we did? After what we did? I've never had a one night stand before."

"I want more because I know how good it will be." Gently, he squeezes my arm and I lift my head. "But intimacy, to me, has always been more than physical, and no matter how good it was, once I get to know you and you get to know me, it will be better than that night. And let me say," he says, nipping at my bottom lip, "I'm glad you've never done that with another man."

"Have you? With another woman?"

"No. I was married to Tabby for fifteen years. Before that I was busy going to school and working. My father always said I'd take over SharperImage, and I never minded because I like PR work. I like picking apart a scenario so terrible, finding what good there is in it, and presenting that to the public. There's good in every situation. My father taught me that. It's being able to recognize it and helping others recognize it."

"That, Mr. Sharpe, sounds like manipulation."

"And when I'm paid, I'm very good at it. Come on, it's getting late and I should get you back to the hotel before you turn into a pumpkin."

He tugs on my hand, and I remember to grab my coffee cup off the railing and set it on the table near our dessert plate that's almost empty.

On the way out, we stop in the kitchen and say goodbye to Riccardo. He smiles warmly, as if thanking me for what I did for Sam. I'm not sure what I did besides wanting to sip on a glass of wine in a hotel bar, but I shake his hand and accept his gratitude. If Sam had been in a bad way, I mean, a really bad way, I'm happy I was able to help.

Instead of going out the front, Riccardo walks with us to the back of the building and we ride in a service elevator to the lower floor. Sam shakes his hand one last time and we step into the cool evening air.

"Want to walk for a couple of blocks?" he asks, linking our fingers together. "Are you okay in your heels?"

"I'll be fine for a little bit."

The sidewalks aren't too busy, and every once in a while Sam pushes me into the niche of a storefront's door and kisses me in the shadows.

At a corner, the limo picks us up, and we ride the rest of the way to the hotel, Sam's arm wrapped around my shoulders.

He walks with me into the Regency's lobby, and we say goodbye near the elevators.

"You were under my nose the whole time I looked for you, weren't you?" he says, referring to my hotel room.

"I'm sorry," I say, kissing his cheek. "I didn't mean to hurt you."

"You aren't the only one to blame. Goodnight, Lily."

"Goodnight."

The doors to the elevator choose that moment to open, and I step inside. He blocks the doors and pulls me to him, stealing one last kiss as an older couple entering the lift laughs in amusement.

In my room, I change into my pajamas and order more coffee. I'm too full of anticipation to sleep.

Sam can look at the bad and see the good.

Maybe he can do that with me, too.

---

"You work fast."

My jewelry is laid out on the dresser in my hotel room and I'm looking for earrings to wear with my green skirt and cream, sleeveless blouse. I pinned my hair up after my shower and my ears look bare.

Keaton didn't let me wear jewelry besides my wedding ring saying I was pretty enough without and that he didn't want other men looking at me. The simple truth was it was just another way for him to control me. The one time I dared defy him, he threatened to rip the earrings out of my ears unless I took them out, and I never wore jewelry of any kind ever again. Like Keaton's jealousy and the simmering violence in his touch, my inability to wear earrings, bracelets, and necklaces is just another thing I'll have to remember to forget.

"What do you mean?" I ask, choosing pearl earrings and a matching necklace.

Janelle huffs and there's a slight edge of envy to her tone when she says, "It's online. I saw it this morning while I was getting Mikey ready for school. You and Samuel Sharpe? Really? How did that happen? Does he know about Keaton?"

Slipping on cream pumps, I freeze. "You . . . saw it online? Already? We went out last night."

"Like I said, you work fast. You've been gone for two weeks and you land the catch of the century. I guess it's that wounded aura around you."

"He's had it worse than me," I murmur, a little put off by Janelle's attitude. We weren't great friends, but Keaton gave me permission to occasionally hang out with her because she's married to one of his detective buddies and it made us look like a normal couple. She never knew Keaton abused me, only that I wanted a divorce and to start over in a new town. I would cut ties, but I need her to tell me what Keaton is up to and if he ever leaves the city to look for me.

"The article mentioned he lost his wife. You looked nice, getting out of that limo. You sure moved up, that's all I can say."

That's all she *will* say, too. She's too bitter to be happy for me. "Do you think Keaton will see it?"

She scoffs. "Don't see why he would. I was scrolling social media while I waited for Mikey to eat his breakfast. Keat don't care about that kind of thing."

She's right about that, at least. Keaton doesn't care for gossip of any kind, and after we were married, I learned quickly to consume it on my work's computer using an incognito window. I wasn't allowed apps on my phone, and my own social media profiles stagnated.

"He's still going to work?" I try to sound nonchalant, not like I'm pumping her for information.

"Hmmm. They caught a murder two days ago and they're working with the NYPD. Looks like it could be a serial killer. He'll be wrapped up for a while, especially if the Feds get involved."

I relax. That's something. Keaton always loved a down and dirty murder to solve. He liked the gore, the way the victims were brutalized. Unfortunately, his grizzly interest in the way murders are performed gives him an edge, and at forty-five, he has the highest closed cases rate in the county.

"Thanks, Janelle. I appreciate the call. Really. But I need to get to work."

"I'd say take care of yourself, but I guess you're already doin' that. Bye, now."

"Bye," I say to the empty air.

I wish I didn't have to depend on her for news and that I had someone else I could talk to, but Keaton effectively cut me off from anyone else I could call, including my parents, and now that I'm not in New York anymore, there would be no point in trying to rekindle those relationships.

The sidewalks are clogged with people going to work, and I join them, waiting at a bus stop near the Regency. I like riding the bus. I can pick out the businessmen, the businesswomen, the nannies, and the college students. The little old ladies meeting their friends for coffee. Before I started applying for jobs, I rode around Carthage to familiarize myself with the city. Not only because I was curious, but also because I need to know where things are located if I ever need to hide. I hope it never comes to that, but in any case, my diligence paid off, and I know the exact bus and the exact route that will drop me off two blocks from Sam's offices.

What Sam will show me is personal.

I needed to see the practical.

The friendly man at the elevator bank who chatted with me yesterday tips his hat and presses the Up button for me.

"Have a good day," he says, and his good mood rubs some of Janelle's acerbic attitude away.

"You do the same," I say, stepping into the lift.

The SharperImage offices are still foreign to me, and I feel like a stranger as I walk to my desk and store my purse. Sam isn't in his office yet, and I head to the breakroom to make coffee. He never specifically asked me to make him coffee in the mornings, but I'm his assistant. I figure that's part of my job, and I don't mind.

I'm waiting for the carafe to fill when Samantha steps into the breakroom and instinctively, my muscles tense. If she doesn't like me or she thinks Sam and I are a bad idea . . . it's only been a day, but I like working here. I like Shiloh and her sense of humor, her willingness to show me things until I understand them because while I can do HR, PR work is out of my repertoire and her patience is a godsend.

"Miss Fowler," Samantha says, leaning against the counter. She's dressed in a dark cornflower blue suit that matches her eyes, and her hair is twisted into a bun at the back of her head. She's slim and a lot shorter than I am, but her features are kind and she carries herself like she cares about people. I wonder if that's the mother in her.

"I think you can call me Lily now," I say, staring at the coffee dripping from the basket of grounds into the carafe.

"Lily. It's a beautiful name."

"Thank you."

"You're welcome. Your date with Sam hit the gossip blogs this morning. I hope he warned you that would happen."

I lift a corner of my mouth. "Not exactly."

She rolls her eyes. "That's like Sam. Since Tabby died, he's been in his own world, and it hasn't been a happy one." Stepping closer, she says, "I know how you met—Sam and I tell each other pretty much everything—"

I wait for her to tell me not to break his heart or if I do, she'll find a way to make me pay, or to warn me off him completely, to tell me that I'm not good enough for her cousin, that I'll never measure up to his dead wife.

"—and I want to thank you for what you've done for him."

I jerk in surprise. "Really?"

"What did you think I was going to say? To stay away from him? I see the way he looks at you, I saw the way he was the week after your night together when he couldn't find you. I like you Lily, and I know you have your own secrets."

Parting my lips to object, she overrides me.

"I don't want to know them. They're between you and Sam, and maybe not even then if they won't affect what you two are building together. I just wanted to say thank you, and well, I hope that one day we can be friends. Tabby was my best friend. Sam wasn't the only one who was hurt when she passed away. She left a hole in our family, and I know for a long time, maybe right up until the second Sam met you, he believed it was too large to fill."

"Loss can feel like that," I agree, pulling SharperImage travel coffee mugs down from the cabinet Shiloh showed me yesterday during our break. I felt like that when my mother and father stopped talking to me, when my friends dropped off because I couldn't see them anymore. Like a tooth that's been pulled, the gums heal, but the hole still remains.

"Yes, it can. Sam's going to resist, but I hope you don't give up on him."

"Isn't it a little early to have a conversation like this?" I ask, pouring coffee.

Samantha looks at her watch, a simple gold timepiece encircling a dainty wrist. "It's not that early. I've already been up for—"

"I don't mean the hour. I mean my relationship with Sam. We just met. Don't you think we should get to know each other first?"

She lifts a shoulder. "I suppose, but I married my husband a month after we met. When you know, you know."

"It's not that simple." I want it to be. God, I would love it to be that simple, but I haven't thought about remarrying. In fact, my mother would call me a fool for jumping into bed with the first man I met, and I don't think she would be wrong. Sam came out of nowhere, and I haven't had time to process anything. Not the way my heart stutters when I see him or the way his kisses make me want more. Not the way he speaks about his wife with such a reverence I'm not sure he's over her, and if he's not, where that would leave me. Where that would leave me in his life, in his company. Maybe the one time in his hotel bed is all I'm going to get, scraps I would be happy to have because at least I know that at some point I'll be able to live my life despite what Keaton did to me.

Samantha looks down at her charcoal grey pumps. "I know."

My hands still over our mugs. "I don't know the way Sam likes his coffee."

"Some cream and a packet of sugar."

"Not black?" I ask in surprise.

"Ever since he was a kid, he's had a sweet tooth. I've never seen him drink a black cup of coffee." She clears her throat. "Shiloh's always late. She comes in after she drops her daughter off at school. Sam and I will be in meetings all day. You'll be all right?"

"I've always been just fine," I lie.

"Somehow, I think you have." She steps toward the break-room door then turns back around. "What are you doing Saturday? Would you like to go shopping?"

I want to decline. I have plenty of things I could do on Saturday, looking for an apartment is one, but making a friend, a true friend, should be high on my list of priorities. "I would like that."

"Good. Talk to you later."

"Yeah."

I carry the travel mugs to Sam's office, and he's pulling his suit jacket off and hanging it on the back of his desk chair. He's wearing a navy blue suit, a red, navy blue, and silver tie, and navy suspenders. Admiring the way his shoulders fill out his white dress shirt, I stumble, and I right myself while he lifts an eyebrow and scratches the back of his neck. "Good morning," he says, his voice laced with amusement. "Is one of those for me?"

"Yes. Samantha told me how to fix it."

"Thank you, but you don't have to. My previous PA made me fend for myself. I don't mind."

"I don't mind, either."

He tips his head in acknowledgement. "Then maybe we can take turns."

"Okay." I try to slip into a more professional role though I don't know what that is yet. "Samantha says you're going to be in meetings all day. I'll be working with Shiloh when she comes in."

"Good. We're trying to form a game plan for Allessandra Biggotti. She's flying into Carthage tomorrow with her handlers, but I have no idea what we can do for her. She's a mess. Maybe if you have time today you can dig around online, get a feel for the girl."

"Allessandra Biggotti, the singer?" She's the popstar of the moment, the radio playing her songs nonstop.

"The one and the same. She's got the energy to light up a thousand stadiums, but underneath it all, she's a burnt out candle flickering in the dark." He sinks into his chair and wiggles the mouse on his plain black mousepad to wake his computer. "Her misery is our gain."

"That's not true. You care about her."

He looks up at me, pain clear in his eyes. "I do, and I'll do everything I can." He pauses. "What are you doing after work?"

I pause. I should go back to the hotel, search for news and double check what Janelle told me this morning. "What were you thinking?"

"Dinner?"

"We already hit the gossip sites," I say lightly, but apprehension slithers around in my stomach again. Janelle's assurance calmed me for a little while, but I can't keep flaunting my relationship with Sam. It doesn't matter if I can't define what we're doing, how I'm feeling, or how he's feeling about me.

He drags his hands through his hair. "Fuck. I knew that would happen. Something lower key then. I told you I'd show you around. Do you like hotdogs?"

Caught off-guard, I laugh. "I could be persuaded to eat a hotdog."

"I'll meet up with you later then to hammer out a plan. Don't go back to the hotel until I catch you, okay?"

"Okay."

I start on the research Sam asked me to do, grateful I have something to keep my hands busy. I don't know if he needs me to, but I begin printing out articles describing Allessandra's wild and heartbreaking ways and collect them in a folder. I've printed out three and I'm drying my eyes when Shiloh hurries into the office and shoves her purse into her desk. "Just let me grab a cup of coffee. I need it!" she says, her hair bouncing around her shoulders, a cute floral scarf poking out from between the curls.

I sit with her for the rest of the day, and while we laugh over a harmless client who's made his share of mistakes, I relax. I'm making friends, Sam cares about me, and I happened to have found a job I like.

Moving to Carthage was the right move, and I pray nothing spoils it.

Shiloh has already gone for the day, but I stand at the printer as it spits out contracts for Samantha and Sam to sign. Together, we went through both Sam's and Samantha's emails and she gave me a list of things I needed to print. She's been holding my hand, and I appreciate it. I'm not above doing Shiloh's busywork.

The last contract is sliding out of the printer when I sense someone approaching me from behind. I'd grown very intuitive at knowing where Keaton was in our house. When we would be on the same floor or in the same room. Cooking was difficult because it meant I was turned toward the stove and it allowed him to sneak up on me. I have a scar on my arm where he crowded against me, and startled, I bumped the rim of a frypan. He wasn't sorry.

Sam presses against me, and stiffening, I struggle not to wiggle away. The printer can't hurt me and Sam would *never* hurt me. He buries his nose in my hair and encircles my waist with his hands.

"Is this appropriate workplace behavior?" I tease, pulling the last contract from the tray and adding it to the thin pile that will go into Samantha's and Sam's inboxes before I leave.

"No." He sounds like a sullen child and it's all I can do not to laugh. "But I want to do it anyway."

He nuzzles the soft skin of my neck and his touch sends shivers all over my body. I resist tilting my head to give him more room. I don't want to encourage him. Well, I do, but I shouldn't.

Finished with the printer, I turn around and face him. Whiskers are beginning to cover his jaw, and somehow, he rumpled his suit. Slight traces of aftershave linger on his skin, and I breathe deeply, scents of citrus and wood filling my nose, the pheromones doing their job, weakening my knees.

His eyes crinkle in amusement, and I think that's my most favorite thing about him. "You're thinking what I'm thinking."

My stomach chooses that moment to growl. I ate lunch with Shiloh and some of the other women in the office, the grumpy HR lady included, and I've never felt more welcome. Not even at the picnics and luncheons and fundraisers I had to attend with Keaton for the department. But lunch was a few hours ago. "I'm thinking about dinner, what about you?"

"Yeah, yeah, dinner. That's *exactly* what I was thinking about," he jokes, and I giggle. I honest to God giggle. What is this man doing to me? I'm not ready for it. "Do you want a ride to the hotel? We're going to walk a little and I think you'd be more comfortable if you changed."

"A hotdog? A walk? Are we going to a park?" I ask, inching away from him. I still have a couple things to do before I can go. Shiloh asked me to finish them, and I said I would.

"Your investigative skills are quite impressive, Miss Fowler. That is indeed what I had planned for tonight. Unless you've changed your mind."

"No, that sounds great, and you're right, I would like to change, but I can meet you. You have to go home and change clothes too."

"That's not—" He stops.

I head toward his office where I put a stack of contracts into his inbox, and with him following me down the hallway, I do the same in Samantha's.

"I think you like riding public transportation," he says when I reach my desk and pull my purse out of the bottom drawer.

I look up in surprise. "Why do you think that?"

"You like the freedom of it. The anonymity. You never rode

a bus where you lived before." His eyes narrow as he stares at me. "He wouldn't let you."

Gripping my purse, I shake my head. It's unsettling how much he knows when I've barely told him anything about my life. "He, he checked the miles on my car every day. He knew how many it took me to drive to work and home again."

The playful arousal flickers out of his eyes, but it doesn't turn them flat. They fill instead with compassion, sympathy, and if I'm not mistaken, understanding.

"Well, then," he says, gesturing toward the elevators, "far be it from me to keep you from something you enjoy. But after you change, can I pick you up? Just me."

Sam pushes the Down button, and the doors immediately slide open. He lets me step in first and then punches the button for the lobby. We start the slow decent, and he's careful to keep a half foot of space between us. We're alone and it would have been easy for him to crowd me, yet he seems to know when he can push and when it would be too much.

I want to thank him, somehow, and I tentatively place my hand in his. He presses a kiss to my temple and links our fingers.

"I would like that. I don't need long. The bus ride is fifteen minutes, then I'll need another fifteen to change."

The elevator doors slide open and we walk across the lobby. We untangle our fingers to use the revolving doors, but he grabs my hand again before I can step toward the street.

His car is idling at the curb, and he hesitates. I know he wants to ask me if I would reconsider, and I might have if my independence didn't mean so much to me. And I *do* like riding the bus. I feel safe sitting on a bench as the city streaks by. I like talking to the children, listening to the grandmothers reminisce.

Reluctantly, he nods, and I appreciate it when he doesn't try to change my mind. "I'll pick you up in forty-five."

"I'll wait outside so you don't have to come in."

"You don't—" he starts to protest, then sighs. "Thank you."

He pulls me to him as people eager to go home rush by us. His driver waits outside the car, his eyes fixed on something that isn't us.

Sam's steady, strong, his grip possessive. Words want to tumble from his mouth—I can tell by the way his lips tremble—and it fills me with immense relief, and not a small amount of disappointment, when he reins them in. The electricity, the spark, more like a lightning bolt, is there between us, but we're not ready. He couldn't have planned meeting me at the bar attached to the Regency. He couldn't have planned how good it would be between us when I let him take me to his room. He couldn't have planned this ribbon of pain would do more than tie us together.

We are unprepared, and I can't, I *can't* let a man bulldoze through my life again. I have to stay in control. I have to have fifty percent of this relationship under my control. If Sam overwhelms me and I lose myself again, I don't know if I'll have the energy to find my way out.

"Lily."

Giving in, I trace his lips, his skin smooth under my finger. "Sam. You're going to see me again in forty-five minutes."

"I'm that transparent, huh?"

"You're lonely."

"That's not the only reason I want to spend time with you."

Ignoring the warning my heart tries to convince me to heed, I whisper a kiss over his mouth. "I know. Goodbye, Sam."

To my surprise, tears fill his eyes. "Never say goodbye."

My own tears burn my throat. "I'll see you later," I amend.

He nods once, briskly, and releases me. He doesn't look back as he trots to the car or when his driver opens the back door. The tinted windows hide him, and I turn toward the bus stop.

His car melds into the traffic and that eerie feeling of someone watching me surfaces again. Maybe I should have accepted a ride after all, but I can't live in fear. Janelle, just this morning, told me Keaton is in the middle of a complicated investigation. He wouldn't be in Carthage spying on me. It's my own nerves, and I push them back.

I'm perfectly safe.

I reach the hotel without incident but five minutes behind. Quickly, I go to the bathroom and change into khaki capri pants, a white shirt I tie at the waist, and fasten my hair into a ponytail. I slip on light pink walking shoes that don't have laces. I don't want to carry a purse, and instead, I shove my wallet, hotel keycard, and phone into a small crossbody bag to keep my hands free. I'm looking forward to walking through the park with Sam. It will be nice to see trees and grass, familiarize myself so I can go alone. In the two weeks I've been in Carthage, I haven't seen the city park, or any park for that matter, and I skip through the lobby. The doorman holds the door open for me and I rush onto the sidewalk at the exact moment Sam pulls up to the curb in the fanciest Range Rover I've ever seen.

I yank my own door open. Keaton was only a gentleman in public.

This earns me as scowl from Sam. "I could have opened your door."

"Next time," I promise, buckling my seatbelt. "I love the color of this truck."

"It was Tabby's favorite color."

I turn in my seat to face him. This is going to happen for the rest of Sam's life. I can either be okay with it . . . or not. "She had good taste." I mean it in every way possible, but he scoffs, then smiles.

"She did."

Rush hour traffic is still in full swing, and we're driving for half an hour before Sam pulls onto a wide road. Trees line the paved path, some raining leaves in oranges and russets, scattering across grass that's a brilliant emerald green. After about a mile, the driveway opens into a large parking lot and Sam parks under a tree. He grabs my hand before I can jump out of the truck.

"You look pretty."

"Thank you. You look nice too. I don't think I've seen you dressed casually. I mean, clothing-wise," I say, fumbling. Naked is about as casual as you can get, but right now he looks especially delicious in dark denim jeans and a black cotton shirt, the sleeves rolled to the elbows revealing his strong forearms.

He chuckles. "Thanks. Let me get your door."

I unbuckle my seatbelt as he slams out of the truck and trots around the back. He opens my door, and we're eye-level. I could spend so much time staring into his eyes, searching out the pain, trying to devise ways to make it go away.

He helps me out with a hand to my arm, and he locks the doors with a fob that he tucks into his pants pocket. We walk close together, our arms brushing.

I look around in curiosity as we start on a paved trail. There are people with their dogs playing Frisbee, and several people running. Two kids and their mother are flying kites, and watching them, I miss mine. I wonder if she heard I left Keaton. If she has, she hasn't reached out, more proof I didn't need she's cut me out of life.

Sam leads me to a clearing full of picnic tables and food

trucks. "I thought we would eat first," he says, tucking a thumb into his pocket and giving me an amused smile. "I don't want to starve you."

"And I appreciate it." There are several trucks, all serving different kinds of foods, everything from tacos to barbecue to pizza. "Are you stuck on hotdogs?"

"I'll have whatever you're having. I'm not particular."

"I have a thing for pizza." I wait for him to tell me it's too fattening or there are better things to eat here. Keaton always had to degrade my choices, even if I chose something he would have too. He made me pick first, just so he could beat me down.

With a hand to the center of my back, he gently pushes me toward the Pia's Pizza truck. "Let's go for it. It's good."

I tamp back a smile and my guard crumbles a little more.

We order huge slices of thick crust, spicy meat lovers and two bottles of Perrier and find a place on the grass near a river, the wooden bridge rumbling whenever a biker would shoot across the planks.

"You said you aren't close to your parents. Why?" Sam asks, balancing his paper plate on a leg while he opens our bottles with a hiss.

I'm going to have to open up about Keaton sometime, and I poke at a piece of sausage. I don't want him calling me a stupid idiot, even if I am. "Because when I met Keaton, I introduced him to her and she didn't like him. She told me he was too overbearing, too arrogant. Asshole, I think she said at one point, but I was in love. All it did was make me mad at her. My dad took her side, of course, but he tried to reason with me."

"When did you meet him?" Sam asks around a mouthful of pizza.

I nibble on the crust of my slice. "We were married for five years, and we dated for a few months before that. So, yeah, I guess six years or so. I was thirty-three. I thought I was old enough to know an asshole when I saw one. I was wrong."

He glances at me. "How'd you meet?"

"I was a PA for a CEO who ran a chain of luxury department stores, and they partnered with the local fire and police departments to throw a huge fundraiser. I was in the parking lot helping supervise a bounce house when I bumped into him. Literally. I fell hard. I don't know what he saw in me. Someone to push around, more than likely, being as how I was so fast to fall on my ass." Yeah, there's some bitterness there. Directed at no one but myself.

"Well, firefighters are supposed to be every woman's fantasy. I should know. I had to watch *Backdraft* so many times I know every line."

He's trying to lighten the mood, and he does, a little. "Keaton isn't a firefighter. He's a cop."

Sam freezes, and nothing but cold rage sparks off his body. "You're telling me a man sworn to serve and protect *hit* you?"

I stare out over park, the setting sun catching the ripples in the water and turning them gold. "It's why I didn't believe my mother. He was a cop, for God's sake. He wasn't going to hurt me. I said he was intense, and tense, because of his work. Who wouldn't be? Being a cop is dangerous, I know that, and it's what made me excuse him time after time."

Sam lifts his hand and pauses near my face. He wants to touch me, but he doesn't want to scare me. I press his hand to my cheek, taking the decision away from him. I don't want to be afraid of his touch, but much worse, I don't want him to be afraid to touch me.

"Was it bad?"

"It wasn't *Sleeping with the Enemy* bad, speaking of old movies. He wouldn't go ballistic if I didn't iron the towels, but one night after a particularly nasty go-around, I realized anytime he put a hand on me, it was out of jealousy. He slapped me if my boss walked too close, or if one of his buddies during a work event talked to me for too long, that was my fault and he'd punish me for it. The worst time, the time that finally convinced me I had to leave, was when our young and good-looking UPS driver delivered a package and asked if he could use our bathroom. I thought nothing of it, but just then Keaton came home and he accused me of having an affair. I couldn't breathe for a month without it hurting."

"Jesus Christ. I'm sorry, Lily. Did you call your mother? How did you get help?"

"My boss knew something was going on, and I confided in him the first day I could go back to work. It was the most horrible day of my life. I had to trust someone, but in my mind, there was no one who wouldn't tell Keaton. He helped me find an apartment and paid his attorney to push the divorce through. Keaton's father was friends with the judge—golf buddies—and the judge managed to stall, ordering mediation meetings that Keaton never attended. That's why the divorce was only final a few weeks ago. He realized he couldn't keep me from divorcing him and finally signed."

I finish my pizza, and despite my depressing and shameful story, it's still good, and the lemon Perrier fizzes on my tongue. I ball my napkin in my fist, prop my chin on one of my knees, and watch the park slowly empty as evening falls over Carthage.

Sam sits, his knee bent, twisting his greasy napkin around his fingers.

We're quiet for so long the silence becomes uncomfortable. "You don't have to see me anymore. I can understand if you changed your mind."

Tentatively wrapping his arms around me, he pulls me to him. "Why would you say that?"

"It's what Keaton said, the last time I saw him. The day he gave me the bruise you saw on my cheek. It was at the court-house and I'd found an empty restroom. Keaton followed me down the hallway, and no one was around. He hit me and said, 'No one will ever want you, Lily. Any man worth a damn doesn't shop at thrift stores. You're secondhand goods, doll. Secondhand goods.' I never saw him again."

Sam sighs and adjusts his legs, framing me with his strong thighs. I rest my back against his chest.

"The day Tabby died," he starts, his voice low, "I laid with her in her hospital bed and the hospice nurses had to call the police to get me off her so they could take her body away. I refused to let her go. Someone, I don't know who, called Samantha. She brought me home with her, and after Tabby's funeral, I sat in her guest room in the dark for over a month. I couldn't eat, I didn't shower."

He stops, and I wipe the tears that start falling down my face.

"Everyone said I would eventually meet someone, that I would move on. It made me so angry. Why would I want to move on? Tabby was the love of my life, and she was gone. Two years went by and some days the hurt felt just as fresh as the day they took her body away. Then one night I go to a bar after work. I didn't want to go home, but I didn't want to bother Samantha and her family. My Mom and Dad mean well, but I'm tired of them fussing. I was looking for something. I don't know what."

The sounds of the park fade away. The children laughing, people chatting as they walk on the trail behind us. I sit. And I listen.

"I saw a woman sitting alone in a booth, staring so forlornly into her wineglass she could have been a mirror image of how I was feeling. I sat down with her, and something happened. I can't describe it. I thought, this woman understands me. I haven't spoken one word to her, but she understands. When she picked up her purse to leave, I had never felt panic so debilitating. I had to ask her to be with me, and miraculously, she said yes. I was a stupid son of a bitch and didn't get her name. Don't ask Samantha what I was like the week afterward." He blows out a breath, his chest expanding against my back. "You're not the only one who's been trampled on. You're not the only one who feels unfit for someone else because of your pain. If you take my secondhand heart, I'll take yours."

---

We finish walking around the park, and he shows me where an outdoor carousel sits near a playground and a small pond where people can buy pellets to feed the ducks.

His words touched me, and I want to believe everything he said. It would be easy to believe them, to make plans, but we haven't known each other long and while we're both in pain from previous relationships, we suffer in different ways that pull us apart as much as push us together.

If Tabby hadn't died, Sam would still be married to her, happily, planning a family through adoption, perhaps, or enjoying time with the families they already have. I still would have left Keaton. There's no changing who he is—violent, angry, abusive—and I would have been on my own.

Two years of mourning may feel like a lifetime to Sam, I know every second you're hurting can feel like years, but I'm more cautious now and don't trust he's over her. I have to protect my own heart. Keaton did enough damage.

Dusk is blanketing the city when we drive back to the hotel. Sam's tense, but there's a weariness under the nerves, and it sets my own nerves on edge. I can't expect every man I spend time with to be mellow or docile, or always in a good mood, but the energy thrumming through him isn't all positive and I twist my fingers in my lap needing space and room to breathe.

He grips the steering wheel and the pressure tightens the muscles in his arms. I choke back fear and lean closer to the door. I need to get out of the truck or I'm going to have a panic attack.

Flicking a glance at me, he frowns. "Are you okay?"

My voice trembles, but I try so hard to keep it from doing so. "You're scaring me."

He coasts to a stop at a red light a block away from the Regency and loosens his hands on the wheel. "I'm sorry. I . . . I'm trying to think of a way to ask if I can go upstairs with you. After what you told me tonight, I don't want to crowd you, Lily, but I . . . I don't want to go home alone."

I didn't know I was holding my breath, and it rushes out of me. I sag into the seat.

The light turns green, and he presses the accelerator, staring straight ahead. He's waiting for me to say no, and why do I feel like if I do, he'll sit up all night watching the lights streak across the walls, waiting for morning? It breaks my heart to picture him sitting in an empty room, maybe a glass of something in his hand, wishing like hell he was anywhere but where he was.

He'll miss the parking ramp if I don't answer him soon. I touch his forearm, his skin warm, his muscles rigid. My skin prickles with unease. Anger and I still have a long way to go before we can live peacefully with each other. "Of course you can. Sam, if there's anything I can ever do for you, all you have to do is ask."

Linking our fingers, he kisses the back of my hand. "Archer can bring a bag to your room, if that's all right. For work, in the morning."

I press my face into his shoulder, trying to hide a smile and failing. Waking up and getting ready for work together sounds good. Way too good. "I'd like that."

Sam turns into the parking ramp of the hotel and finds a parking spot on the second level. We sit in the dark between two SUVs, the fluorescent lights flickering above us. He unlashes his seatbelt and turns in his seat. "Thank you."

"There's no need for that," I say, slightly shaking my head.

"Maybe not, but I always want you to know I appreciate what you're doing, what you're giving to me." He brushes his lips over mine but opens his door before I can ask for more.

Anticipation crackles between us as we ride in the elevator to my floor. I'm tidy by nature, and I don't worry about him seeing a mess. I always hang up my clothes, put my jewelry away, throw wet towels into the hamper. House-keeping came while I was working earlier, and the bed is made, the carpet vacuumed. The room has a vague scent of air freshener when I push the door open, but I don't have time to analyze it.

Sam nudges me against the wall and covers my mouth with his, shoving his hand under my blouse, along my ribs. Keaton never brought violence to our bed, and if there's anything I can be grateful for, it's that. I can understand Sam's rough urgency for what it is: desire.

I kiss him back, letting his tongue slip into my mouth. There's a hint of pizza mingling with a taste that's all Sam. Slowly, I unbutton his shirt and splay my hands over his chest. He's strong, cut in a way you wouldn't think looking at him in a suit, and I would bet my first paycheck that after Tabby died, all he did was work out to the point of exhaustion in the hopes of a little sleep.

Reaching for the top button of my shirt, he drags his mouth away from mine. "Is this okay?"

"Yes," I hiss, raking my fingers through his hair and tugging his face closer to mine. "Kiss me."

He chuckles against my lips while undoing the buttons of my blouse. He unties the knot at my waist and with my shirt hanging open, cups one of my breasts through the satin and lace of my bra. I tip my head back and press into his touch. Heat and my own desire course through my body, and I can't think of anything but having him inside me.

"You don't know what a gift it is that you like me touching you," he murmurs, moving his fingers to the button of my capri pants.

"You don't know what a gift it is that you like touching me without wanting to hurt me," I counter honestly. "I didn't think I would want to be with someone so soon, but it's so easy with you."

"Christ, Lily," he growls, and he ravages my mouth, our teeth gnashing together.

Somehow, we make it to the bed, and he kicks his jeans across the floor while I peel the capris off my legs. He stands at the foot of the bed in his boxer briefs and black shirt that's hanging open and I have never seen anything so sexy before in my life. Keaton worked out to the point of obsession, but he never did to me what Sam does now, looking at me with his blue eyes full of awe and gratitude.

He swallows. "You'll tell me if I do something you don't like? I knew Tabby's body like I know my own—" Embarrassment reddens his neck and cheeks. I guess it's not very romantic to bring up your ex at every turn, but I forgive him. Keaton and what he did is never far from my mind, either, and it may be like that for a long time. I can't think it would be any different for Sam.

I push his shirt from his shoulders, and he lets out a shuddery breath. "Have you forgotten we've done this once before?"

"That was different. I didn't know what we were doing would turn into something so much more. And then when I couldn't find you, I—"

I press a finger to his lips. "We did find each other, and that's what matters most. But we have to be prepared for the fact this might not work. Tabby is always the first in your thoughts, and Keaton isn't that far behind in mine. If anything, he taught me to be realistic. It doesn't hurt so much then, when things go sideways."

He grips my shirt in his fist, wrinkling the cotton. "Lily."

"Please, Sam." I don't want him to promise me things he'll never be able to give me.

"No. There's no 'Please, Sam.' I know what I want. I've known it since the minute I asked you to the suite I keep upstairs. If you have doubts, if you need to go slow, then say so, but don't put this on me because I was married for longer than you. Our marriages both ended in disaster, and yes, we're both still healing, but why does that have to break us up? Why can't we heal together and let it bring us closer?"

All I can do is stare. He sounds so sure. So sure after a few days with me.

Drawing my blouse down my arms, he says, "Look, if you need an out, I'll give you one. Take the same three months we're giving you at the office. Temp-to-hire. If, in those three months, you don't think it will work out there, or here with me, go. You leaving me can't hurt any more than I've already been hurt. But, if you think it will work, sign on the dotted line and *stay*."

He drops my shirt onto the floor and I'm standing in nothing but my bra and panties, my hair pulled back until he tugs the elastic from my ponytail and the waves fall around my shoulders.

"Christ, you're beautiful," he says, and reaches around my back and unhooks my bra.

The only light in the room is seeping around the edges of the curtains, and it's just enough for him to see by. He's hard, staring at my semi-nude state, and with his eyes boring into me, I undress the rest of the way, wiggling out of my panties and tossing them near the rest of my clothes.

He throws the extra pillows onto a nearby chair and yanks the comforter halfway down the mattress. The only thing left are his briefs, and he takes them off and throws them on top of his shirt.

I swallow, having the same reaction I did before. Sam's *huge*, and in the light, it doesn't seem real he can fit inside me, except that he has, and it felt right. He never hurt me, my body accepting him like he was made for me.

I don't realize I'm frozen to the floor until he says, "We've done this before," with a quirk of his lips.

That urges me forward, and I crawl into bed with him, the smooth, cool sheets feeling luxurious against my skin. Sam reaches for me and cuddling me close, nudging my thighs apart, not wasting a second. His fingertips flutter over my seam, delicately exploring, until he finds what he's looking for, wet and hot.

I don't want him to have all the fun, and as he pushes his fingers inside me, I hold his cock, squeezing his rigid length. He hisses out an impatient breath while I moan.

His thumb finds my clit, and I try to move away. "Sam."

He stills. "You don't want to come?"

"Not yet, not so soon."

"You want to play?" he asks and licks at my lips.

"Like what?" I'm guarded. Games mean different things to different people.

Sam settles onto his back and nudges me on top of him, his

cock nestled between my legs. "I've always preferred mission-ary. I like doing all the work, and when I have a woman under me, I feel protective, but maybe it's time I try new things. Lift up."

I raise myself up onto my knees, and he positions the tip of his cock at my opening.

"Like this? Is this okay?" I ask, slowly sheathing him. He stretches me, and I sink, inch by inch, his fingers digging into my thighs as he tries to keep control.

"Only a fool would say no," he mutters, squeezing his eyes shut. "Give me a second, sweetheart."

I wiggle, adjusting around him, my hands braced against his chest. It's been many years since I've been on top during sex. Like Sam, Keaton needed the control, but not to feel protective. He wanted the power, knowing I was trapped underneath him. The tip of Sam's cock pushes against the center of my body in a way that hurts but feels good, too.

His eyes flutter open and his hands move from my thighs to my waist. "I could get used to this," he says, yanking me down as he thrusts his hips upward.

I gasp, the pain quick and sharp, and he stops. "Did I hurt you?"

"Yes. No. Just a little." I rise on my knees and then slowly sink down, letting my body adjust to his size.

Sam moves his hands higher and gently tugs at my nipples. The slight pleasure-pain zings to my core and my muscles clench around his cock. "Do you like that?" he asks through clenched teeth.

"Yes," I say, my breasts heavy, my nipples stinging.

"Good. I want to watch you come," he says, moving my hand from his chest and positioning my fingers between our bodies.

"Sam, I've never—" I've never gotten myself off in front of

anyone before, and embarrassment stains my cheeks. I hope he can't see it.

"There's nothing to be ashamed of. Feel me inside you. Feel what you do to me, Lily."

I explore the base of his shaft, my mound swollen with arousal and his cock buried inside me. My clit is slick and huge, and I circle it while bearing down, filling myself with Sam. He focuses his attention to my breasts, pulling and rolling my nipples, squeezing them.

"Make yourself come all over my cock. I want to feel how much you want me."

I tip my head back and rub my clit as I ride him.

The shame of pleasuring myself in front of him disappears when he says, "You're a goddess, Lily. Gorgeous." He jerks his hips upward, slamming the tip of his cock into my core, and the pain sends me over.

The orgasm almost hurts, Sam's cock filling me to the brim.

He doesn't give me time to catch my breath. The second the last wave of my climax rolls through me, I'm on my back, Sam's arms braced alongside my head, and he's moving in long, even strokes, building and building until he's hammering into me. I want to feel him come, and I lift my hips, encouraging him to go as fast and as hard as he needs to.

With a hand under my ass, he holds me still and comes, shooting hot gobs of semen deep inside me. He groans, and a drip of sweat runs off the tip of his nose and lands on my cheek.

I give him more time than he gave me, skimming my fingers up and down his back as he pants. "There's something to be said for trying something new," he finally says, his voice raspy and amused.

"You always did missionary?" Trying to keep out the past will be our downfall.

"Always. Tabby needed . . . that part doesn't matter. What

about you and good ol' Keaton?" Still connected, Sam lowers himself onto me, careful not to crush me. "He did make love to you, didn't he?"

"When does having sex stop and making love start?" I ask, brushing his damp hair off his forehead and out of his eyes.

"The second you start to feel things. Like the way I started feeling things at Sargento's. I knew that night the next time we did this, it would be making love."

My eyes fill with tears. "Sam."

"You and Keaton?" he prompts.

"Then I don't think he ever made love to me. He felt things, but nothing like this."

"I'm sorry." He softly presses his lips to mine, lowering his body even closer. His cock grows inside me, and while he's on top, we make lazy, tender love.

I wrap my arms around his neck. I'm too spent to come again, but he does, though this time not as forcefully, and when he pulls out, I whimper. I'm sore and the friction burns.

"Did I hurt you?"

"No. It wasn't you. I'm not used to it."

"I was too rough. It's been a long time and I forgot to be gentle. I'm sorry. It won't happen again."

I reach out and touch his arm, not liking what's slithering in his eyes. "No. I liked every single second."

My words don't soothe him, don't reassure.

"There's nothing you can't tell me, Lily. I mean that. I need to know if I hurt you so I don't do it again." He tucks me into his side.

"There's nothing you can't tell me, either. I'd rather know the ugly truth than be told a pretty lie."

"I promise."

He falls asleep, his lips pressed into my hair.

Trying not to disturb him, I set my alarm on my burner

phone for six. I don't know what time he wants to be at work, and in the morning, we'll have to share a bathroom.

I'm dozing, and my hair and pillow muffle his voice. I'm not sure if I hear him correctly when he says, "I love you . . ."

I try to forget about it, write it off as our pasts that can't leave us alone, but it eats at me.

My name didn't sound like my name. It sounded like he said, "I love you, Tabby."

I remind myself what I told him. I'd rather know the ugly truth than be told a pretty lie. I just didn't think he'd take me up on it so soon.

Sometime before the sun comes up, we make love, and it feels like a dream, Sam filling me, his lips on my skin, but I'm sleeping in the next second. When I wake again, it's to the scent of coffee and the shower running.

Sam sips on a cup of coffee while he shaves and dresses in a crisp suit his driver left at my door sometime last night. I'm still lying in bed trying to wake up enough to drink a cup of coffee without sloshing it all over myself.

He sits on the edge of the bed and offers me a slice of bacon. "You're okay getting to work? I know you like taking the bus, but I can send a car for you. As my PA, you have the right to one anyway."

I narrow my eyes. "You just made that up."

Laughing, he pushes the piece of bacon between my lips, and I have no choice but to open my mouth. "I did, but I'm the boss so it's my prerogative."

Crunching, I say, "Go. I'll be fine."

"If you're sure. Remember, Allessandra Biggotti today. And please, don't ask for her autograph."

I mockingly gasp, a hand to my heart. "I'd never be so crass."

"Just thought I'd throw it out there. Not everyone has class —or common sense. I'll see you later."

I'm not offended. I'm sure most new hires *are* starstruck during their first weeks at SharperImage. I catch his arm. "Did you really mean what you said? About no goodbyes?"

He leans over and kisses my forehead, inhaling deeply, then exhaling, his breath fanning my face. "I've said enough good-byes to last a lifetime. I don't want to say them anymore."

"Nothing lasts forever. You'll see Tabby again one day."

"Then I hope to God she forgives me." He crushes his mouth to mine, but before I can adjust, sink into the kiss, he's gone, the door clicking shut behind him.

---

I shower with a sinking heart that I try not to let get the better of me. This relationship will be a journey. I can hear my mother telling me in her not-so-subtle way that I don't need any more journeys, and if I do go on one, go alone. I lean against the shower wall, steam billowing around me, the scent of Sam's body wash permeating the wet air.

She wouldn't be wrong. I needed more time to myself, but I'm in it now. When Sam told me he was making love to me, I wanted to believe it with everything I still had because I was making love to him, too.

I dress with care in a teal pencil skirt and a sleeveless blouse that has matching teal buttons running down my back. I don't want to look like a stick in the mud around Allessandra and her team. They chose SharperImage because they're trendy, know what's coming, and can spin black and white into neon color. I'm part of the team now, if I choose to be, and I don't want to let Sam down. I wear my hair in a twist and have a heavier hand with my makeup. My heels are a little higher too, but I pack flats in a larger bag the color of my skirt just in case I need to change. Despite it being my third day on the job, I feel like a professional who has a handle on things, and on the bus, I tip my head at tired businessmen who won't waste good money to take a taxi to work every day. Those are the men I should be after, my mother would say. Men who earn a steady paycheck and know the value of a savings account. Who want to play t-ball with their kids, who get excited for family road trips to see the Grand Canyon.

Keaton blew me away with his looks and dangerous charm. I only saw the outside, not the inside, where things matter most.

Shiloh isn't in yet when I step into the office suite. Samantha careens around a corner, her heels skidding, and disappears into Sam's office. He's already been here for an hour, and after storing my purse, I go to the breakroom. The carafe is barely warm, and I start a fresh pot, grateful I have something to do.

Sam didn't say how big of an account Allessandra Biggotti is or if SharperImage caters to clients even more famous than her. I know, just from listening to gossip and being a fan of her music, she's on par with Britney Spears, Ariana Grande, and Taylor Swift, and to me, that's pretty damned big.

I fix Sam's coffee the way he likes it and carry two travel mugs to his office. His door is open, and he's hunched over his desk, Samantha peering over his shoulder, pointing to something on a piece of paper.

"I brought you some coffee," I say, hating to interrupt but not knowing what else I should do.

Sam gestures for me to step into the room. "Thanks. Mine's cold. Thanks for the work you did yesterday and the articles you printed. Driving while intoxicated, smashing into a car that had children inside. She's lucky she didn't kill anyone."

I set his coffee on his desk, and he gulps, downing half the mug. Samantha looks between us as if trying to gauge our relationship, but he's too focused on Allessandra's file to give off any vibes.

"*We're* lucky she didn't kill anyone," Samantha corrects. She smiles faintly at me. "You look nice."

"Thanks." I smooth my skirt with a damp palm and sip my coffee.

The elevator dings its arrival to our floor, and we can hear the doors slide open.

"It's showtime," Sam says, standing from behind his desk.

"What? Now?" I ask, startled. I was under the impression they were flying in from somewhere like New York or LA.

"They came in yesterday afternoon. Allessandra's horrible to deal with on a good day. No one does business with her when she's jet-lagged. Even by a couple of hours."

"Oh. Good luck." I wish I had more to contribute, but I know next to nothing about public relations and what Sam's plan of attack consists of.

"You're with me."

"What?" My tongue is glued to the roof of my mouth.

Sam quirks an eyebrow. "Didn't I tell you that part? Well, I'm telling you now. Come on."

I look at Samantha, but all she does is shrug. She doesn't seem angry Sam's including me, but if given the choice, I would have bowed out.

"Gary, nice to see you again, though I wish it could be under more pleasant circumstances," Sam says, striding across the empty floor and greeting a rotund man sporting thick, black-framed glasses and a goatee. "Allessandra."

It's then I get a glimpse of the young girl. Waif-thin, dirty blonde hair hanging down to her waist, she hides behind Gary, whoever he is. Her manager, maybe. Two older people also step around the corner, and Sam pauses.

"Mr. and Mrs. Biggotti. I wasn't informed you'd be here," Sam says, shaking their hands.

Allessandra moves off to the side, and I want to wrap my arms around her. She looks like she doesn't belong, when really, this whole thing is for her. Because of her.

"We have refreshments set up in the conference room," Samantha says smoothly, shaking everyone's hands, including Allessandra's.

It's difficult for me to believe this is the girl who sets stadiums on fire, though I don't mean literally—arson wasn't on the list of things that has gotten her into trouble. Her tickets sell out in minutes. Scalpers resell them online for thousands of dollars. A world tour hangs in the balance while she awaits a court date. And she stands there, chewing on a fingernail.

I lag behind the group as we walk down the hall to the conference room. A conference room I've only seen in passing my first day on the job.

Allessandra eyes me, her Converse sneakers scuffling along the carpet. Her jeans have so many holes I'm surprised they stay on her legs. She's wearing a sweater I saw in a fashion magazine's ad, holes in the material that are supposed to be there, and I shake my head in bafflement. Her outfit costs more than what Sam will pay me in a month, and I signed on with a very lucrative salary.

Neither Sam nor Samantha sit at the head of the table, preferring to sit across from each other. Allessandra's parents sit next to Samantha, and Gary claims a chair next to Sam. That leaves me at the end of the conference table with Allessandra. I take a chance she likes coffee and pour her a mug from the service that has somehow appeared in the middle of the table. A large tray of donuts, danish, and coffee cake is positioned near the coffee carafes, and using the plastic tongs provided, I add a donut iced with chocolate and covered in colorful sprinkles. I serve them to her and push a cream and sugar service in her direction.

Samantha and Sam wait, and he meets my eyes. As his assistant, pouring coffee is my job, and I do, filling all the mugs at the table like the waitress I was in college, my hand steady. When I move to the head of the table to fill Sam's and Gary's mugs, Sam brushes my wrist with a slight touch of his fingertips.

"Thank you. This is Miss Fowler, my new assistant. She's sitting in to get her feet wet. I hope you don't mind." His tone suggests he doesn't care if they do. This is a side of Sam I haven't seen, haven't needed to see. He's all business.

Allessandra adds cream and so much sugar to her coffee I wince. I slide into my chair and give her a small smile. She doesn't return it.

Sam covers his fist with his other hand and rests his chin on his knuckles. "Allessandra. What can we do? We want to help you."

"Your job," Allessandra's father spits, "is for you to get rid of it, and get rid of it now. She has a world tour in two months. Two months, and no one will show up with that fucking video everywhere. People are already refunding their tickets, and after this, no one will insure us. No one. Say goodbye to another tour, Allessandra, because that's where this is headed."

I watched the video he's referring to, the one a passenger in another car recorded once he realized the drunk driver was none other than Allessandra Biggotti.

The video has been viewed millions of times all over social media inducing outcries of support as well as demands for justice for the family whose lives she almost destroyed.

"We can't make this go away—" Sam starts.

"That is *not* what we pay you for!" Mr. Biggotti's face turns red.

"You need to take a deep breath—" Gary says, holding out his hands.

"Where were you?" Mr. Biggotti hollers, saliva flying out of his mouth. His wife cowers by his side, and I want to mimic her in an ingrained reaction to a male's anger. "You're her manager for Christ's sake. What are we paying *you* for, if you can't handle a twenty-one year old girl?"

"I have other clients—" Gary tries to defend himself.

Mr. Biggotti scoffs.

I inch my chair toward Allessandra who's watching everyone, her eyes darting from person to person, her hands wrapped around the black SharperImage mug.

"We're not going to get anywhere until we understand what's going on with her," Samantha says. "If we don't talk to her, we'll find ourselves in a similar situation all the sooner."

"You'd like that, wouldn't you?" Allessandra's father says, jabbing a finger in the air. "I'm aware of your client roster. We're your biggest moneymaker."

Sam sets his jaw. "I don't know how you can possibly accuse us of such a thing after what Samantha and I just said."

Allessandra's eyes fill with tears and I can't listen to this anymore.

I stand and hold her clammy hand in mine. "Excuse me. I'm going to show Allessandra the cafeteria. I think she needs some air."

Mr. Biggotti drills holes in me with his hateful stare. If looks could kill, I'd be nothing but ash on the floor. "Who in the hell do you think you are?"

"She's my assistant, and Allessandra has no business listening to this." Sam meets my eyes. "Go."

I tug on Allessandra's hand, and she pushes away from the table and follows me out of the conference room.

Two bodyguards I didn't notice earlier flank the elevator, and they escort us to the cafeteria on a lower floor. I've only been once with Shiloh, but I find it easily and a few moments later we're seated at a window table sipping hot chocolate and poking at chocolate chip muffins. The guards stand by the cafeteria doors allowing us to talk in private.

"I'm sorry about that," I say, dipping a spoon into the mound of whipped cream in my mug.

"Don't be. I'm used to it." Her voice comes out in barely a whisper.

"Your dad," I ask carefully, "he's in control?"

"It's always about money. More money, and then more. Do you know how I got started in this business?"

"I have to admit I don't." I didn't get that far into my research.

In mock shock Allessandra slaps her hands to her cheeks and lets her mouth drop open. "Someone doesn't know? Holy shit. I'll tell you. I was a weirdo in kindergarten, singing, joking, always trying to make people laugh. My dad saw it and thought I had a chance to make it big, so we moved to LA from a little bumfuck town in Michigan. We found an agent and started making the rounds, and it wasn't long before I was cast as the little sister on *McKayla and Me*. Have you heard of that, at least?" she asks, but she doesn't sound mean about it. I'm just another adult who doesn't know much about anything.

Nodding, I say, "Yeah." The series catapulted the girl who played McKayla to fame, and she fizzled out just as quickly as several other child stars.

"After that, I was in, and I haven't had a day off since."

"Like Miley Cyrus and *Hannah Montana*."

"Yep."

Allessandra leans her head against the window, Carthage spread out before us.

"What would you do then? If you had the freedom?"

She glares at me. "Besides take a fucking vacation?"

"In addition to that."

"I've been lucky, thanks to my dad, I guess, but he's never let up, not for one fucking second. I always felt like he was living through me, like *he* was the one who wanted to be the star." She sighs. "I never did small concerts. I envy those singers who start out in the food courts at the mall, state fairs, the dive bars. Places where I could talk to people. Where they'd treat me as a human being and not some freak on stage."

"You're not allowed to do small concerts? Because of the money," I guess.

"Yeah."

"What does your manager say?"

"He wants me to do the huge concerts, of course."

I rip a piece of muffin off with my fork. "Do you do any charity work?"

"I think my dad gives some money away." She shrugs.

"What if you did small concerts—"

Her eyes light up.

"—but," I caution her, "at first they probably won't be the way you want. Carthage has a large children's hospital and their cancer center is full right now. I bet the patients there could use a pick-me-up. What if Mr. Sharpe could work out that kind of thing for you? I know it's not what you had in mind, but if you can do some good with the smaller shows, it would be a win for everyone."

Allessandra taps her feet under the table. "I would really like that. Everywhere has a hospital, don't they?"

"They do. Gary could arrange other kinds of smaller bene-fits for you, like foster kids who need help and kids with terminal sicknesses who would like to meet you as their last wish through the Wishing on a Star program. There are so many ways you could do good."

"I love it!"

She hops off her seat, runs around the table, and gives me a hug. She feels bony in my arms, and I'm reminded she's just a child. Only, she's not.

"Mr. Sharpe will spin this, you know. He'll have to. What you did has severe consequences, and people might accuse you of doing these concerts to get out of trouble. If you want to be treated like an adult, you're going to have to start acting like an adult. If you want people to listen to you, then you have to speak like an adult."

Allessandra sits in the chair next to me instead of across the table. "I know, but you heard them. How can I get them to listen to me when they won't listen to each other?"

"I think today is about damage control. Your dad and Gary aren't unreasonable all the time, are they?"

A corner of her mouth pulls down. "I guess not."

"If you're serious about being heard, you'll have to show them you're growing up. You've been in trouble off and on for years. It will be up to you to teach them that you're trying to be different, and they'll come around. It won't be easy, and it might take some time, but have patience and things will work out."

She reaches across the table and slides her muffin to her. "Mr. Sharpe likes you. He couldn't stop staring at you up there. Are you sleeping with him? He's hot." She wrinkles her nose. "But he's too old for me."

"He gave me a chance when he didn't know if he could count on me. He trusts me and I don't want to let him down," I tell her honestly. I don't want her to think everything will be perfect when she's older.

"Why would you do that? Let him down, I mean."

"My ex-husband convinced me I wasn't any good, just like the adults in your life have made you think you aren't worth anything but the money you bring in." I'm guessing, but the tears that fill her eyes confirms I hit my target. "He's trying to help me see I'm worth something as a person, that I can be valued even if my ex-husband didn't. You're more than your voice, Allessandra. You have the power, grow up and use it."

Her voice trembles. "Will you help me?"

"I'll help you, and so will Samantha and Sam."

A bodyguard approaches our table, the earpiece fitted into his ear barely visible. "They want you upstairs."

"We're ready, aren't we, Allessandra?" I squeeze her hand.

"Yeah. Yeah, I am." She smiles at the bodyguard. "Thanks, Tim."

His eyes widen and he steps back.

She looks at me, chagrined. "I've always hated them. That's another part of growing up. Learning to accept that they've kept me out of trouble because I wasn't grown up enough to do it for myself."

"Nice start." Collecting our dishes, I flick a glance at Tim. "We'll be right there."

He nods.

The conference room's atmosphere has cooled off, and while I stand by her side, Allessandra outlines what we talked about in the cafeteria. The smaller concerts, especially for sick children. That she's more than just her voice, and if they'll treat her as more than that, she'll treat them like peers. That she's burnt out and needs a vacation. That she's lonely, something she adds on her own, and somehow needs time, space, and opportunities to date.

The entire time I stand by her side, my hand resting on her

shoulder, and as she speaks and everyone in the room listens, her confidence grows.

"What she needs—" her father starts, and I bristle, his arrogant attitude rubbing me the wrong way.

"Is an advocate," I say, glaring at him and her mother. "She's your daughter. When is enough going to be enough?"

"Miss Fowler's right," Sam says, leaning back in his chair. "Allessandra can sing for the rest of her life. She has the spark and the drive. Stevie Nicks, Pat Benatar, Joan Jett. But if she burns out and lands in jail, *prison*, it's over. Give her a break, Mr. Biggotti, or you'll regret it."

Mr. Biggotti and his wife have the grace to blush, and Allessandra relaxes.

"We can put together a concert at the children's hospital for later this afternoon. We'll have to spin it, Allessandra. Your intentions are pure, I get that, but for now we have to use that to our advantage too, okay?" Sam says mildly, meeting Allessandra's eyes.

"Miss Fowler warned me you would have to do that. It's okay. I'll be doing it because I want to, but it will look like I'm just trying to save my reputation."

"Good." Sam looks at me. "Shiloh knows the drill, and after you explain what we need, she'll walk you through how to put something like this together."

"Sure." I sweep the table. I'm dismissed, but I want to say goodbye. "It was a pleasure meeting all of you."

Allessandra grabs my arm when I step toward the conference room door. "Thank you, Miss Fowler. And your ex-husband sounds like an asshole."

I laugh. "He was. You're going to be okay, sweetie. Take care of yourself."

I let myself out of the room and once the door clicks behind me, I sag against the wall. It's been so long since I've stuck up for myself, or for anyone, and my blood pressure spiked going toe to toe with Allessandra's parents and manager. I couldn't let them trample all over the poor girl. Sam would have done what he could, but they needed a fresh perspective, and I was more than happy to give them one.

Shiloh's sitting at her desk, and after I explain what we need, she conferences me in on a phone call to the children's hospital. They're only too happy to accommodate Allessandra Biggotti and a benefit she's willing to do for the patients, even with such a last-minute notice. After that's scheduled, Shiloh shows me how to email Sam and Samantha the contact information for the PR director at the hospital and the time we agreed upon. She helps me type up what I remember from the meeting in a meeting notes template—also what Allessandra and I talked about in case we need it for future reference—and after we finish, we both sit back and sigh.

She's so friendly and unassuming, but I ask tentatively, "You don't mind I was included in the meeting?"

Waving a hand, she says, "Not in the slightest. I've been Samantha's assistant for years and I don't want a promotion. I've seen it all and don't need any more than that. I understand why Sam wanted you in there, and it sounds like you did the entire company proud. I'm happy for you, Lily."

"Thanks."

"In fact, after we order lunch for them, let's go celebrate. They'll be in there until they have to leave for the hospital and won't need us for the rest of the day."

"Are you sure?" Leaving, even for lunch, doesn't feel right, but it makes sense they'll be busy putting other aspects of Allessandra's damage control into motion.

"Positive."

"Then I'm in."

Shiloh shows me how to order food for the group and how

to bill it to the expenses account, and after we let the delivery staff into the conference room and everyone is settled into the working lunch, Shiloh and I walk down the street to a fancy little coffeeshop.

On the way back to the office, she answers a phone call from her child's school, and I think back to the morning I debated doing the interview at SharperImage. Where would I be now if I hadn't? If I'd told Dottie I didn't want to work in PR? The idea swims sickeningly around in my stomach. I may not have seen Sam again. I may not have discovered PR could be so rewarding. I got a thrill helping Allessandra, and I want to keep doing more of that.

What if I hadn't moved to Carthage at all? What if my mother and I hadn't been fighting and I hadn't needed to move here to feel closer to her?

I sit with Shiloh for the rest of the afternoon, pushing down a feeling of dread. I *did* go to the interview, and Sam *did* come back for me after he threw me out of his office. I *did* move to Carthage in the first place, and it opened up a whole new world. I can stop feeling queasy. Things are good.

The group bursts out of the conference room a little after three. Allessandra spies me stepping out of the restroom and she swoops into my arms for a hug. "We're stopping at the hotel so I can change, then we're going to the hospital. Thank you for everything you did, Miss Fowler. I think we're finally going to start listening to each other."

"That's great. Go get it."

"Thanks."

She darts off, speaking animatedly with Gary.

Sam disappears into his office, and Samantha hides in hers, muttering, "I need a drink."

Shiloh and I laugh.

A moment later an internal message pings Shiloh's computer. *Can you send Lily in here, please?*

*Right away, Mr. Sharpe,* she messages back.

I swallow. I overstepped, and now Sam's mad. "Time to face the music."

Shiloh frowns. "Why do you say that?"

"Because I stuck my nose into his business. I had no right to talk to Allessandra and her team that way."

"You know Sam's not like that, Lily. If he hadn't wanted you to talk to her, he wouldn't have let you take her to the cafeteria alone. It's okay."

I try to see reason in what she said, but I'm a panicky mess when I reach Sam's door. I poke my head around the doorjamb, and I scuttle into his office, the apology tripping off my tongue. "I am so sorry—"

"Shut the door."

My hand shakes as I do what he says.

He stands, rounds his desk, and leans against the edge. "Come here."

"Sam, I can explain—"

"Come here, Lily," he says softly, and tentatively, I approach him. "Farther."

I'm standing in front of him, and I can't go any farther unless I stand between his legs.

"Come."

My skin blazes with his command. It's not what he means, but unbidden, images flit through my mind of us making love this morning before work.

I study the planes of his face, his tired eyes, his strong nose, the clean lines of his jaw. He's handsome, sexy, and he scares me to death. "No."

He closes the gap, gently wrapping an arm around my waist

and resting his hand on the nape of my neck. My heart thrums in fear, and a trickle of sweat runs down my stomach from underneath my breast. I'm trying so hard not to shake, to not look like I'm afraid.

Keaton always knew when I was, and he twisted it, played with it. The ultimate game of cat and mouse.

I can't stop it, and a tear drips down my cheek.

Sam nudges me closer and kisses the tear away. "Do you know how difficult it is to see you all day and not be able to touch you?" he murmurs against my skin. Maybe he doesn't know how freaked out I am, or maybe he does and he doesn't want to give my fear validation by acknowledging it. He rubs the pad of his thumb over my jaw as he holds me.

I shake my head. I can't speak. Tears and terror are bottled up in the back of my throat.

"When I'm angry, I'll use words, Lily. I've never raised my hand to anybody or anything, ever. Do you know why I asked you to come into my office?"

I stare at our feet, trying to block him out.

"To ask if you wanted to go to the children's hospital with me to watch Allessandra sing."

In shock, I lift my head. "That's it?"

"That's it. I'd ask you to dinner too, but I'm not sure how much of your time I should be claiming for myself. I'm sure you have things to do when you're not at work."

"I thought you were mad I interfered."

"No. She's performing because of you. We never would have gotten that far with her if it hadn't been for you. Her father is an overbearing asshole and we wouldn't have been able to have a civil conversation if you hadn't taken her to the cafeteria. You did good."

"I'm sorry." This is Sam. I don't have to explain.

"There's nothing to apologize for. We haven't known each other long and I'm rushing you. If this is going to work, we need to talk to each other. I will always, *always*, tell you when I'm angry, and you always need to tell me if I'm crowding you. Please."

I nod, and feeling like I need to repay him for his kindness, for his patience, I reach for the buckle of his belt. My body is the only thing I can give him.

He stops me, lifts my hand to his mouth, and kisses my fingertips. "I've never made love in my office, and you're not in any frame of mind to have sex, make love, or anything in between. I'll never take when you can't give."

With a cry escaping from between my lips, my adrenaline crashes and I sag into his body. His strong arms are the only thing that keep me on my feet.

His hand rubs gentle circles over my back. "Shh."

Time slips by as he holds me, but eventually, I feel his body shift. "We need to go if we're going to be on time. She stopped by her hotel room to change. If we leave now, we'll arrive at the hospital a few minutes ahead of them. Did you want to go?"

I lean away and wipe my damp palms over my face. "I would like to go. And dinner, if that's still an offer?"

He tilts his head. "It is, but as tempting as it will be to spend the night again, I'll go back to my own place when we're done." Sighing, he says, "Why does it feel like we've known each other for a million lifetimes? And why doesn't that scare me more?"

"Because there are worse things to be scared of."

"And you and I both know what they are. Be brave?" he asks, his lips centimeters from mine.

I don't understand the request as I don't have anything to fear from him, but I say, "I'll try."

"Good girl. Let's go." He brushes his lips against mine.

Shaky, clammy, my stomach still churning, I follow him out of his office.

On the way to the hospital, he holds my hand, and there is nothing he could have done that would have reassured me more.

---

The children's hospital is an enormous building, a gigantic statue of Alice in Wonderland sitting in the pristine yard near the main entrance.

News vans are packed in the visitors parking lot, but not a reporter or cameraman is to be seen. They're all inside waiting for Allessandra to appear. Shiloh and I were the ones who called the news stations. As much as Allessandra wanted it to be a small, private concert, everything she does until her reputation is back on track will be examined, weighed, and tallied in the pro or con columns.

Sam parks in one of the last remaining spots and we enter the children's hospital through the front doors. There's an excited electricity buzzing around the corridors, and we follow the brightly colored signs to the cancer wing.

We take an elevator to the fifth floor where nurses rush by us wearing cheerful scrubs, and even some children dressed in pajamas "walk, not run" down the hallways, joyous smiles on their faces, their feet wanting to move so much faster than their manners will let them.

In the middle of the wing, the hallways open up to a large sitting area near floor-to-ceiling windows and a coffee bar positioned against the wall.

Children are already waiting impatiently and expectantly for their popstar idol to appear and treat them to the concert of a lifetime. They sit in wheelchairs, some eagerly perch on cushioned chairs meant for visitors, and others too sick to stand or sit are wheeled into the area lying in their hospital beds. Kids of all ages are here, from toddlers cuddled in parents' and nurses' laps to older teens leaning against the walls trying not to look impressed. They all have similar qualities about them: ashen skin, fatigue, and hope that is slowly fading as the days and months go by and treatment does little.

I recognize the bleakness and turn away. They remind me too much of myself when I was at my lowest—a place I never want to go again.

"This must be the highlight of their month," I tell Sam, but I step back before the words are finished leaving my mouth.

His skin has turned a sickly pallor and a sticky sweat covers his face. His throat works like he's trying to swallow but can't. His eyes are wet, his lips tremble. He stares at a young girl who's sitting in a wheelchair, an IV attached to her arm. She's wearing a pretty nightgown and matching robe, a white teddy bear in her lap. She looks no older than fifteen, but she could be any age, really. She's too thin, her blonde hair lackluster and limp, and her skin seems almost transparent under the fluorescent lights, stretched tightly across her bones.

"I can't do this," he says, stumbling away from me. "I can't be here. I'm sorry, Lily. I need a raincheck for dinner."

Before I can say a word, he turns and rushes toward an emergency exit. He pushes the fire door open and disappears down the dimly lit set of concrete stairs.

I don't have time to wonder what just happened as Allessandra chooses that moment to appear out of nowhere wearing a short black skirt, sequined top, and a matching bowler hat. Gary's with her, as is her father. Samantha's with them as well, and she smiles at me from across the gleaming waxed floor. Her eyes search the spaces next to me, and when she doesn't see Sam, she weaves around the nurses and excited children to my side.

"Didn't you come with Sam?" she asks.

"He left. He said he couldn't be here."

"Oh, fuck," she mutters under her breath. "I'm such an insensitive bitch. Tabby had breast cancer. It's no wonder he couldn't stay. This must have brought back a lot of memories. Shit. I'm so stupid."

"Do you want to go after him? I'll stay and let you know how things turn out." Sam never told me how his wife died, and I feel sick inside knowing he saw these children and pictured his wife in their places. "He probably shouldn't be alone."

The director of the children's hospital quiets the group and introduces Allessandra. Maybe the kids don't know about her personal drama, or maybe they don't care. She receives a warm welcome, and surprisingly, she starts her set a cappella, singing a song I've never heard before.

"No," Samantha whispers under Allessandra's voice. "He wouldn't want me bothering him now. He's always licked his wounds better in private. I'm glad he has you, Lily. I would have worried a lot more if this had happened before he met you. You're good for him."

Allessandra's song melds into another about lost love, something a twenty-one year old girl would know little about. "Do you think it would be okay if I checked on him later?" Samantha would know better than me, but I want to see for myself that he's okay.

"I think that's a great idea. Be there for him if he wants to talk. You have such a calmness about you, tension just oozes out of him when he's with you. Here's his address." She scrawls it on a piece of scrap paper she slides out of the file she's holding, and I shove it into a side pocket in my purse.

There's more to Allessandra's concert than just her singing. Samantha walks me through talking with the director of the hospital, introduces me to their public relations person, and we chat with Gary and her father, who has significantly calmed down. Mr. Biggotti apologizes for how he treated me earlier, noting the look on his daughter's beaming face that she was allowed, *encouraged*, to do the impromptu benefit.

After an hour of signing autographs and taking pictures with the staff, patients, and their parents if they attended, reluctantly, I agree to a late dinner. Samantha prods me and reminds me it's for SharperImage, standing in for Sam since he's not here. When she turns it into a work assignment, I have no choice, and I ride with Samantha to a trendy restaurant located in downtown Carthage.

Allessandra attaches herself to me and asks Samantha if I can be there when she gives interviews to the paper and bloggers the next morning. During their working lunch and subsequent meeting, they decided on a game plan for Allessandra to open up about mental health, the importance of taking care of yourself even when you feel like you can't, and making time for relationships. The morning will busy with her speaking to the news outlets before flying out to California to await her court hearing.

"Of course she can," Samantha says, sipping a cup of coffee. "We're so glad you two connected in such a positive way. Never hesitate to reach out, Allessandra, all of us at SharperImage want to help you."

Allessandra looks chagrined, and she blushes. "I never believed that until Lily, I mean, Miss Fowler. I hope we always stay in touch."

I'm honored this mixed-up girl thinks so much of me, and I slip her my cell phone number while we say our goodbyes in the restaurant's lobby. "It's only a burner phone. I don't want a cell phone plan until I know my ex-husband will leave me alone. If I ever change the number, I'll tell you. I promise."

"Thanks. I'll see you in the morning!" Ignoring the paparazzi who take her picture and shout questions at her, she darts out of the restaurant and toward a waiting limo. Her bodyguards hustle her inside, and Gary and Mr. and Mrs. Biggotti follow.

Samantha and I stay behind and wait for the car service. She insisted I take a company car to Sam's penthouse. "You made more progress with her in one day than we have in all the years she's needed our services," she says, waving off the doorman and opening the glass door herself to step onto the sidewalk. The streets are empty now that Allessandra's gone, and we stand at the curb undisturbed.

"I told her a little about my ex-husband. I think it helped when she realized even adults have problems and if you don't speak your mind and fight for what you want, you'll always be crushed under someone else's shoe. It's not a fun place to be. My ex stole five years of my life and I'll never get those back. All I did was remind her that she has the power. That without her, Gary and her parents have nothing."

"I guess we all need to be reminded of our own agency," Samantha murmurs as two sleek black town cars pull up to the sidewalk, their headlights glowing in the evening's dusk. "I never thought of approaching her like that. I'm glad you did. See you in the morning. I'm beat."

"Have a good night," I say as the driver of my car opens the back door for me.

I slide onto the leather seat and glance out the opposite window to the other side of the street. A man is standing on the corner wearing dark slacks, a black trench coat, and mirrored sunglasses, staring in my direction.

My heart trips in panic.

It's Keaton. He looks exactly like Keaton.

But it can't be. Yet . . . I was stupid and didn't follow up on what Janelle told me about the murder investigation. I didn't follow up because I was too involved with Sam.

A large delivery truck blocks my view, and when it rolls through the intersection, the man is gone.

Stupid. Samantha's not the only one who's stupid. I should have looked online, made a couple of phone calls and checked that Keaton was actually in the middle of an investigation, checked that what Janelle said was true and there was no way he had time to track me down.

The car glides into the sparse traffic, and I settle into the plush seat, searching the sidewalks though I know I won't see him again. The driver doesn't ask for an address. Samantha must have told him where I wanted to go because a few minutes later the car stops in front of a skyscraper, the city lights glinting against the glass.

"Mr. Sharpe's building, Miss Fowler," the driver says, meeting my eyes in the rearview mirror before climbing out of the car and holding the door open for me.

"Thank you." I step onto the sidewalk in front of Sam's building. A doorman is watching us, his uniform crisp.

"Will you be needing me further, miss?" he asks, slamming the door shut.

Sam may ask me to spend the night, but even if he doesn't, I can catch a taxi to the hotel. "No. Thank you."

The driver nods and touches the rim of his cap. "Good evening."

"Good evening."

I search the sidewalk in both directions. I don't see the man who stood on the corner across from the restaurant, but that does little to ease my apprehension. It wouldn't be difficult for Keaton to find me. He's hunted down some of the most gruesome killers New York state has ever seen. It would take him less than an hour to figure out where I am.

The doorman holds the door open for me, and I step inside the lobby saying a quiet, "Thank you."

A distinguished man wearing an expensive suit stands behind a desk, and he motions me over, a pen in his hand. "How can I help you this evening?"

"I'm here to see Sam. I mean, Mr. Sharpe."

"What is your name, please?"

"Lily Fowler."

He taps a few keys on the computer in front of him and slowly shakes his head. "You're not on his guest list. I'll need to call for his approval."

"That's fine. Thank you."

He lifts a receiver and dials a number. This is all so new to me, but I should have known I wouldn't be able to waltz right into Sam's penthouse. Even security measures at the hotel prohibits the front desk agents from confirming that I'm a guest or telling anyone what my room number is, and I felt safe checking in knowing my information was protected.

"You can go up," the concierge says, hanging up the phone. "His private elevator will take you to his floor."

"Thank you."

"Enjoy your evening."

I step inside the empty elevator. I'm glad it's private and I can let my guard down. Being Allessandra's person of the moment and seeing someone who so much resembled Keaton has exhausted me. I'm looking forward to sitting with Sam, maybe drinking a glass of wine, and letting him hold me as we both decompress after the stressful day.

I've had so little affection in the past few years it isn't any wonder I fell so easily for him.

Sam's waiting as the elevator doors slide open, and I try to keep my eyes from widening in disbelief. I've only known him a short time, but even when he's talking about Tabby, I've never seen him this haggard, and that includes the evening we met at the bar. A grey t-shirt that's too large hangs off his shoulders and grey sweatpants sag around his hips. Stubble covers his jaw, and his eyes are bloodshot. It doesn't look like he's combed his hair since this morning.

"Sam—" I say, alarmed, reaching out.

"What are you doing here?" His voice is gruff, and I push back my fear. Sam said he's never hit anyone, and I believe him. He's not going to hurt me.

"I wanted to make sure you were okay."

"I—" He blocks the doors open, but he doesn't invite me into his penthouse. I'm trapped in the elevator. "I thought I could do this. I thought I was ready, but I'm not. I'm sorry, Lily. I can't be with you."

Keaton rarely beat me badly, not the way a lot of abusive husbands go at their wives, but the one time after the UPS driver used our bathroom, he left me in a pool of blood, trembling in shock. I'd lain on the floor of our bedroom, in the dark, not moving, my mind an ugly mess of hurt and denial. He came in later with a wet washcloth and an ice pack for my broken nose and told me he was sorry, that he couldn't imagine another man touching me. He told me he loved me, and my heart wanted so much to believe him because I still loved him. I never thought I'd know that kind of pain ever again, the man I loved hitting me.

This pain is worse. I fell in love with Samuel Sharpe, and I didn't want to admit it to myself because I knew this would happen. I knew I wasn't good enough to replace his dead wife, but I hoped, God, I hoped. I need him as much as I want him, and for some idiotic, irresponsible reason, I was counting on him to keep me safe from Keaton.

It's a hard lesson learned that I'm the only person who can take care of me.

I try to smile, but I can barely lift the corners of my mouth. "It's okay. You were right in your office earlier. We went too fast.

I'm not ready for something like this, either. I'm scared of my own shadow and I have nightmares that Keaton is coming for me. I don't have much to offer if I can't get over what he did to me. I'm sure there's no woman in the world who can give you what Tabby did when she was alive. I wish you well. Goodbye, Sam."

I say the word without thinking. It's such a natural thing to say, after all. Goodbye. I never had someone say it to me on their deathbed. The goodbye I told Keaton had been mixed with relief and hate. Tabby's goodbye to Sam had been full of love, regret of time lost, and it was permanent. It's fitting then, that I say it now.

We tried, and we're done.

He stares at me, his jaw clenched.

The elevator can't move if he doesn't release the doors.

"Let me go."

Sam drops his arms to his sides, and the metal doors slide shut. With a shaking hand, I push the button for the lobby, and I press my cheek against the cool panel as the lift carries me back down to street level.

The doorman hails a taxi for me, and I hold it together until I'm sitting in the back, the driver ignoring me in favor of the music he's playing through his earbuds.

Doubling over, I press a hand to my mouth to hold back the sobs.

It's better this way. I had no business trying to be in a relationship so soon after my divorce. I need to learn to stand on my own two feet. Keaton robbed me of my dignity and self-esteem, and moving to Carthage was supposed to be a fresh start, a fresh start I'd be making on my own. I need to learn to be strong alone or I'll never be able to offer anyone anything.

I pay the driver in cash and step onto the sidewalk in front of the Regency. An elegantly dressed couple is coming back from their night on the town, her silver gown sparkling in the lights attached to the hotel's stone wall, the man's tux just rumpled enough I can guess what they were doing in the back of their limo. They're laughing, his arm around her.

At a distance, I follow them and avoid using the same elevator.

My room is dark but for the desk lamp's hazy orange light. The air is scented with a crisp fragrance, and housekeeping made the bed and vacuumed. Everything is as it should be, but there's something off, something that sends shivers down my spine.

Other things weigh more heavily on my mind and I push the feeling away. I drop my purse on the wing-backed chair near the bed and with a grateful sigh, kick off my heels. I never did put on my flats and my arches will pay for it tomorrow. It's too late to run a bath, and I wash my face and change into pajamas.

Sam wasn't a part of my life long enough to get used to it, and for that, I should be thankful. I brush my teeth, comb out my hair, and haul my laptop into bed with me. I bring up the employment agency's website and log into my account. Using their messaging system, I write to Dottie and explain I need a different position. I can't work with Sam after this, and no matter how professional I want to be, I can't finish my three months. It will be too difficult.

Hopefully, when Samantha finds out what happened between Sam and me, she'll let me out of my contract. I can ask her to call Dottie on my behalf and explain I tried but I wasn't a good fit. I feel like a coward, but it will be easier on Sam, too, if he doesn't have to see me every day.

Letting out a shuddery breath, I email Samantha. I haven't learned that much, and they haven't invested many resources in my training. It's better for her to find someone else before more time goes by.

I take off the jewelry I'm slowly starting to get used to wearing again. I set the pieces on the dresser where the rest of my necklaces, bracelets, and earrings are, but something doesn't look right. I search for what's missing, but everything is right where I left them.

I'm just tense because I saw someone who looks like Keaton.

He made no threats, didn't indicate he'd come after me. I'm jittery . . . and sad. I didn't expect Sam to break up with me, but then, we weren't really together. No promises were made. People sleep together all the time without commitment. I don't know why I thought Sam and I were different. He took from me, and I gave. I took from him, too. I'll have to make do with that.

I stay up another hour looking through the employment agency's open positions. The bank's CEO still needs a PA, and that looked like it had potential. SharperImage still needs an HR director, but I'll steer clear of that, even if Samantha offers me the job. I scribble a few notes of other positions that sound good, and I finally go to bed at midnight feeling like I might have dodged a bullet.

Sam did me a favor. I can be mature enough to recognize it.

I should have listened to my mother all those years ago. Live for yourself, do for yourself. If you only count on yourself, no one can let you down.

I don't want to go in to work tomorrow, but I made a commitment to Allessandra. I assure myself as I drift off, if I can face Keaton's fists, I can face Sam's sad eyes. Except, I expect the latter to be much, much harder to bear than the former.

# CHAPTER SIX



Their sad, hollow eyes. The scent of death. Everyone acting normally, like they can't smell it over the lemon disinfectant, but I can. Standing with Lily while my mind is at my wife's side as she lay dying, it's too much, and I have to get out of here.

I trot down the stairs two at a time, and I'm lucky I don't break my neck.

I don't calm down until I'm outside the children's hospital, the wind blowing against my face, cooling my skin.

Bracing my hands above my knees, I lean over and drag in deep breaths. I should go back, but I can't. The little girl in the wheelchair holding that teddy bear reminds me so much of Tabby during her final days. She isn't going to get better, just like we knew after the cancer spread that Tabby's days were limited. I sat by her side for hours holding her hand, reminiscing about the years we had together.

Never once did she ask me to stay single after she was gone. That was a vow I made to myself the second she drew her last breath, and if I hadn't met Lily, I think I could have kept that promise.

Damn her to hell for sitting in that bar alone.

I'll spend the rest of my life cursing the weakness that made me approach her.

My cell buzzes, and I think it's Samantha asking where I ran off to. It's like her to worry, even if she thinks I'll be mad.

A text from my father-in-law lights up the screen. I haven't spoken with Ardith or Cyrus for a few weeks now. I was so consumed with Allessandra's damage control, and, let's be honest, meeting Lily, that I forgot to check in with them. After Tabby died, we visited her grave every Sunday after church. I wasn't a churchgoer before I met Tabby, but when we married, I attended because it made her happy. It wasn't until recently I stopped going with her parents. I have a very complicated relationship with God and sitting in Sunday morning services did not give me the peace Tabby's parents found.

*Come to dinner tonight. It's been a while,* his text says.

*What time?* I reply.

*Anytime. Ardith is looking forward to seeing you.*

*All right. I'll be there at 6.*

*Sounds fine.*

My father-in-law is a man of few words, and the exchange lasts a mere minute. I only have an hour before they're expecting me, and I use the time to shower and stop by the florists to pick up an autumn bouquet to give to my mother-in-law.

Cyrus and Ardith are old-fashioned, insisting on Sunday afternoon dinner after church. He and I would watch football while Tabby and her mother puttered around in the kitchen. I don't like football, but it was expected, even more so during the holidays when Tabby's brothers would come with their families. More often than not, she would find me with a sleeping child in my lap, and she would meet my eyes across the living room, hers full of wistfulness and longing. Her body wasn't strong enough to support a pregnancy, even before she was diagnosed with breast cancer, and I talked her out of trying many times, something her primary care physician would thank me for at every six-month exam.

"I have everything I need, as long as I have you," I'd say, and I'd show her all night as I made delicate love to her until the sun came up.

Her parents live in the same house they did when Tabby and her brothers were children, located in a quiet neighborhood just outside Carthage.

For years after I married their daughter, Cyrus and Ardith tried to persuade us to move into a house in their neighborhood, always telling us when something came up for sale. I never wanted to, and as Tabby's condition worsened, it wouldn't have been safe for her to live outside the city. We needed quick access to her doctors, and after impatiently explaining that to Cyrus, he stopped asking. Tabby loved the penthouse anyway. She said she felt like a princess, and I always made sure to treat her like one.

The road is empty, and I park in their driveway near a maple tree, the leaves turning a brilliant red that reminds me of Lily's hair.

I can't linger in the truck. A few minutes of quiet would have soothed my nerves, but Cyrus and Ardith are already at the front door waiting for me to come in.

With Ardith's bouquet in hand, I shuffle up the walkway.

Cyrus greets me with a firm handshake, and Ardith sniffles a little when I give her the flowers.

Their house smells the same, a mixture of lemon Pledge and a roast in the slow cooker. Nothing has changed, not the couch or loveseat, not the old TV that sits on the floor with the rabbit ears, not the drapes.

"How have you been?" I ask, slipping off my shoes as I have always done at Ardith's request.

"The same, the same," Cyrus says, leading us into the kitchen. A stack of newspapers is piled in the middle, and Ardith places the bouquet next to them.

I sit in the same place I always have whenever Tabby and I would stop by, and while I usually find solace in these visits, today I don't. Cyrus is holding back his temper, and Ardith doesn't have time to uncap a beer for me before he's shoving one of the newspapers turned to the society pages under my nose.

"We want to know what this is," he says, his voice rough with anger, his finger jabbing at a grainy black and white photo in the center of the page.

It's a picture of Lily and me at the park yesterday. She's sitting between my legs, her back pressed against my chest. My arms are wrapped around her, and I can hear her telling me about her cop husband who liked to slap her around. I can smell her hair, hear her breathe, feel my heart give a little more as I devour our picture with my eyes. "She's . . . I met her a couple of weeks ago. Why?"

"Why? Why would you destroy our daughter's memory like this? It isn't right. We counted on you to do the right thing, Sam."

Silently, Ardith sets the beer bottle on a napkin in front of me, and I guzzle half its contents before answering him. "Tabby's been gone for two years, Cyrus. What do you want me to do?" Guilt, jagged and sharp, cuts at my heart.

"Respect her. Mourn appropriately. You stopped going to church with us. You stopped going to the cemetery, too. Don't deny it. Did you forget her the day we put her in the ground? Is that it? Fifteen years of your life with our daughter gone between some woman's legs?"

"No!" I choke, appalled.

"Then what are you doing? Everyone who looks at this picture will know you're sleeping with her. No one is that comfortable if you haven't tasted what's forbidden." Cyrus leans over the table and braces his hands near the stack of papers. "There are other pictures. You've been spending time with this woman. Who is she? Where did you meet her?"

"I . . . was having a difficult night and I met her at the bar attached to the Regency."

"You fucked her that night," he says, his face red.

"Cyrus!" Ardith protests. "That language is not necessary."

"Yes, it is. There can't be love between Sam and this woman. If there's no love between a man and a woman, then they're screwing, rutting like animals. You're better than that, Sam. If you weren't, we never would have given you our blessing to be with Tabby."

The night I asked Lily up to my room, and last night when we went back to hers, that wasn't rutting. I'm in love—but I've been very careful not to call it that. Since the moment I met her, Lily has meant more to me than a quick fuck, and that's Cyrus's point. She shouldn't. She should mean less than nothing because I should still be in love with his daughter.

I am, oh God, there are days I miss Tabby so much I'd rather be dead with her than live one more day alone. Then I see a redheaded beauty sitting in a bar by herself, a bruise on her cheek, sorrow in her eyes, and I think maybe someone is hurting as much as I am. Maybe I can share my pain with someone who understands what it's like to hurt.

That night on the rooftop at Sargento's, the wind rustling her hair, chocolate cake on her lips, I found something I hadn't had since Tabby passed away, but that something doesn't belong to me.

"What do you want me to do?" I can't tear my eyes away from our picture. We *do* look comfortable with each other. We look like lovers.

It hasn't been three hours since I last saw her at the hospital, and I already miss her.

"Remember Tabby. You're forgetting about her." His voice cracks, and Ardith rests a hand on his arm. "Go to church with us on Sunday and afterward, we'll visit her." He sinks tiredly into the chair next to me and rubs his forehead. "I wish God would have blessed you with a child. Ardith and I prayed every night that God would see fit. He must have had a plan, and we trusted Him, but it broke our hearts when you didn't conceive."

My throat is too tight for me to say anything.

"Don't see that harlot anymore," Cyrus says, gathering the newspapers, including the one with the picture of Lily and me at the park. "She's only after your money. At least you know Tabby loved you for you. She loved you before you took over your father's company."

"Yes, she did."

I could tell Cyrus that after Lily asked me if I was truly a billionaire, she never brought up money again, but that wouldn't change his mind. Lily is what Tabby isn't. Alive.

Ardith kisses the top of my head. "You have us, Sam. You'll always have us. Tabby would have wanted it this way."

After a silent dinner seasoned with blame and remorse, I wander up to Tabby's old room. They left it exactly as it was after we married, and if we had a late night planned, we'd sleep in her room rather than drive back. There are pictures of us everywhere, and I pick up the one propped on the nightstand. It's Christmas and we're sitting in front of the tree. One of the gifts I bought her was an engagement ring, and I asked her to marry me that night, outside, as the snow fell.

We look so young, my arm around her, the back of her hand to the camera, showing off the ring. Even then I understood how traditional her parents are, and I asked her father's permission first.

He knew I was an up-and-coming PR executive, that I could take care of Tabby, and he made me swear on a Bible I would never hurt his daughter. I found it amusing, but I did what he asked. It's not so amusing anymore, not when I can't touch Lily without her flinching. I was naïve, thinking we had the world at our feet.

But the only thing we had were doctors, sickness, and death.

Cyrus is right. I don't belong with Lily.

Tabby was mine, and I owe it to her memory to be alone. It's the only way she's going to live in our hearts. If I keep mine empty, there will always be room for her.

It's dark when I park in the underground garage, and my phone has remained oddly silent. Lily must have told Samantha I left Allessandra's concert. Samantha knows why those kids got to me, but I don't know if Samantha would have told Lily.

Whether she did or not, I'll have some explaining to do tomorrow at the office. I'll tell Lily I can't see her anymore. It hasn't been that long. It won't hurt that much.

The second I step into the penthouse, I go for the whiskey. It slides down my throat smooth and hot, burning, attempting to thaw me from the inside out. I down another and one more, the alcohol loosening my muscles, softening the pain. I pour another and carry it into the bedroom, the pictures of Tabby and me I left hanging mocking me, as if to say I'll never be able to replace what I had with her with anything, anyone, else.

I just finish changing out of my suit and into a pair of sweats and a t-shirt when my landline rings. No one uses the number except for the concierge downstairs, and it's not a surprise that Lily is in the lobby. I should send her away, give me time to think about what I want to say, but the quicker the better. I'm sloshed, and it won't hurt, the whiskey numbing me, doing its job spectacularly.

"Send her up," I slur.

When she reaches the penthouse floor, I'm nervous and sweating, but I'm also tired, so tired. Dinner with Tabby's parents pulled me right back to where I was the night I met Lily at the bar. The mourning is like a comfortable shroud, and instead of it suffocating me, I let it cocoon me.

Grief is the devil I know.

Tabby's memories are all I have left, all that I'll have left, and no one can replace her.

The doors slide open, but I block Lily from stepping out of the elevator. I can't let her into the penthouse. This was Tabby's home, and I can't let Lily into what used to be our sanctuary.

"Sam—" she says, her eyes wide. She steps forward and reaches out a hand.

I must look like complete shit to elicit such a response. "What are you doing here?" My voice is gruffer than I meant it to be, the alcohol letting out my fear.

She drops her hand. "I wanted to make sure you were okay."

I search her face. Shadows rest under her eyes and the makeup she wore to the office this morning is gone. Her hair is coming loose and I need all my willpower not to tuck those pieces behind her ear. She's still wearing the same clothes she wore to the hospital. How easy it would be to invite her in and lead her to the bedroom. The same bed I slept in with Tabby. I can feel her presence behind me, her hand on my back urging me to make Lily leave.

Is that Tabby? Or her parents? Does it matter now? I can't honor Tabby's memory if I'm with another woman, and I say the only thing I can say.

"I—I thought I could do this, I thought I was ready, but I'm not. I'm sorry, Lily. I can't be with you."

Blood drains from her face, turning her lips white, and I want to call the words back, but I can't. What she does next hurts me more than anything else besides Tabby's death. She gives me one of her slight smiles, the ones where she's trying so hard to be happy.

"It's okay," she says, her voice so thin I can barely hear her. "You were right in your office earlier. We went too fast. I'm not ready for something like this, either. I'm scared of my own shadow and I have nightmares that Keaton is coming for me. I don't have much to offer if I can't get over what he did to me. I'm sure there's no woman in the world who can give you what Tabby did when she was alive. I wish you well. Goodbye, Sam."

The word hits its mark. She knows what it does to me. It's the last word Tabby said to me before she slipped into a coma and never woke up. The word triggers emotions that I will never be able to outrun, and she says it now because she knows how final this is.

I stand in front of the elevator, and I can't move. Her voice, that word echoing in my heart, the only thing there besides Tabby's ghost.

"Let me go."

Her command trudges through the booze and up to my brain and I drop my arms. The doors, free of their obstruction, close, hiding Lily from my sight.

My body shakes like I have the chills, but my skin is hot to the touch. What am I going to do without her? I've known her for two weeks, and already she's infiltrated my life.

More whiskey slides easily down my throat. We're old friends.

I haven't changed the penthouse much since Tabby's death. Her little knickknacks still adorn the bookshelves in the living room. She had a thing for unicorns, and they sit, porcelain, glass, bronze, next to her favorite books. The kitchen is still full of the cookery she used, the wine closet stocked with her favorite red. The bathroom closet still contains her favorite shampoos and conditioners, body scrubs and lotions. I sleep on the sheets she picked out, the matching comforter worn. Her dresser still sits in the bedroom, full of her clothes. Her dresses still hang next to my suits.

I buried her with her wedding ring, the engagement ring from the photo part of the set. My own ring matched hers, but I leave it in a drawer in my office now.

Pouring more whiskey, my head swims with booze, fatigue, and guilt.

I can hear Cyrus: "You did the right thing."

I bring the whiskey bottle and glass with me to bed.

Tabby's side is empty, and it's as if my body, my heart, knows it still belongs to her. I've never rolled onto her side. Not once.

I drink until I can't stand to even walk to the bathroom to piss, and my last thought before blacking out is I wish to hell I could drink myself to death and finally be done with all of it.

---

"What did you do?"

Samantha's voice echoes in my head and I cover my eyes. The cleaning crew opened the blinds in my office and sunlight streams through the sparkling windows, icepicks ramming their way behind my eyes and into my skull.

Slouching in my chair, I try to block her out. I can't tolerate anything anymore.

My gut roils sickeningly with stale booze, and my skin is covered with sweat. Though my suit is crisp and smells faintly of dry-cleaning chemicals, underneath the starch, I stink.

It's eight in the morning.

I can't drink a cup of coffee because I know as sure as I know anything, it will come right back up.

"What?"

"Jesus Christ, Sam. Are you okay?"

"I would be if you left me the fuck alone."

I don't completely mean what I say. After Tabby passed away, those first few months were hellish. Samantha looked out for me, made sure I didn't do anything stupid. I don't think I'd be sitting here if it wasn't for her, her husband, and kids. My parents. They rallied me, kept me sane. Pushed me into the shower, cajoled me to eat. Reminded me there were people on earth who loved me just as much as Tabby ever did.

Samantha ignores me. "What did you say to Lily? I have an email from her asking me to call her employment agency and tell them it's not working out. She sent it last night. Did she go see you? Why would she do that?"

You know when you think things can't get worse? Don't tempt Fate. She's happy to prove you wrong. "Let her go." I gag, the bitter taste of whiskey filling my mouth.

"Why? The way she handled Allessandra, what she did for the girl, I was going to ask if we could talk about promoting her to a junior executive instead of your PA. She has compassion and sympathy, and we've been missing that in the way we handle clients."

Her voice hits me the wrong way, and anger, fucking *fury*,

surges through the pain and whiskey. I stagger from my chair and shove my desk phone, blotter, computer monitor and the plastic in/out trays onto the floor where they crash into a heap, paper fluttering all over the carpet. "What the fuck did I just say? If she doesn't want to work here anymore, let her go! Christ, Samantha, can't you get it through your fucking head? Leave me alone."

I fall back into my chair and cover my face with my hands. Tears leak from my eyes.

I've never yelled at her like that before, and I expect her to trip over herself to get away from me. Instead, she kneels in front of my chair and wraps her arms around my waist, resting her cheek on my chest. "Sam," she whispers.

Crying against the top of her head, I sob, "I can't do this anymore. It hurts so much."

"I know it does, I know it does," she murmurs in the way she comforts her sons.

The door opens and through my tears I see Lily, her hand on the doorknob. "We heard a crash— Oh. I'm sorry for interrupting." She backs out and closes the door softly behind her. She looks beautiful today, her hair plaited into a braid, wearing a green sheath dress and matching heels. I didn't get a good look at her face, but I'm an asshole to admit I want her to feel as badly as I do.

Samantha leans away and asks, "Can you tell me what happened?"

"I went to see Cyrus and Ardith yesterday. They saw a picture of Lily and me in the paper."

"The one of you two in the park. It was nice to see you close to someone again. I'm guessing they didn't agree."

"No."

She's always furious when she defends me against my in-laws and their beliefs and I tense for an outburst, but she says quietly, "I don't understand what they want from you. Do they want you to be alone for the rest of your life?"

"They think I haven't grieved long enough, and there are days, nights, I agree with them. It's been two years and it feels like yesterday we put her in the ground. I see her everywhere, *feel* her everywhere, and being with Lily . . . Sometimes I can lie to myself and think that's what Tabby would want, for me to move on. But how do I know? How do I know she would be happy for me? I'm in love with her, and it scares the shit out of me."

"Because the only thing that hurts worse than losing someone when they die is losing someone who's still alive."

"Something like that," I say, but it's exactly like that. When Tabby's doctors told us her cancer spread and there wasn't anything more they could do, I had time to prepare. Nothing truly can prepare you for the death of a loved one, but when you know it's coming, it's easier to bear, somehow. We said the things we needed to say to each other and did the things we wanted to do. A trip to Paris while she still felt strong enough, time with her family. Evenings watching movies she wanted to see. Long talks about how our marriage had been perfect and there was nothing we would have changed.

Telling Lily goodbye was a different kind of hell. She's still here, living, breathing. I'm able to touch her, hold her, make love to her, and I can't.

"You should go home," Samantha says, rising to her feet. "You're in no shape to work."

"I don't want to go home." It's not home. It hasn't been home since Tabby passed away.

"And I know why. It's what I've been telling you for the past year. You see Tabby around every corner. Sell your penthouse."

"And what?" I ask bitterly. "Move into something with Lily?"

Samantha scoffs. "Of course not. You've known her for two weeks, and one of those weeks you thought you were never going to see her again." With her hands on her hips, she surveys the damage I did to my computer's monitor and the rest of my things. "I'm not going to break her contract. She can finish out the three months *and* I'm going to offer her a junior exec position along with education reimbursement for the classes she's going to need if she accepts. You need to apologize and explain why you told her you couldn't see her anymore. Tabby's parents are unfair and unreasonable. They think it's okay for you to be alone because they aren't. They still have each other. You have a right to date and remarry, and they can support you when you do or get the fuck out of your way."

I never thought about it that way. Cyrus can tell me he doesn't want to see me with another woman, but at night, when I'm alone, he has Ardith. Actually, that's not a picture I want in my head, and I chuckle, pressing the heels of my hands into my eyes. I have a horrible headache and nothing is going to make it go away except lying in a dark room after drinking a gallon of water and swallowing a double dose of ibuprofen.

"You can promote her, and I'll apologize, but I can't see her. I'm not ready to date."

Samantha crosses her arms over her chest. "Fine. Don't date her. Let Cyrus win. He planted the seed you should be alone for the rest of your life and that's bullshit. You're always going to miss her. Always. She was your wife for fifteen years. But can you love someone else and miss her at the same time? Yes. And if Lily is the woman you think she is, she'll understand and support you. If she expects you to go on as if Tabby were never alive, then she isn't the one for you, but I don't think that's true."

I don't think it's true, either, but I don't say anything.

She wrinkles her nose. "Go home or go to my place. Use your room at the Regency, but go *somewhere* and shower. You smell."

"Thanks."

"Ah-huh."

"No, I mean it. Thank you," I say, emotion rubbing my throat raw. I fucked up and instead of making me feel worse, she gave me a shoulder to cry on and advice I needed to hear.

"Anytime. I mean that, too." She turns and lets herself out, and I'm staring at the mess on the floor, tempted to leave it for the cleaning crew tonight, when someone lightly knocks on my door and pushes it open.

"Samantha said you need some help," Lily says, stepping into the room.

I sigh. "Yeah, I guess I do."

She kneels on the floor and begins to gather the papers that flew out of the in/out trays. Maybe she's familiar enough with the clients she knows what belongs where. Her hands are steady, her fingers long and graceful. Her nails are painted a light beige and she's not wearing any rings.

"What did you do with your wedding band after your divorce?" I ask.

"I put it on his dresser when I left. It didn't mean what I thought it meant."

I pick up my monitor and set it on my desk. The cables attached to the back look twisted and bent in their sockets, but the screen flickers on when I wiggle the mouse. I may need to have IT replace it.

"I stopped wearing mine a year after Tabby passed away. Some people thought it was too soon, but I couldn't look at it on my hand anymore." I rub at the empty spot, feeling the weight of the gold that had represented so much to me.

"Mine started to feel like the proverbial ball and chain. He claimed me and there wasn't a way to escape. After a while, I hated looking at it. I felt like a prisoner." She picks up my trays now straightened with paper and sets them on the edge of my desk. Dropping to her haunches, she reaches for my leather blotter and centers it on the shining surface.

My phone is lying on its side, the receiver off the hook. I grab it and put it back in its usual place.

The only thing left is a container of paperclips. They scattered when I pushed it onto the floor, and I kneel with her as we push them into the plastic box one by one. Being this close to her and knowing I can't touch her is torture, and I concentrate on the paperclips.

The time to say something is slipping away, but when she rises to her feet, I can't get the words past the stickiness in my mouth. I want to say I'm sorry, I want to tell her I'm in love with her, I want to tell her I can be in a relationship despite missing Tabby so much my heart is shredded with it, but I can't tell her any of those things. It wouldn't be fair.

She pauses when she reaches the door. "Is there anything else?"

"No. Thank you."

"You're welcome." She stops and sucks in a breath. "You don't look like you're feeling very good, Sam, and . . . when I was at my lowest, I would have done anything to escape what Keaton was doing to me. Anything. If my boss hadn't helped me, if he would have turned on me and told Keaton, fired me, anything but what he did, it would have been easy to find another way out. You know what I'm talking about. Don't let it get that far. Talk to Samantha, or me, or a therapist who deals with grief. The pain you feel missing Tabby? Don't do that to the people who care about you."

"You know me, don't you?"

"You sat next to me at the bar, but, Sam, I let you."

I don't go back to the penthouse after Lily leaves, Sammie mentioning something about her supporting Allessandra during her interviews. I sink into my chair, the headache still clawing away behind my eyes, my neck stiff, my back aching. I stink, and I'm too nauseated to eat. It's what I deserve for trying to drink myself to death, and I'm not surprised Lily saw right through me.

Despair.

Hopelessness.

Torment binds us together, and until I can turn that into happiness, we'll never have a chance.

I summon Archer into my office and it's not ten minutes later he's standing in front of my desk. He's younger than me but experienced in things I've never begun to dream of. I pay him for that experience, my safety and that of my family top priority. We don't have many shady clients, but sometimes even the ones who we think won't give us trouble surprise us on a level we didn't anticipate. I pay Archer to think ten steps ahead, and he earns every penny.

"I want dossiers created for Lily Fowler and her ex-husband," I say, hitching an ankle onto my knee and trying to look like I haven't been hit by a semi-truck. "I don't know much about him. His first name is Keaton, and he lives outside New York City somewhere. He works homicide. Violent. He used to beat on her, and it won't happen again."

He nods, hearing what I haven't said.

"Slimeballs like that don't disappear and he let her go too easily for me to trust it. I want a detail on her twenty-four hours a day, seven days a week. She's staying at the Regency."

"Anything else?"

"I don't want her to know."

"Done."

"That's it."

"I'll have the information on your desk by tomorrow morning."

"Thank you."

*I have nightmares that Keaton is coming for me.*

I was too ravaged by what I was doing to listen to what Lily said to me in the elevator last night. She's still afraid of him.

Even if we don't end up together, I'll make sure he never hurts her again.

Better yet, I'll make sure he never hurts *anyone* ever again.

It's a little after two o'clock when I stagger out of my office. Lily's back and she and Shiloh are standing near the elevator. I approach them, my vision slipping sideways. I need that water and a nap, but I won't be able to rest unless I speak to Lily first.

"Can I talk to you for a minute?" I ask her.

She looks to Shiloh, who says, "I'll wait for you in the lobby."

"Thanks."

She meets my eyes, her gooey irises soft and warm like the caramel brownies my grandmother used to bake before she died.

"What is it?"

I clear my throat. I didn't think of what I should say, and as a PR man who makes millions spinning mistakes into miracles, I should be able to do that with my own life. Fortunately, I haven't needed the practice.

"I want to take back what I said last night, but you and I both know there's more truth there than lies. That doesn't mean I don't want to spend time with you, explore where this is going. I know I hurt you, and if you don't want to give me another chance, I'll understand."

"Sam—" She stops and sighs. "I want something with you, but if we ask anybody if we're a good match, they'd say no. We're too damaged, too broken, to have anything left over for anyone. There was a lot of truth to what I said last night, too. I was counting on you—"

This time, I'm the one who flinches.

"—to be something that isn't your responsibility. It isn't only you who can mess us up."

My heart sinks with every word she says. She's going to hold me to what I said. Which is her right, and probably wiser than I want to admit. I let Cyrus inside my head, and I fucked up. He could do it again. The guilt is still there, the need to be with Lily stronger than my grief Tabby is gone. It's ripping me in two.

Desperately, I grab her wrist and pull her down the hallway. Her heels click and squeal against the tile as she tries to keep up without landing on her ass. I find an empty conference room and drag her inside, the door closing with a soft bump. The blinds let in enough sunlight that I don't bother flicking on the overhead bulbs. In the shadows, I crowd her against the wall, my hands on either side of her head.

Her pupils dilate, and her breath comes out in sexy little puffs.

"What about this, Lily? What about what we have?"

She pushes on my chest, but I don't give her an inch. "Sex? You're bringing sex into this?"

"No. I'm bringing chemistry, arousal, and desire, into this. Every time I see you, I want to bury my cock so deep inside you, you can't think about anything but crying out my name. I want to twist my fingers in your hair, pin you to the bed, and make you feel how much I want you."

"That's not love," she whispers, tears running down her cheeks. "That's not love."

"Christ, Lily. It is to me." I seal my mouth over hers and extinguish the mewls of protest. She stands rigid for a moment before pulling me closer and moving her lips under mine.

I sag in relief. I almost lost her. I would have deserved it, and I never would have stopped fighting to get her back if I had, but the shitty situation I created between us is a lot easier to handle with her acquiescence.

She drags her mouth away. "You can't keep doing this to me."

"What? Pulling you into an empty room and having my way with you?" I try to joke, but it falls flat.

"No. Saying you don't want me then crawling back on your hands and knees. You *hurt* me last night, and what's worse is everything you said was true. You're not ready to be in a relationship, and if I let you have your way, this will happen again."

I rake my hands through my hair. "Then what do you want me to do? I fucked up. The minute the words left my mouth I knew I had. I can't promise I won't fuck up again. I'm human, Lily."

"I know that." She slides her hand down the front of my shirt. "I can't promise it, either." Pausing, she bites her lip. "Samantha talked to me about a PR position instead of being your assistant. Will you relax and slow things down if I take it?"

Hiding my face in the sweet curve of her neck, I whimper. "How do you know what I need before I do?"

"I need it too. I need you, Sam," she whispers in my ear.

"Thank God."

Leaning away, she asks, "Do you feel okay? Will you tell me what happened last night?"

I rub my thumb over her lips. "Yes, but not now. Shiloh's waiting for you. Are you going to a late lunch?"

"No, just a coffee break. I ate earlier with Allessandra and her team."

"Thank you for doing that. She's got a long road ahead of her and every little bit of help she has will count. I'm going home to shower and get some sleep." Going to Samantha's would be the coward's way out. If I can't face the penthouse where I lived with Tabby, then I don't deserve to have Lily in my life.

"Okay. I meant what I said. Don't hurt yourself." She squeezes my forearm and opens the door of the conference room.

I won't tell her how close I came last night, hoping a case of alcohol poisoning would take it all away, but she probably already knows. Wrapping my arm around her waist, I pull her to me. The hallway is empty, but I don't care who sees us. "When can I see you again?" I'm shaky, and I'll be able to rest knowing we have plans.

"Tomorrow at work isn't good enough?" she asks, molding her back to my front and leaning her head against my shoulder.

"No. I need more than that."

"Then you tell me."

"Tomorrow evening. Let's—" I want to spend time with her, but not at the penthouse. Not yet. My room at the Regency is too impersonal, and if I suggest her room, she'll think I want room service and sex. Which is true and sounds pretty damned amazing, but it's not all I want.

"We'll go out. Carthage is beautiful in the fall. I'll—" *Take you to one of my favorite restaurants.* Except I don't have a favorite restaurant that I don't share with Tabby. "I'll figure it out."

She turns. "Spending time with me is going to be complicated for you."

If I try to deny it, she'll see right through me. "Yes."

"You may find spending time with me will be complicated in other ways, too," she says, and the small amount of joy I gave her when I came for her disappears.

"I have a feeling my demons are bigger than yours." I kiss her cheek. "Go now, before Shiloh leaves you claiming caffeine withdrawal."

She lifts a corner of her mouth in one of her sad smiles. "I can only hope that's true."

"I guess we'll find out."

"I guess we will."

She walks down the hallway, her shoulders sloped, her steps slow and heavy.

Keaton isn't the only thing she's scared of, and I'll have to do better to keep myself from being one of them.

---

The next morning I'm feeling more like myself, and right at eight, I meet with Samantha in her office. Noting my eyes are clear and I don't stink like a bar, she dives into updates on Allessandra's case. This is another thing I have to thank Samantha for. Yesterday, while I was hungover and heartbroken, she and Lily were still doing the work. Since Allessandra's impromptu concert at the children's hospital, with Lily's help, she's met with several bloggers and interviewers and appeared on two local morning talk shows sharing a message of hope, self-care, and mental health awareness. Samantha shows me a clip, and the popstar looks like a different person.

"She looks good. Healthy. Nice turnaround." I nod, satisfied. After a week of positive publicity, no one will remember her car accident.

"That's all due to Lily," Samantha says, putting her phone to sleep and setting it aside. "We forgot Allessandra's our client, not her father or Gary. We've been in this business for so long all we care about is sweeping up the broken pieces. Lily reminded me that sometimes those pieces can be glued back together. She accepted the position. Will that be a problem for you?"

I shift at the small table Samantha uses to answer email and drink coffee instead of at her desk. It's positioned in front of the window, and Carthage, in all her fall glory, sparkles beneath us in the autumn sunlight.

"No. Well—"

Samantha tenses. Unless Lily told her, she doesn't know that Lily and I literally kissed and made up yesterday.

"—I'll need another PA, and Shiloh won't feel slighted?"

Samantha shakes her head and sips her coffee. "No. I've offered her a PR position several times. She likes what she's doing."

"Okay. Then that's a done deal. You aren't going to mind that Lily and I have something going on the side?"

"I just want to see you happy. The second that stops, then I'll mind."

"Fair enough. What do you have going on this weekend?" The normalcy of the question hits me. It's been too long since I've cared about mundane things like weekend plans.

Samantha's eyes widen. She knows it too. "I invited Lily shopping Saturday, but you know what? With the cooler weather, it will be nice to spend it outside. Why don't you two come to the house? Clint can barbecue and she can meet the boys."

That sounds too much like the way Tabby and I would spend our weekends—Saturdays with Samantha and Clint, Sundays with Cyrus and Ardith—and a refusal is fast on my lips.

"Too soon?" she asks, searching my face for evidence she said the wrong thing.

"No. If we can eat dinner at Sargento's, we can go to your place for a barbecue. I'll talk to her about it tonight."

Samantha stands, ready to get on with her day. "Oh? Are you seeing her after work?"

"Yeah."

"Good. With Allessandra under control for the moment, I'm going to check in with some of our other clients."

"I'll be in my office."

"See you later. And Sam? I'm glad you and Lily worked it out."

"Yeah. Me too."

I know Lily's here, there's a fresh mug of coffee on my desk sitting next to a plain brown folder. Archer has come and gone. I worry for a moment Lily saw the file, but even if she did, she's not the type to snoop and there's no way she could know I asked Archer to look into her history.

I sit and open the file. Archer's summary is on top, typed into neat paragraphs.

Keaton Kessler, 45.

A decorated homicide detective with the Honeywell, New York, Police Department. I scan the cases he's closed, and on paper, he's a competent and celebrated detective. Which probably explains why he was never prosecuted for domestic violence. They watch each other's backs.

Clean driving record.

Donates to charity.

Archer dug deep, and Kessler's net worth, including his 401k, is listed along with assets such as a house, speed boat, ATV, and SUV. Kessler likes to play when he's not beating up women or working.

He's dating a little bunny, Amanda Isaacs, 25.

Almost half his age. Nice.

His parents also live in Honeywell, along with a sister and her family.

I flip the paper over and reveal Kessler's department headshot. His dark brown hair is cut into a no-nonsense style and his blue eyes are hard. His lips form a strong, serious line. Under the professional persona, I have a difficult time seeing the kind of man he would be in private, but I have a feeling he isn't that different off the job than he is on. He needs to be taken seriously, will get offended if you don't. I've worked with types like that, who get into trouble because they feel disrespected and lash out. Lots of pride, big egos. A little kid made fun of Kessler on the playground and he never forgot it. Created a chip on his shoulder bigger than the Grand Canyon and will take it out on anyone who reminds him it's there. I bet he's the department PR's biggest nightmare.

I flip to the next photo and suck in a breath. I wasn't prepared for the emergency room's photo of Lily's face. Split lip, black eye, bruised cheek. A medical report paper-clipped to the photo indicates she fell down a flight of stairs in their home and hit her head against a stack of packing crates at the landing.

I don't know how any self-respecting doctor could sign off on such a blatant lie.

Dr. Morrison won't have a job when I'm through with him.

I can't stand to see anymore, and instead I skim the personal information Archer found for her. Her parents, Francine and Edward Fowler, live in Honeywell.

She said her mother grew up in Carthage, but I didn't ask Archer to dig into her parents' lives and there isn't anything about them besides their ages and previous occupations. They're both retired now. Lily's an only child, and I bet that made it even more difficult when they stopped speaking to her.

She must have felt so alone, abandoned, while Kessler was abusing her.

At least her prior employer stepped up. There are still some decent human beings in the world.

Online, I search for Francine Fowler, and I find her maiden name easily enough. With a few clicks of the mouse, I dig up a couple of old *Carthage Chronicle* articles. One is about a high school class band trip detailing the competition between the Carthage Cadets and a high school located across the state. Her mother played flute. In another, the same class is documented visiting a museum in north Carthage that's still there, a class photo taken on the wide steps in front of the building. I search the faces looking for Lily's mother, but the photo is in black and white and too grainy to decipher any features that may resemble Lily. Only the caption at the bottom of the photo assures me that Francine is part of the group.

That gives me an idea of what Lily and I can do tonight. She wanted to see her mother's childhood city. What better way than to show her places her mother had gone to? We could visit the museum and then eat dinner at a restaurant close by.

I don't see Lily all day, and I focus on work in a way I haven't since Tabby died. The past two years have been consumed by sadness and grief, and everything I turned my attention to was covered by a thick, grey veil.

It wasn't until the day Lily stepped into my office for a job interview that I could finally *see*, and the light was blinding.

At five, Samantha pokes her head around the doorjamb of the connecting door we share. "Are you good?"

"I'm good," I can say honestly, and Samantha waggles her fingers and leaves to go home.

Lily's sitting at her desk and glances up at me when I lean against the edge. "Hi."

"Hi. Are you ready to go?" I ask.

"Yes. I'm just finishing up some paperwork Samantha asked me to fill out. Am I okay dressed like this or should I go back to the hotel and change?"

"You look great, but if you want out of those heels, we can stop by the Regency. It's up to you. How long do you plan to stay there?" I ask as she puts her computer to sleep.

Her hands still. "I'm not sure. I want to look for an apartment, but living in a hotel, I can make a quick getaway if I need to. You know?"

I hate the sound of it. I hate thinking she could disappear in the middle of the night and I would never see her again. "Don't do that."

"Don't do what? Run if I need to run? I'll do what I have to do, Sam."

"Okay." I brush a soothing hand down her back. "Okay. I'll comp your room and you can stay as long as you need to stay to feel safe."

She takes her purse out of the bottom drawer, rolls her chair away from her desk, and stands. I guide her past Samantha's office and down the hallway toward the elevator. "What do you mean, you'll comp my room? I can afford to pay for it or I wouldn't stay there."

"I don't know anything about your finances, but it would be a waste of anyone's money to stay in a hotel indefinitely. At least let me count it as a business expense since you're working here now, and one day, when you're tired of hotel living or you feel safe enough to sign a lease, whichever comes first, I'll help you find a place to live."

Pressing her lips against a cry, she pauses and swallows before she speaks. "It would be nice if just once I could take care of myself without depending on other people's charity."

"Hey." I raise my hand to her face. She tries not to show it, but she still winces. After looking at the photos Archer included in her dossier, I can't blame her. I can't blame her one bit for thinking a man's hands would have anything but anger and violence festering inside them. I cup her cheek and rub my thumb over the spot where the bruise had been. "You are, by far, one of the bravest people I know. And do you know what else is brave? Accepting help if it's offered when you need it. You may not need me to comp your room, but I never want you to feel like you have to check out when you're not ready. Promise me, if you need to run, run to me."

She turns her head and kisses my palm. "Thank you."

"You never have to thank me for giving you what I want to give you. Now, let's go. You asked me to show you around the city, and tonight we're going to do a little sightseeing."

"Will there be food?"

"I guarantee it."

"Then I'm yours."

I press the Down button and slant my lips over hers. I want to say something witty, something funny or romantic about us belonging to each other, but the past has a hateful way of sneaking into the future so I don't say anything at all.

---

I decide to drive, and the elevator carries us down to the underground parking garage. It's brightly lit, but Lily trembles and presses herself into my side. "Are you okay? Bad memories?" I ask, leading her to the dark green Range Rover I drove when we went to the park. It was Tabby's favorite car, and after she passed away, I had it detailed to get rid of the scent of her perfume. I should have sold it, but I couldn't find the energy to bother.

"No. Well, I parked in a garage like this when I worked for the man who helped me. Keaton would wait for me sometimes, leaning against my car, checking the mileage, and if he was off shift, he'd follow me home, preventing me from going anywhere else. I could never walk with anyone because I didn't want them to meet him."

"You didn't have any friends?" I ask, but I already know the answer. In a relationship like that, I'm sure Kessler was quick to separate Lily from everyone close to her. Then he could say, "See, no one cares about you like I do," and she would believe it.

"I keep in touch with one woman since I moved, but I wouldn't call her a friend. She's married to a cop who works with Keaton and he let me talk to her sometimes. Besides her, no. People forget about you pretty quickly when you're not available to do things. After I married Keaton, the invitations dried up because I always had to say no. He never wanted me to do anything, go anywhere, without him, and at the time, I thought it was romantic. Now I see he was isolating me so I would feel like I didn't have anyone to help me. Luckily, we needed my income to live how he wanted to live, and I had to work. It saved me."

I unlock the truck and open the door for her. I wait until she's sitting in the passenger seat and then ask, "Have you spoke with him? The man who helped you?"

She shakes her head and clenches her purse's straps that's laying in her lap. "I'm too afraid to stay in contact with anyone from there, besides Janelle who promised she wouldn't say anything. I don't think Keaton knows Owen helped me. I'd been saving, planning, hoping, but Owen found an apartment for me and paid the deposit and first month's rent. Without his help, I couldn't have gotten a divorce, but if Keaton ever found out, he'd want revenge."

"Then maybe you should let him know you're okay. Use a pay phone in the lobby. He'll know you're in Carthage but nothing more than that, okay?"

Her gaze slams into mine. "You'd let me do that?"

I lean against the side of the truck. "Relationships, real ones, not the shit Keaton dragged you into, are partnerships." I hold up a hand, and mirroring me, she holds up hers. "Two halves that create a whole." I lace our fingers. "Common courtesy is to be expected. Don't run in the middle of the night without telling me where you're going. I won't drink myself to death. If you have coffee with Tyler, one of the junior executives, I'll know it's only coffee and shop talk. If I smile at Shiloh, you'll know it's because she's Samantha's PA and I'm only being friendly. There's a dark, thick line between common courtesy and blatant disrespect. All I ask is if you don't want to be with me anymore, you tell me. No need to lie, no need to hide, no need to cheat."

"I haven't had that in a long time," she whispers, her eyes on our entwined fingers.

"And I had it for so long I took it for granted. Call Owen tomorrow, okay? I bet he would like to hear from you."

"Okay."

"Okay."

Reluctantly, I let go of her hand, round the truck, and slide behind the wheel.

"Where are we going?" she asks as I navigate out of the underground parking and onto the street.

"It's a surprise."

"I don't like surprises."

"Not the kind you're used to getting, but you'll like mine."

"That's . . . bold," she says, staring curiously out her window.

"Because it's true."

She laughs, and I hold her hand again. Lily, the real Lily, is under there somewhere. Kessler didn't beat it out of her, not all of it, and it will be a pleasure to draw out the pieces of herself she's forgotten.

The Carthage Institute of Art is located in the north part of the city down a wide street full of businesses, cafés, and trendy retail stores that can afford the high rent that comes with the historical location. I find a parking spot on the street and kill the engine.

I help Lily out of the truck, stealing a moment to press my lips to the soft curve of her neck. Her scent is something I'll never tire of. Honey, maybe. Almonds. She smells sweet, and I draw in a deep breath.

"I didn't take you for a museum-goer," she says, letting me hold her hand while we across the street.

"I'm not, normally. You said your mother grew up here, and I did a little snooping. Your mother visited this museum with her high school class. There's a picture of them on these steps, but I couldn't tell which one was her. If I show you the picture, maybe you can point her out to me."

She stops mid-step, her hand skimming the black handrail. "My mother came here?"

"Yes, she did. Let's look around."

"Sam, I don't know what to say."

It makes me sad that such a small amount of kindness could leave her speechless. "Say you'll go to Samantha's Saturday afternoon for a barbecue instead of shopping. You can meet her husband and kids."

"I would like that."

"Good. If you're up for dinner after we walk around, there's a bistro down the street that I heard serves good steaks and a mean dirty martini. Do you like those?"

She wrinkles her nose. "Not really, but I like the chocolate ones."

"Then we'll order you a chocolate one. Come on." I tug her hand.

The museum is empty when we step inside, the hardwood floors sparkling in the light drifting down through the skylights. A large spiral staircase in the corner leads to more artwork upstairs, but for now, with my hand to the small of her back, we walk around the first floor. White walls create a stark backdrop for the large canvases, and we stop at one, the wildflowers bursting in a bright array of color. The work is so intricate, I can hear the bees buzzing, darting from one flower to the next. If this had been a gallery instead of a museum, I would have purchased it on the spot.

"Will you tell me what happened?" Lily asks, staring at the painting, too scared to look at me.

Pretending I don't see her flinch, I tuck a curl behind her ear. There's nothing that calms me more than burying my face in her hair. "Tabby's parents saw our picture in the *Chronicle*. Someone took our picture while we were at the park the other day. They're upset I'm seeing someone."

We step aside to another painting. This one is of a forest at dusk, and creatures that have white, glittering eyes peer from behind thick tree trunks. It's creepy, foreboding, and resembles too much of real life. Someone is always watching what I do.

"Do they think it's too soon?" She doesn't look at me.

"They don't want me to date at all. They want me to stay single to honor Tabby's memory."

"They told you to stop seeing me."

"Her father crawled under my skin. The kids at the hospital reminded me of Tabby's last few months, and Cyrus chose right then to text and invite me to dinner. His timing was good. For me, not so much. I let him convince me I was disrespecting Tabby by moving on and after a good couple of drinks, when you stopped by, I did the only thing I thought I should do."

"That's what Janelle accused me of, too, and when you ended it, I thought it was for the best. Keaton made me dependent on him, and it's been difficult to adjust to being alone. I tried to convince myself it was better if I had time to myself."

"Do you want that time, Lily?"

She nuzzles her nose against my cheek. "Is it bad if I say no?"

"Not any worse than me being glad if you say it."

"Then, no, I don't."

I brush her lips with mine and lead her to the next painting.

"What changed your mind?" she asks.

How do I put into words the misery that slammed into me after I sent her away? How my love for her and my love for Tabby played tug of war, Tabby's memories and Cyrus's hateful words winning, even when knowing if I lost Lily, it would kill me.

"I didn't want to lose you. Samantha helped me see that losing you would hurt worse than when I lost Tabby. With Tabby, I had warning and we had time to say our goodbyes. With you, after I told you I couldn't see you anymore, I had mere seconds to memorize your features before you disappeared. The guilt that it was true ate at me. I was an easy target, and I'll regret the look I put on your face for the rest of my life."

"Oh, Sam," she says, and she wraps her arms around me.

At this, I press my face into her hair. "I haven't told them I'm not going to stop seeing you," I murmur. "I don't know what it will do to our relationship."

She leans away, and I miss her warmth. I've been starved for touch since Tabby died, and it's another reason I fell into bed with Lily. I need her body just as much as I need her heart.

"They're afraid of losing you."

I step to the next painting, this one of a prairie, golden hay bales dotting a harvested field. "What do you mean?"

"They're afraid of losing you. You're their only connection to Tabby now. You were their son-in-law for fifteen years. What do they think will happen if you start seeing someone else? Remarry? They're afraid you'll forget Tabby, yes, but they're afraid you'll forget them, too. Maybe if you explained that you'll always think of them as family, that if you consider the next woman in your life part of Tabby's family, it would be easier on them."

I scoff. "Lily, there's no woman on this earth who would even think about doing such a thing. You're kind, generous, and have a forgiving nature I've already taken advantage of, but even you wouldn't do something like that. He called you a harlot, accused you of going after my money. Why would you want to meet a man like that? And more, consider him family?"

"Oh, I don't know. Maybe I *am* a harlot after your money."

Laughing, I nudge her to the next painting. "The last thing you're after is my money."

Amused, she pokes her tongue into her cheek and asks, "Why do you think that?"

"After the time you've had, money isn't what you want. Love, kindness . . . he could be the richest man in the world but if you knew he wouldn't treat you well, you'd walk away. The things you need in your next relationship are priceless."

Tears shimmer in her eyes as she studies the next painting. One drips down her cheek, and slowly, I raise my hand, showing her my intention to wipe it away. She still flinches, and my heart hitches.

"Would you really want to meet them?"

"One day. If they want to meet me. They're still mourning, and you'll need to convince them you have a right to stop."

"Were you close to Keaton's parents?"

"No. Long before he met me, he alienated them with his temper. They attended our wedding, and just before the ceremony started, I was standing in my dressing room at the church wearing my gown thinking that despite what my own mother and father said about him, this was the happiest day of my life. Then his mother came into the room. She took my hand and said, 'Good luck, Lily. You're going to need it.' In the five years we were married, the only times I saw her or his father were if we happened to bump into them at the grocery store."

"She knew what her son was and didn't warn you." My voice trembles with anger.

"I hated her for a long time for that, but you know what? It wouldn't have mattered. I loved him, Sam. I wouldn't have believed a word she said. Why would I believe her if I didn't listen to my own mother? My mother knew what he was, and she did everything she could to make me listen. I thought my wedding day was the happiest day of my life. It was her saddest. She said my father gave me a way to a devil wearing a tux."

"Do you think about reaching out? Now that you've left him?"

"The first time he hit me and I didn't leave, they disowned me. They said if I wasn't smart enough to leave a man who was capable of doing something like that, they couldn't support me. I've tried to look at it from their point of view, if I had a daughter and she was in the same situation. It would be like watching her slowly kill herself. When he was off duty, Keaton kept his service weapon on the kitchen counter. He wanted me to see it. Wanted me to know he'd use it. Sometimes I want to blame her for failing me, but I can only blame me because I failed myself."

"That's not true. You're here."

The more she talks about him and what he did to her, the

more relieved I am I put a detail on her. Even now Archer is around here somewhere, keeping watch of the entrances and exits, noting who's coming and going. If Kessler steps foot outside New York, I'll know, but it's what I'm going to have to do to lock him up that turns my blood to ice.

"I am, aren't I?" Lily says, looking slightly shocked at the realization.

"You are. Let's finish looking around, and we'll celebrate at dinner."

The sunlight glimmering through the window catches her skin. She looks like an angel, a ravaged, damaged angel, rediscovering she has wings. One day she may decide she's strong enough not to need me anymore, and in that pain of loss I'll be thankful I had a hand in helping her fly.

# CHAPTER SEVEN

*Lily*

We finish touring the museum, and when we step outside, the sun is setting, casting the sky in brilliant oranges and pinks. There's a chill in the air, and Sam drapes his suit coat over my shoulders as we walk to the bistro down the street.

He orders a dirty martini and a chocolate one for me, winking as he relays the request to our server.

Over the steaks he promised, our topics of conversation turn lighter: Allessandra, the barbecue at Samantha's, and PR classes. It's nice not talking about such serious things, and on the way to the Regency, I'm feeling almost content. I'll never be able to completely relax with Keaton out there somewhere, waiting like a snake to strike, and knowing I can stay at the hotel for as long as I need both relieves me and breaks my heart. I want a home. I want to find a place where I can settle in, meet my neighbors, and not worry about Keaton finding me and ripping it all away.

At the intersection near the hotel Sam says, "Invite me up."

I don't hesitate to ask.

---

We make love, and I can call it that because that's what it is for me. Maybe it's too soon, maybe he'll never feel the same way, maybe it can't last because Keaton won't let me have it, but I love him. I try to show him with my body because I can't say it with words. I don't want to pressure him into saying it back or think I'm trying to trap him in a relationship.

He's on top the way he likes, and I don't mind. I feel safe, him over me, his tongue tangling with mine. His cock is huge and hard, and he moves in and out of me with languid thrusts. Leisurely, Sam enjoys me, his finger lazily circling my clit until I feel like I'm going to explode from impatience.

Only when I orgasm and the pleasure is coursing through me does he let go, riding on the waves of my release. He buries his face in my hair, and I hold him close, his skin slicked with sweat.

His shuddering stops and his breathing slows. He rolls off me, and with a kiss to my lips, falls asleep. I know the feeling. It's difficult to sleep when you feel like your world is crumbling around you, and after he broke up with me, that must have been what it felt like. I know it did for me.

I indulge for just a moment, rubbing my fingers over his scruff, giving him another kiss he doesn't participate in. I want to call Tabby's parents and give them a piece of my mind for adding to Sam's suffering when he's already mourned long enough. It's not my fight, but I'm angry they'd use his love for their daughter against him.

My phone buzzes on the nightstand with a text from Janelle. *Call me.*

Glancing quickly at Sam, I slip on my robe and pad to the

other side of the room. It's not a suite like Sam's upstairs, and to have total privacy I would either need to go in the bathroom and shut the door or step into the hallway. I don't have anything to hide from him, but the less he knows about Keaton and his potential to bother me, the better. Keaton isn't a threat to Sam—I'm not worried about that—but I don't want him to feel as if he's getting more trouble than I'm worth.

I slide to the floor near the loveseat and lean my back against the wall. I bring up Janelle's number and hit Connect. It rings several times before she answers, her voice low and tense.

"You and your rich man flaunting it again." Jealousy makes her tone brittle. There's a burst of chatter behind her, and a band plays music in the background, a cover of an old U2 song.

"We're not flaunting anything. I have a right to live my life," I whisper furiously.

"Paparazzi don't care about *normal* people, Lily. You looked fucking fancy tonight in your pretty dress and heels, his jacket over your shoulders like you're some goddamned queen. That was tonight, right? What were you doing? Expensive dinner? Was the wine more than what Keat makes in a year or what?"

I squeeze my eyes shut. Pictures of us walking to the bistro are online. Why does anyone care what Sam's doing? Because he's a rich widower and the second Tabby died, he became Carthage's most eligible bachelor. Of all the men to fall into bed with . . . Of all the men to love.

"How's Keaton handling it?" I murmur, my head low, hoping I don't wake Sam.

"How do you think? We're at the Showdown, and he made Amanda give him a blowjob in the john. He said he's going to fuck her real good and pretend she's you. He's pissed, Lily. Pissed."

Amanda. I didn't know he was seeing someone.

"What about the case?" I grapple for something positive that would make him happy, and he's happiest when people are kissing his ass. "Did he solve the case?"

There's another burst of laughter in the background, and I can picture the Showdown, a popular police hangout where off-duty cops go to drink and wind down after a long shift. One of the bartenders watched Keaton slap me in the back hallway and didn't say anything. No one will report him, it doesn't matter how he treats Amanda.

"No. They hit a dead end and the chief told everyone to go home and get some rest. The boys are too wound up to sleep and they came out here to blow off steam. Someone started passing their phone around when you popped up online. He's taking some real shit, people saying you left him for a rich guy."

Sam rolls over with a gentle snore, his hand reaching out looking for me. He'll wake up soon if I don't go to bed.

"But he's still in Honeywell." I need to know for sure.

"He's still here, I see him right now, and he has his hand up Amanda's shirt. She's a little cutie too, met her at a sandwich shop when he stopped in for lunch. Blonde, big boobs. She worships the ground he walks on, unlike you, who never appreciated anything he did for you."

I ignore her. I appreciated the days he didn't treat me like a punching bag. "Is she safe with him?" It's a stupid question. No one is safe with Keaton.

"Of course she is. He treats her good. And who knows, she probably likes it rough. Don't you? I heard him say you liked his belt against your ass. I gotta go. Check in real soon, ya hear?" It sounds like a threat, but before I can answer, she disconnects.

Keaton never brought violence to bed, only used me for his own pleasure, rolled over, and fell asleep. If he'd been cruel, I wouldn't have been able to sleep with Sam as quickly as I had.

Keaton never whipped me with a belt or anything else, but if he's doing that kind of thing with his new girlfriend, his behavior is escalating. I wish I could tell someone. I wish there was a way to stop him.

I rest my forehead on my knees. There's nothing I can do. When I fled, I wasn't thinking about the women he'd date, or, God forbid, marry, after me. I was only thinking about myself and how to put as much distance as I could between his fists and my body.

It's selfish to say I don't want to worry about Amanda or the way Keaton's treating her. Maybe she has a stronger support system than I did, and if she needs help, she'll be able to find it.

I crawl into bed, and the second I slip between the sheets, Sam puts his arms around me. He mumbles something intelligible in my ear. I wouldn't be hurt now if he said he loved Tabby while making love to me. He loved his wife and by some miraculous thing, he's turning that kindness, compassion, and passion toward me. Scraps? No. But I'm willing to share him with her.

I'm not too proud to thank her for shaping him into the man I spend time with.

Even with Sam in my bed, I have nightmares. Only this time, I'm not alone.

I'm running from Keaton with a woman named Amanda, and we can't run fast enough.

---

Friday goes by in a haze of paperwork, a company tour from top to bottom, and meetings. It's difficult to believe I've been working at SharperImage for only a week, but with the way Allessandra and her case turned out, my new coworkers respect me for stepping up only days on the job. Elated, Sam and

Samantha invite everyone in the office out to celebrate Allessandra's new image, the win for the company, and the weekend, and after drinks and dinner, when Sam drops me off at the Regency— "I don't want to take up all your time, sweetheart. I'm sure you have things you need to do. I'll pick you up at one o'clock to go out to Samantha's" —I'm buzzing with champagne and a feeling I never thought I'd have again.

Happiness.

Things are falling into place better than I ever thought possible, the only thing dampening my joy is the fact I can't reach out to my parents to tell them. When my mother said she and my father couldn't talk to me anymore, couldn't watch me hurt myself, she meant it. Their attorney mailed me a certified letter stating they'd written me out of their will. Keaton read it, said, "Good riddance," and threw it into the trash.

He threw the only family I had into the garbage, and I didn't bother to retrieve it. There was nothing I could do to change their minds. I chose Keaton over them, and they were making me pay for it.

No, not making me pay. It wasn't a form of revenge or justice. They were simply erasing me from their lives, and it didn't matter what happened afterward. They wouldn't care. The only way I can be close to my mother now is to keep exploring Carthage and try to see the city through her eyes.

The Regency's lobby is busy with people checking in, and I stand in a packed elevator. I appreciate Sam not wanting to crowd me, but if he would have asked to come up, I would have said yes. This is week three in the hotel and I should look for my own apartment. Maybe I'll feel more at home and enjoy my evenings alone. The only thing keeping me from doing it now is what Janelle said about Keaton. The more Sam and I show up in the paper and on the social media sites, the angrier Keaton is going to become until eventually he'll explode and hunt me down.

The hotel offers some security, and I can ask Sam for a company car. He's already offered, and if I tell him why I changed my mind, he'll provide me one with no strings attached.

But I don't want to live the rest of my life in fear. It's why I left Keaton in the first place.

With the pay bump I'll receive accepting the promotion, I can find an apartment that has security like Sam's—a concierge who won't let anyone up without my consent. SharperImage's security is top-notch, too, not that either of those things will protect me. It would be different if Keaton wasn't a cop. He can flash his badge and gain access anywhere, anytime. I've seen him do it.

If he decides to come for me, there is nowhere I could run where I would be safe.

No one gets off on my floor, and I walk down the quiet hallway alone. I use my keycard to open the door to my room, and immediately I feel something is off. Once again, housekeeping has been in, and my bed is made and there's a delicate scent of lemongrass and cucumber lingering in the air. I flick the light on. My clothes are tidied, the trashcan under the desk empty. From here, I can't tell if my jewelry has been tampered with, but in the past, housekeeping has moved my things only to dust and then moved them back into their places.

I'm about to shrug it off when I see it.

A man's footprint pressed into the vacuumed carpet's piling.

Someone has been in my room, and I swallow back a moan of fear.

It could have been Sam. He owns the hotel, after all, and

has access to my room—has access to every room in the building.

Maybe he forgot something when he spent the night last night and came back to pick it up. I wish he would have asked me first, if that's the case, but he had all day to mention it and he never said anything. Not at work, not during dinner. Not when he dropped me off. He had numerous chances to tell me, and it's not like I would have gotten angry.

I breathe through my nose trying to stave off a panic attack.

It could have been the manager of the hotel. A male on the housekeeping staff.

There's a reasonable explanation, especially since I talked to Janelle just last night and she assured me Keaton is still in Honeywell.

Unless she's lying to me. She gave me a play-by-play of what he was doing at the Showdown, but was she reporting what she saw or making it up? She didn't send me photo evidence. There's no way for me to know.

I make use of all the locks on the door, engaging the chain and the deadbolt. I don't want to let paranoia get the better of me, but I give in and block the door with the chair next to the bed. Overkill, my brain tells me, but it's enough to calm me down. I order a glass of wine—undoing all my security measures to let him in—and run a bath in the large garden tub after he serves it to my room with a smile and a, "Goodnight."

A hot soak and a good night's sleep will help me see things clearer in the morning. A male on the housekeeping staff who assisted in cleaning my room or the hotel's manager who needed to check on something seem the most likely, and only a woman who has a rocky past would think anything sinister of an unexplained footprint in a hotel room's carpet piling.

The warm bathwater and scented salts help me relax and

the joy of the day trickles back to me, keeping me company while I get ready for bed.

Tomorrow I'll spend time with Samantha on a personal level. Besides asking Owen for help, I've never crossed the line from professional to personal with any of my bosses. I'm sleeping with Sam, but it doesn't feel like I'm sleeping with my boss, though technically that's what I'm doing. Maybe because Samantha's been doing the bulk of the work at SharperImage while Sam's been grieving, but she feels more my superior than he does, and I've been reporting to her all week.

I like her. We get along, more for the fact that I pulled Sam to shore than the way I do my job, I suspect, but she wouldn't have offered me a promotion so quickly if I hadn't impressed her that way, too. I'm looking forward to tomorrow. I want her to like me as much as I like her. She's strong, competent, carrying a professional load and still managing to take care of a family. I could have been her if I hadn't tangled with Keaton.

Now my biological clock rarely ticks and all I want to do is live a life where I'm not looking over my shoulder every second.

My phone buzzes, and a text from Sam pops up. *Goodnight, beautiful. See you tomorrow.*

A smile plays with my lips, and I press my fingers over my mouth. I'm pathetic if something so small like Sam thinking about me can weaken my knees.

I consider playing hard to get and not replying, but I picture him sitting in his dark penthouse, maybe sipping on something like I am, feeling lonely and down. Scared, too, maybe. Not of a stupid footprint in his carpet, but of spending his life alone, navigating his way without his wife by his side.

*Goodnight. I had fun tonight.*

He sends me a red heart, and I send one back along with the tired emoji to keep the mood light. Both of us lonely after a long day could turn into some heavy texting, and I don't want that right before bed.

He returns it and I wait for a moment, but there's nothing more.

I crawl into bed, and a wave of homesickness hits me. It's one thing to be homesick for a home you know, it's another to be homesick for a home you've never had. Giving in to my own loneliness and fear, I call Sam.

"Are you okay?" he answers without saying hello.

Tears clog my throat. "I'm just a little sad." My voice quakes.

He sighs. "Honey, I am too. I miss you."

My laugh is half a sob. "I miss you too."

"Talk to me."

I do. We talk until two in the morning when we both fall asleep, our phone lines still open. At seven, I wake up to go to the bathroom and I hear him lightly snoring. Grateful I have someone like him in my life, I don't disconnect, and I fall back into a heavy sleep until almost noon.

---

"I haven't done that since high school."

"What's that?" I ask, a bouquet of flowers on my lap and three bottles of red wine at my feet. Sam's driving us to Samantha's, and I suggested we stop for flowers on the way.

"Falling asleep talking on the phone."

"Oh?" I like hearing Sam's stories, these little glimpses into his life, and I'm looking forward to Samantha telling me what it was like growing up with him.

"Yep, Mary Jane Johnson, senior year of high school. She said she couldn't fall asleep without me telling her a bedtime story."

I quirk an eyebrow. "Is that code for phone sex?"

He taps my nose. "There's a reason Samantha promoted you. She made these cute little gasps when she came."

"And you? Did you get yourself off under the covers?"

He laughs. "Hell, no. I sound like an idiot when I come."

"Don't be too hard on yourself. I think you sound rather sexy, snarling in my ear. I'm sure Mary Jane would have thought so too."

"I never got to find out, unfortunately. She used me for my storytelling abilities. For the real thing, she looked elsewhere." He *tsks*, shaking his head, his hands relaxed on the wheel as he drives down an empty two-lane highway.

Smothering a laugh, I say, "Somehow I think you did just fine."

"Well, it wasn't long after that I met Tabby."

I turn in my seat and face him, the seatbelt pushing against my hipbone, the cellophane around the bouquet rubbing against my vest. "How did you two meet?"

"You really want to know?"

"Why not? You know how I met Keaton."

He tips his head. "Looking back, it actually wasn't that spectacular, though when it happened, I knew my whole life was about to change. I went to the University of Minnesota, Carthage. It's not Columbia or Harvard, but it's a family tradition and I liked the idea of staying in the state, being close to my family. At the time, Cyrus was the custodial and maintenance director. He still is unless he retired and didn't tell me. I was on campus, minding my own business when this golden-haired nymph floated by me. I turned around and tailed her until she stopped at her father's office in the facilities management wing. She twirled around and confronted me. Luckily, her father was still supervising a job or he probably would have had me kicked out for stalking. I just gaped at her, you know?

Mr. PR major tongue-tied. I asked her out, and for some strange reason, she said yes. We were never apart for long after that."

I know why she said yes. For the same reason when he asked me up to his room after sitting with him for barely an hour and I followed him, a woman with my history, without blinking an eye.

"Quick," I comment.

"Yeah," he says softly, his mind in the past now, standing in that university hallway.

He turns into a residential neighborhood and slows down for a few kids playing near the street.

"Samantha's a lot like me that way, too. Clint asked her to marry him on their first date. She lasted a month before she said yes."

"Well, luckily for us, we've been there, done that," I say, hoping it sounds like a joke. I don't pretend I'm the sort of woman a man marries. Well, not the kind of woman Keaton turned me into.

He turns into a large driveway and stops in front of a three-stall garage that's attached to a massive two-story house. "Didn't like the t-shirt?" he asks, shifting into Park and killing the engine.

I hide my face by leaning over and grabbing two bottles of wine. "Not particularly."

Reaching for them, he says, "I don't blame you there, but maybe you should try a different store."

"Haha." I open the truck's door holding the flowers and the last bottle of wine tucked under my arm. "No thanks."

I slide out before he can say anything, and with a hand to my lower back, he guides me up the front walk.

Sam narrows his eyes at me as he rings the doorbell, and I'm about to ask him what he's thinking when a tall, burly Black man wearing jeans and a grey and black sweater swings the door open. I stand frozen, craning my neck to stare into his face.

Beside me, Sam stiffens.

Samantha comes up behind Clint, and she too, stills at my reaction.

I finally find my voice. "You're Clint Pearson, number twenty-eight, Minnesota Vikings."

Clint laughs, wagging his finger at me. "Not for a long time. You don't look like the type to follow football."

"Not me. My ex-husband. Some things you can't avoid no matter how much you try. Sam didn't mention you played ball."

Sam nudges me into the entry way and hooks an arm around my neck. "Because I like to be the famous one in the family. Hey, Clint. Hi, Sammie," he says, kissing Samantha's cheek.

I laugh. "What makes you famous?"

He rubs his fingertips with his thumb. "That's all I need, baby." He winks.

Samantha rolls her eyes. "The sad part is, he's right."

I share a tolerant smile with her. "Here, we brought these for you."

"Thanks. Flowers were always Tabby's wheelhouse." She sucks in a breath. "Sorry."

Tangling my fingers with Sam's, I try to find strength and not a little bit of courage. I hadn't considered that Sam and Tabby probably did this every weekend, and it will be just as awkward for them as it will be for me. "It's okay. You don't have to avoid talking about her around me."

Sam clears his throat. "I'm being rude. Lily, this is Clint, but you knew that, Clint, Lily Fowler. She moved from New York to Carthage a few weeks ago."

Clint squeezes my hand and says, "Samantha's told me a lot about you already. It's nice to meet you."

"It's nice to meet you, too. You have a beautiful house."

"It's a pain in the ass on good days. We'll have the demons show you around if you're interested."

"I'd love that. Oh, and this too," I say, holding up the bottle of wine I'm still carrying.

"You really went all out. That has to be your doing. Sam isn't that thoughtful."

Samantha playfully elbows her husband. "We're set up in the backyard. The boys are playing on the trampoline."

Clint and Samantha lead us through a huge living room and into a backyard that has to be at least three acres of land. A large trampoline that has protective netting around it sits toward the back and two little boys jump in the center while a golden retriever barks from the sidelines.

"Boys," Clint hollers, his hands cupped around his mouth. "Come say hello to cousin Sam's friend."

They stop bouncing and slide off the trampoline. The dog chases after them as they run across the yard.

"This is Cole and Carter. This is Miss Lily, say hello." Clint turns to me. "You're not scared of dogs, are you?"

"No, not at all. Hi. It's nice to meet you," I say to the boys, kneeling and letting the dog lick my face.

"Her name is Goldie," Cole says, his eyes squinting behind a pair of black-framed glasses.

"We named her ourselves." Carter's wearing a Viking's jersey that has his dad's number on the front.

I grin. "You did a great job. It fits."

"Thanks! Can we go play now?" Cole asks, shifting back and forth on his feet with impatience.

"Yeah, yeah. Go." Clint waves them off. "Come sit and we'll pour some wine. A little day drinking never hurt anybody. I can put the steaks on soon, if you two are hungry."

I glance at Sam and shrug. "Whatever works for you."

We sit at a picnic table covered with a red and white checked tablecloth. Clint and Samantha already put out wineglasses, huge wooden bowls full of chips, crystal dishes filled with what looks like dip, and a vegetable platter.

Sam straddles a bench and pulls me to him. I lean against his chest, sitting in the V of his thighs.

Clint uncorks one of the bottles Sam and I brought and Samantha digs around in a cooler at her feet and pulls out a bottle of beer, uncaps it and sets it in front of Sam. It's the same brand he drank at the bar the night we met.

Their yard is full of trees and flowers, white and navy blue wicker furniture on the porch. A fire pit is built into the ground off to the side and cozy chairs are positioned in a semi-circle around it.

"How come you don't live in a house like this?" I ask Sam, kind of over my shoulder as he has his arm laying on my belly holding me close.

"Tabby needed to live in the city. It was a lot faster to get her to the doctor in an emergency."

I feel stupid for asking. "I'm sorry. I shouldn't have said anything."

He sips his beer and kisses my cheek, his lips cold. "It's okay to ask. She would have loved a house like this, but it wasn't practical."

A lull falls over the table and Clint says, "Sammie and I lived in the city before the boys came along. There are perks to both. We spend a lot of time on the road, to and from work, especially since right now my construction site is on the other side of the city." He pops a chip into his mouth. Crunching, he continues, "We wanted the boys to have a yard, and being able to adopt a dog was an extra bonus. Having to get up at stupid o'clock to make it to the site by eight isn't great, especially in the winter when we do interior work, but weekends like this remind us why we do it."

"How did you go from football to construction?" I ask, choosing a chip for myself and nibbling on the edge. Sam's chest is strong against my back, and his flannel shirt is scented with fabric softener. I turn my head and the soft cotton brushes against my cheek. Casually, he slides his hand under my shirt and his fingers graze my skin.

Samantha watches him and a tender look crosses over her face.

He catches it and pats her hand.

"Back when I played ball, I found some trouble. Brawling in bars, booze cruises, hotel parties. My reputation took a beating, and the team's manager hired an outside PR firm to straighten me out. I was a sullen jackass thinking I didn't need anybody talking me up in the press, but then Sammie walked into the conference room. Somehow, she knew right away this wasn't about parties, it was about me playing ball. While I was growing up, my mom worked two jobs and took in laundry besides, and football gave me something to do after school. I didn't plan on it, but I went all the way and signed with the Vikings for more money than I ever thought possible. My mom didn't have to work anymore. I could put my sisters through school."

"And you started to feel like a paycheck," I murmur, remembering my talk with Allessandra.

"You got it. My worth as a human got tangled up with my worth as a football player. They didn't get along and I grew resentful. Sammie helped me see I had already made so much money I didn't have to play anymore if I didn't want to, but it took a while for that to sink in. Football had been my entire life since I was ten years old. In fact, I had to get my head bashed in during a rough Thanksgiving Day game against the Steelers. I woke up on a gurney with a severe concussion and I knew that was it. I was done. But the first thing I thought of wasn't getting out of the game, it was Sammie's face. I asked her out, and over cheeseburgers and French fries, I asked her to marry me. I didn't know how this would go down," he says, lifting up her hand and gesturing between them, pointing out the differences in their color. "I wasn't sure she could handle this hunka hunka burnin' love, but she came around."

Samantha slaps his arm and he grins.

"But construction?" I prompt.

"Oh, when I was in college I majored in construction management. Starting my own business seemed like a no-brainer. I had the money to invest and Sammie and Sam helped me with the business end of it—tax IDs, hiring people, office space, you know. Me getting that going, and with her at SharperImage, we were busy and put kids off for a while. Once things quieted down, we built the house, I knocked her up, and here we are." He holds out his arms as if embracing the backyard and the house then helps himself to another chip.

"That sounds so romantic," Samantha says sarcastically, pouring more wine into her glass. "Drink up," she says to me, nudging the wineglass I haven't touched, too enthralled by Clint's story to remember she poured it for me.

"Hey," he says, turning to her and cradling her face in his hands. "Everything I am, right now, this second, is because of you."

Behind me, Sam stiffens, but he presses his lips to my temple.

Clint follows suit, kissing Samantha's forehead. "I'm going to round up the demons and we can play a couple games of cornhole before we put the steaks on. Sound good?"

"Yep," Sam says, taking another swig of his beer. "You?" he asks me, his lips close to my ear.

"It's perfect."

The afternoon floats by in a haze of games, wine, and satisfying conversation. Before we eat, we decide to play touch football, and Cole, Carter, and I team up against Clint, Samantha, and Sam. The kids and I trounce them, and the boys go crazy doing a touchdown dance every time they're able to dodge Sam. Goldie joins in on the fun, barking her encouragement, and at one point, getting in Clint's way. He trips over his own feet to avoid hurting her.

The boys howl with laughter, and Samantha chases them through the yard, yelling playful threats of retaliation. I fall onto my butt in the grass, tired from running, a hand to my heart.

"Hey, are you okay?" Sam asks, trotting over to me. "Do you need to rest?"

I suck in a breath. "No. I just haven't been this active in a long time. Cole and Carter have way too much energy."

Clint drops to his haunches and watches us, his hand on Goldie's head.

Sam wraps his arm around me and helps me stand. "Come sit. You don't want to overdo it."

"I'm okay." I say, but I walk with him to the picnic table and he pulls a wet bottle of water out of the cooler, uncapping it and setting it in front of me.

Gratefully, I swallow the cool liquid.

Clint declares himself too hungry to play anymore, and Samantha shoos the boys inside to play video games while we talk.

The steaks are perfection, golden corn on the cob tastes like heaven, and I fill up on grilled garlic potatoes I would never get tired of eating. The home-cooked meal is fabulous and reminds me that's another reason why I want to find my own apartment.

Room service is nice but I'd rather live in a place with a kitchen and cook for myself.

The sun starts to set and the temperature dips.

"I'm going to clean up. We can start a fire, if you have time to stay for a while longer. The boys love s'mores," Clint says, stacking our empty plates.

"I have time if Sam does," I say, rising from the bench intending to help Clint clear.

"You're not tired?" He rests a hand on my hip.

"No. You?"

"No. We can stay for another hour or two."

I smile at Clint. "I'll help you clean up."

"Lily—" Sam starts.

"She's fine, Sam," Samantha says. "Help me get the fire going."

Sam frowns and I brush my fingers over his cheek. "Are you okay?"

His eyes drill holes into mine before he says, "Yeah."

"Okay."

I follow Clint inside the house, my hands full of empty wineglasses. Clint sets a stack of plates in the sink.

"Do you know what's wrong with Sam all of a sudden?" I ask, carefully placing the glasses near the edge of the sink.

He turns to me, his eyes sad. "It's the way the boys tired you out after football. Tabby had a weak heart, among other things. It probably brought back some hard memories."

"Oh. I'm sorry. He doesn't talk about her very often and I don't know much about their marriage. Her parents don't like him seeing me."

Clint fills the sink with water and adds a squirt of dish-washing liquid. He scoffs. "I'm sure they love seeing your pictures in the paper. Sammie lets out a little squeal every time you pop up online. She's been so worried about him and was afraid he wouldn't snap out of it. But if I can offer some advice?"

Pushing my sleeves up my arms in preparation to wash, I say tentatively, "Sure?"

"He's going to have knee-jerk reactions like the one he had this afternoon for a long time. I don't want to say humor him, but try to understand, okay? Sammie said you two have hit the sheets. You noticed he likes missionary?"

My cheeks flame and I busy myself with a sponge and one of the wineglasses. "Mostly, yeah."

"It's the only way Tabby could be intimate. Her heart wouldn't let her get that into it, and Sam did all the work. He told her all the time he didn't need sex to be happy, but you know, she liked it too and didn't want to give it up."

"I see." I did. I wouldn't want to give up sex with Sam, either.

"She had asthma, allergies, and various other issues. He cares about you, and the things he's been conditioned to watch out for with Tabby, they'll bleed a little into your relationship. I hope it doesn't get to a point where it will annoy you."

Clint rinses the wineglass I just washed and dries it with a hand towel.

"Was she always . . . fragile?" I ask, washing another glass.

"Yeah. Tabby told Sammie her mother had a difficult pregnancy and said if she'd been the first born, she'd be an only child. Anyway, I know his reaction to the boys wearing you out confused you, and I wanted to shed a little light on why. Like you said, Sam doesn't talk about her much, but if you don't know, you can't understand."

"I appreciate that."

"Do you, though?" Clint asks, huffing a laugh and putting the wineglasses inside a cabinet.

"He's struggling. We both are. I don't know where we'll end up, if I'm being honest with you. The way we met is a bit unconventional, and I don't know if we can build a future on that, or if I want to try. My past is, well." I shrug. "I don't want to drag Sam into it, you know? He's already gone through enough."

"I get it," he says, rinsing the plates I just washed and slotting them in a strainer to dry, "but Sam never does anything halfway. Once he reaches the point of no return, dealing with your troubles will be easier than living without you. The Sharpes fall hard, and they fall fast. Luckily for me. Talking about dragging someone through some shit. If Sammie wouldn't have fallen just as hard as I did, I don't know if we'd be married."

"You guys are great together."

"Thanks. She definitely brought more to the table than I did, but if she heard me say that she'd disagree. Anyway, I didn't mean to get that heavy with you. It just means a lot to Sammie that Sam accepted the invitation. He hasn't spent an afternoon out here like this since Tabby died. I'll grab the chocolate bars and marshmallows. The graham crackers are under here if you can grab the box for me." He points to a cabinet that's near the floor with his toe.

"Sure."

We spend the next hour around the fire, and Cole and Carter show me how to toast the perfect marshmallow. I'm tired but content when Sam announces it's time for us to go, and the goodbyes are heartfelt and sincere when we say we have to do it again soon.

"Have fun?" Sam asks once we're on the highway headed back to the city.

"It was great. They're a lovely family." I yawn.

"But you're okay?" He laces his fingers with mine.

I lift his hand to my mouth and kiss his knuckles. "I'm okay. Tired. All that fresh air did me in. I'll sleep well tonight."

He's pensive during the drive, and it's not a surprise when he doesn't ask to come up to my room.

"I have things I need to do tomorrow. See you Monday?" he asks, parking in front of the Regency.

"I'll be at work, if that's what you mean."

"It's not, but it will do for now. Let me get your door."

Sam jumps out of the truck before I can tell him I can open my own door and trots around the front, the headlights illuminating his tired features and glinting off his blond hair. With a hand to my arm, he helps me out of my seat.

I'm reluctant to go upstairs alone, afraid of what I'm going to find. Another shoe print? My jewelry in a mess? My clothing not quite right, as if my skirts, blouses, and dresses have been rifled through? I can't ask him to come up. I can't be a burden. My conversation with Clint was uncomfortable, but it also shed a lot of light on Tabby and Sam's marriage. He took care of her for fifteen years. He needs a break.

I force a smile. "I had fun today. Thanks for inviting me."

"You're welcome. I liked having you there. Goodnight, Lily."

"Goodnight."

He brushes a kiss over my cheek.

The doorman opens the door for me, and I look over my shoulder. Sam is standing on the sidewalk watching me. I give a slight wave that he doesn't return.

Upstairs, I gingerly open the door to my room, but nothing is disturbed. There's the slight scent of lemongrass and cucumber air freshener that housekeeping uses, the familiar vacuum tracks in the grey carpet. My bed is made, my personal things moved, allowing the housekeepers to dust, and moved back again, in the same places, but not.

Last night I was overreacting.

I change into pajamas and wash my face, and drag my laptop into bed with me. It's time to start looking for an apartment. Spending time in Samantha and Clint's home made me realize that even if Sam is comping my hotel room, I want a space I can call mine. My name on a lease, paying rent I can afford with a job I earned on my own. Maybe not entirely on my own, but I'd gotten my promotion through my own grit and I'm proud of that.

I open the HR package in my email that details how much I'm going to net every week once I start getting paid and begin to cross-reference that sum with available apartments that have rents in my price range. I'll have to ask Sam which parts of the city are nice neighborhoods and which areas I need to avoid.

I stay up way too late spinning dreams of the future, picturing Sam in my apartment letting me cook for him, spending the night, waking up together. If given a chance to look back, I would have cursed myself for being so stupid.

Women with pasts like mine don't get futures like Samantha's.

And I was an idiot for thinking I could.

# CHAPTER EIGHT

*Sam*

Sunday mornings are for sleeping in. Breakfast in bed. Reading the paper while sipping on coffee. Dozing as sunlight pours through the window.

If I admitted a dislike for anything during my marriage to Tabby, it would be Sundays with her family. I knew before I married her she was a God-fearing woman, and part of me liked that. She was kind, a good person, she believed in God and lived in His name, attended Bible study without me on Wednesday evenings. She wasn't afraid to die saying she would be resting in God's arms for eternity. My parents didn't bring me to church, though I was taught to believe in God. That little bit of faith helped me tolerate the Sunday morning services, but resentment bubbles up in my throat sitting in a pew this morning next to Ardith and Cyrus without Tabby.

I don't want to be here.

Members of the congregation remember me, giving me both a side-eye for showing up in the papers with a woman who isn't Tabby and telling me over and over how much they miss her and they're so sorry for my loss. Tabby was too special to remain on earth. God called her home before I was ready and I should find comfort in that.

I didn't then and don't now. I'd like to know if His plan aligns with Cyrus's—me living alone and turning my penthouse into a shrine until loneliness kills me.

I don't need to be guilted into missing her. I do every goddamned day, and I won't apologize for swearing in church. God knows what He did to me the minute he "called Tabby home."

Grief has taken up such a large portion of my heart it will be strange to live without it. If I can get to that point. Spending the day with Lily, Clint, Samantha, and their boys was a good start. I missed those afternoons and it will be nice to have them back.

I shift on the hard bench, the program crinkling in my hand. Lily scared me, getting winded while playing with the kids. It brought back difficult days when Tabby would sit on the porch, a blanket laying in her lap watching Clint, the boys, and me roughhouse in the yard. Samantha would usually sit with her, talk about shopping, SharperImage, gardening and cooking. Women stuff.

Lily sharing in the fun felt strange for everyone, and Clint knew I was overreacting when she had to stop and rest, something any normal person would have needed to do after playing an aggressive game of ball. She never said, but I'm sure he laid it all out in great detail while they washed dishes why something so harmless could send me over the edge.

Cyrus elbows me, and I focus on the sermon. The message is a good one, forgiving those who do us wrong as it's not our place to seek retribution. I can see where Cyrus and Ardith are coming from, I really do, and I might be able to forgive them for the things they've said to me because of their own pain, but when Keaton Kessler steps into my path—and I know he will—I will make him pay for what he did to Lily and I won't feel sorry for it.

We linger in the foyer after church, fellowshipping with Ardith's and Cyrus's friends, chatting with Pastor Greenwood who said he was glad to see me and that his door is always open if I ever need to pray. The room is stuffy, and I tug at my tie. Sweat drips down my back, but I don't know if it's from the heat in the room or because I know after Ardith is done speaking with an old friend of hers we're going to the cemetery to pay our respects at Tabby's grave.

"Sam," Cyrus says as she says goodbye, "it's time."

I rode with Cyrus and Ardith to the church, leaving my own car parked in their driveway. I could blame the queasiness on motion sickness, sitting in the backseat of the Mercedes minivan Tabby and I bought them for their anniversary a few years ago, or it could be because this will be my first time visiting Tabby's grave since meeting Lily and taking her to bed.

It might be a little of both, I think, as Cyrus slams on the brakes instead of running a yellow light. We never visit Tabby empty-handed, and we stop so Ardith can buy a large bouquet of pink roses. Traffic lightens as we get closer to the cemetery and Cyrus relaxes behind the wheel. I lean back in my seat and my mind skips around from Lily, Allessandra and other cases, my parents and what they're doing this weekend, to what I want to say to Tabby.

Cyrus turns onto the long gravel road and rocks crunch under his tires. Several people are taking advantage of the mild weather to visit loved ones who have passed. He parks half on the grass and half on the path in front of the section where Tabby's grave is located.

We're silent as we shuffle over the grass to her plot. I know every gravestone on the way to hers. Loving Parents, Missed Daughters, In Memory of Treasured Grandparents. A little girl, hit by a car, gone before her time. In my darkest hours, it would console me, knowing that Tabby and I had a happy life together. Not as long as we wanted, certainly, but longer than what some people are blessed with.

Ardith kneels the moment we reach Tabby's grave and starts tending to the immaculate grass. There aren't any weeds that need to be pulled, but she fusses and replaces flowers that look hours old with the new bouquet.

The inscription on the headstone never fails to lodge a lump in my throat.

Tabitha Grace Sharpe<br>
May 5, 1980-June 20, 2019<br>
Loving Daughter, Devoted Wife<br>
May she rest in the arms of Jesus.

The plot next to hers belongs to me, a macabre thing couples do when they think they're going to grow old together. We hadn't planned on Tabby needing hers so soon and my stomach rolls when I look at the empty granite.

Ardith starts to cry, and tears run down Cyrus's face. Tabby was daddy's little girl, and I had to prove over and over again I would be a good husband before he walked her down the aisle to meet me. It helped I came from a solid family with means and I was able to pay for the best care money could buy. Tabby never worked a day in her life, and Cyrus and Ardith had always been grateful.

A breeze blows gently over the cemetery, and I push my hands into my pockets. I miss her with a craving unrivaled by anything I've ever felt before. The scent of her skin, the taste of her lips, the feel of her arms around me. Yet, the hunger for her is fading, lost to thoughts of Lily and the kind of life we could have. It would be a different life. Not better, but different. While I never once minded living in the penthouse, Lily and I could build a house outside the city. We could go on holiday without me having to worry if she was getting enough rest. We could walk a dog in the evenings, and maybe down the road, somehow, have children, if she was open to that. She was so good with Cole and Carter. Tabby broached the subject to me once, not having our own, but fostering, adopting. A live-in nanny could have made it possible, but I didn't want to put her through any added stress and I told her I wanted to keep her all to myself. It wasn't a lie. During the fifteen years we were married, I didn't want or need anything else to be happy.

"Please stop seeing her." Cyrus's voice is rough, ragged with grief.

I never would have described him as cunning, but asking me to cut Lily off now, while we're standing on his daughter's grave, drops him to a new low I didn't think he was capable of.

"This isn't the place, Cyrus."

"Like hell it's not the place. Damn straight it's the place to tell you to stop seeing that hussy. Tabby wouldn't have wanted it, you *know* that."

"We didn't talk about what I'd do after she was gone." We avoided it.

"You didn't need to. You know what the right thing is, Sam. She wouldn't have wanted this."

Squinting in the bright sunlight, I meet his eyes. "You think Tabby, your kind, generous daughter, would have wanted me to spend the rest of my life alone. You really think that?"

His gaze flicks over my shoulder. "Yes."

He's lying. Out of church not half an hour, and he's lying to me. "What do you get out of this? You and Ardith? If I live the rest of my life a widower? I'll never be with another woman, never have children. I'll live alone in that penthouse with nothing but my memories of Tabby, driven to drink because I miss her, yet not allowed to move on. What do you get out of that?"

"You'll always have us, Sam. Come back into the fold. Start going to church with us again. Pastor Greenwood welcomed you back with open arms. We'll visit Tabby as much as you need. Every day, if it will make you feel close to her again. Spend Sunday afternoons at the house. We're still your family."

"I'll always be part of your family, even if I decide to remarry. Lily—"

"Will *never* be a part of our family," Cyrus says with such fury Ardith's eyes widen and her lips part in shock. "She's nothing but a gold digger, a whore, hanging on you for what you can give her. I know who she is. The paper printed her name and I researched her online." His pauses. "Don't you think there's a reason her ex-husband hit her? That maybe she deserved the punishment?"

Violence isn't the answer. Cyrus may claim to know what Tabby would have wanted, but I know without a doubt she wouldn't want me beating her father to a bloody pulp in the middle of the cemetery.

"Cyrus—" Ardith starts, scrambling to her feet.

"No, Ardith. He misses Tabby. We all do. Someone told me you can demand I stay single because you two still have each other. Maybe that's true. Maybe you have no idea what I'm feeling and what you're asking me to live with until I die too. On the other hand, maybe it's out of pure selfishness you don't want me to see Lily anymore. When I stopped by your house the other day, you guilted me into breaking up with her and it worked. But you know what? After I sent her away, I tried to drink myself to death because I'd rather be dead than live the second half of my life with only Tabby's ghost. Do you think she would have wanted *that*, Cyrus?" I suck in a much-needed breath of air. "I think you should go."

Ardith pauses, fighting between what her husband wants and how Tabby would have wanted her to treat me. "Do you need a ride?" she finally asks, stepping forward.

I narrow my eyes, pushed to my limits. "I won't need anything from you, ever again. I had the best part of both of you and she's gone."

Ardith gasps and Cyrus squares his shoulders. They turn, and without another word, wind their way around the gravestones. I stare until they climb into their van and go, Cyrus focused on the gravel path and Ardith, her face buried in her hands.

The second they're out of sight, I drop to my knees, clutching at Tabby's headstone for support. Eighteen years of my life are gone. Ardith and Cyrus may miss me because I'm the last link to their daughter, but I severed the only living ties I had left of her. Her parents had become a comfortable albatross around my neck. I needed them while they choked the life out of me. Now their hold is broken, but I still can't breathe.

"Christ, Tabby, tell me what to do," I beg, the cellophane wrapped around Ardith's flowers crinkling under my knees. "I miss you so much."

I sit with her, waiting for her to speak to me, until the sun starts to set, casting a golden glow over the stones. She would want me to move on. I believed it with all my heart when I asked Lily out the first time, and I believe it now. Maybe she would be envious of the things Lily and I will have—our walks, holidays, even touch football with Cole and Carter—but she would want me to have those things. She was always saying how sorry she was she couldn't give me more when what she was already giving me was perfect.

"When Lily's ready to move into an apartment, I'll sell our

penthouse," I tell Tabby. "If she can commit to a new life, then so can I. But I need your approval, baby. Some kind of a sign letting me know you're okay with it."

I sit for a few more minutes, waiting, for what I don't know. Lightning to strike or an idiotic rainbow, but nothing materializes that I would take as a sign from Tabby. Birds fly overhead, bees hover around flowers planted at some of the gravesites. I'm about to call Archer and tell him I need a ride when a pathetic mewling comes from behind Tabby's gravestone.

Bottle-green eyes peer at me around the granite, and moments later a grey cat with black markings, no more than a year old, skinny, shaking, and scared as hell, crawls through the grass, her belly low in fear. She approaches me, her nose twitching, her hunger winning.

I stretch my hand out and let her sniff. After a second's hesitation, she crawls into my lap. "I don't need this right now. Fuck."

Gingerly, I rub her head.

Tabby isn't going to send me a sign. If I want to be with Lily, that's a choice I'm going to have to make without anyone's help.

I call Archer. "I'm at Tabby's grave. I had a fight with her parents and you'll need to send someone to pick up my truck at their house. I'm stuck at the cemetery and need a ride back into the city and an overnight bag. And also . . . cat food."

"On it." Archer disconnects. He doesn't question the unusual request.

While I wait for him to pick me up, I sit with Tabby, my anger with her parents slipping away. At one point I would have considered apologizing, asking them if they still wanted to be a part of my life, albeit small one, but Cyrus's comment about Lily's ex-husband is unforgivable. There must be public record of Lily's abuse, and if that's the case, I need to ask my attorney to find the information and scrub it. I won't have Lily's privacy violated like that, not when I can do something about it.

Forty-five minutes later, Archer drives down the gravel path, but when he parks in front of the section where Tabby is buried, I'm reluctant to go. I always feel like this when I visit, like I'm abandoning her all over again. Archer waits patiently, knowing this is how I am and giving me time to push back my grief so I can pretend everything is okay. Each time I come, the pretending is a little easier, and today instead of a stab of sorrow and guilt, my "I'll be back soon" is bittersweet.

A bag of kitten kibble is sitting on the backseat along with my leather overnight satchel. I should call Lily and ask if she's in her room, if it's okay that I stop by and stay the night, but I don't want her to say no. I need her after the day I've had. I need her soft voice and barely-there smiles that still make my knees tremble and my heart quake with anger at the bastard who taught her to smile like that in the first place.

"The Regency, please." If Lily's not in her room or doesn't want me to stay, I can sleep upstairs. I'd rather sleep in an impersonal hotel room than go home. My nerves are too raw for that.

Archer parks near the curb and helps me out of the car. My hands are full of cat, food, and my things, and amused by my load, the doorman opens the door for me. I mumble, "Thank you" for his help.

The elevator's empty and thankfully I don't have to stop on the way to Lily's room. The cat squirms, not trusting me, and she hisses when I don't let her go, digging her claws into my arm.

"Hold on," I say, clutching at her and the plastic bag of food.

A little desperately, I knock on Lily's door, needing to put something down, preferably the cat before I lose a limb. I sense her on the other side, looking through the peephole, and she opens the door, alarmed. "What is it?"

"Cat. You've never seen one before?" I don't want to sound testy but rescuing this furball hadn't been part of my agenda.

She lifts the cat out of my arms, gently unhooking her claws from my suit jacket.

"Yes, I know what a tabby cat looks like. Where did you find her?"

"At the— What did you say?" I freeze just inside her room.

"I said I know what a cat looks like—"

"No, the other part."

"You mean a tabby cat? My mother loves them. She's always had two or three for as long as I can remember, and this one is gorgeous. Look at those eyes." Lily presses her nose to the cat's. "Let's get you some food and water, huh? And maybe a bath. You're filthy."

Lily picks up the bag of cat food off the floor and sets both the bag and the kitten on the desk.

I shake my head and look up at the ceiling. "Well played, Tabitha Sharpe. Well played."

***

Lily putters around the room with the cat, and I change into lounging pants and a t-shirt and order whiskey from room service. I lie on her bed, sipping the drink while I watch her struggle to bathe the cat in the bathroom sink. Despite being in a hotel room, it feels like home, and the tension Tabby's parents pushed on me drains away.

"We need a litter box."

"What?" I ask, her voice jerking me away from the cemetery.

"A litter box. Can you do that? This cat is going to pee all over the place if it doesn't have a box."

"How do you know she'll use it?"

"How do you know it's a she?" Lily lifts an eyebrow as she wraps a towel around the soaking wet cat.

"Good point." I call down to the front desk and request a litter box and litter. They'll do it because it's me, but this hotel is also pet-friendly and they might have a plastic box with a bag of litter sitting around somewhere.

Lily plops the wet furball onto the bed and starts rubbing at her with the bleached-white towel. "You never said where you found her."

"At the cemetery. I visit Tabby on Sundays."

I look at her to see if she's hurt, or, though it would be unlike her, jealous. She simply says, "I don't know how a cat would end up at a place like that unless she was dumped. Poor thing. Are you going to keep her?"

"Nope. She's yours."

Lily stops rubbing. "But I . . ."

I sip my drink. "What?"

She wraps the cat in the towel and lifts the squealing bundle to her chest. She kisses the top of the cat's head as two tears drip down her cheeks. "Keaton wouldn't let me have a cat."

Someone knocks on the door, and I roll off the bed. I press a kiss to Lily's temple. "I'll buy you a hundred cats if it makes you happy."

She sniffles. "I want to name her Tabby. Is that okay?"

I want to say no, that it's off limits. I can't say it all the time, her name on my lips every second because of a cat, but I asked for a sign and I got one. "It's perfect."

It's the first night we sleep together but don't make love. I lie on my back, an arm crooked above my head, and talking to the ceiling, tell her most of what Tabby's parents said and that I couldn't tolerate it anymore. "They didn't want me to move on. I think your theory about them wanting to hang on to me was true, but after I told them I couldn't be a part of their lives if they couldn't accept how I wanted to live mine, I realized I was hanging on to them too. They were all I had left of her, and I thought I needed the connection. All they were doing was keeping me in the past."

Lily turns to me, the cat sleeping between us. "You still love her, Sam. Sometimes it's okay to live in the past."

"Not if it's going to cost me my future." I rub my thumb over her cheek. The room's dim and I don't see her flinch, but I feel it, the slight jerk of her head expecting a slap instead of a caress. "I didn't think I'd have a second chance at this kind of happiness."

"You don't think we're moving too fast?" she asks, her voice soft, her breath hinting of mint.

"I feel like if I didn't, I'd lose you. When you stepped into my office for that job interview and I kicked you out . . . Rushing downstairs to see if you were still outside, scared you weren't but terrified you were, it seems like I'm still rushing, racing against the clock to keep you here. I don't know why there's such . . . it's not anticipation, that's too positive of a word, but foreboding, maybe. Urgency. Do you feel it?"

"Yes. But I'm not running to you, Sam, I'm running from Keaton and the things he did to me. I'm running from the lost relationships with my family, my friends. Maybe it's not me you're running to, but away . . . from Tabby's death. Her family. Your lost future with her. The things we're running from can't be outrun. We just don't know it yet."

Lily drifts into a troubled sleep, but I lie awake listening to her breathe.

She's wrong.

Tabby's gone, my ties to her parents severed. Not as neatly as they could have been, but severed just the same. I have nothing holding me back now except our memories I will never forget, regret we weren't able to grow old together, and shame I moved on as easily as I have, which wasn't *that* easy, I can hear Samantha point out. Those feelings I can deal with, and I will. With the help of Samantha, my parents, and Lily.

What Lily's running from isn't much different. She can repair the relationship with her parents, and I'll encourage her to make friends here. With eyes on her, Kessler will never bother her again, though eliminating him permanently will satisfy me a lot more, and I'm sure Lily will sleep easier.

It will help when Lily signs a lease in Carthage. It will help when I sell my penthouse. It will help when the time is right and I ask her to marry me.

I'm running too fast, and she can't keep up. One thing at a time.

She's keeping the cat. She won't run if she has the cat. With the way she doted on her all evening, she would never leave her behind, and trying to run with her would be too much work.

If her feelings for the cat outweigh her feelings for me, I'll take it.

For now, I'll take it.

---

Archer packed me a suit, and in the morning, I shave while Lily showers, her sexy figure a smokey silhouette behind the frosted glass. My cock does his thing under the towel wrapped around my waist, but I tell him to calm down. I finish quickly and move into the bedroom before she sees. I don't want her to think our relationship is about sex, and last night I was more than content to sleep beside her without it.

We dress in silence, and she wiggles into a russet-colored sheath dress and snakes a dark orange belt around her waist. "Do you think we should tell housekeeping about Tabby?"

"What about her?" I ask absent-mindedly, tying my tie in the mirror.

"That she's here?" she asks, nudging my hands aside and straightening out the knot. "Will they scoop her litter? Feed her?"

Oh, the cat. I'm going to need time to get used to that. Tabby's namesake.

Lily did a better job on my tie than I did, and I tuck my shirt into my pants. "We can ask the concierge to do that."

"Is that person usually a male? Does he have a reason to go into people's rooms?"

Buckling my belt, I ask, "Why?"

"Because the other night there was a shoe print in the carpet and I told myself it was hotel staff and not to worry about it."

I pause. "No one should have access to your room."

"I know, but any of the staff can come in here, right?" She shrugs. "Maybe it was housekeeping."

"Housekeeping wears tennis shoes. Even the males. I'm checking into this, Lily."

She pulls a cardigan out of the closet and leans over to pick her purse up off the floor. The cat brushes against her legs and she scratches behind her ears before standing.

"I don't want to be any trouble."

I cuddle her to me, my hand to her lower back, and raise my other hand to her face. Will there ever be a day when I don't have to warn her before I want to touch her? I hope so. "Your safety," I say firmly, grazing by thumb over her jaw, "will never be trouble. Never. I couldn't save Tabby from the breast cancer that took her life and I couldn't fix her weak heart, but I did what I could with the resources I had and she lived as peacefully and as happily as possible. I will do the same for you."

"Sam," she says, her voice a breathy puff of disbelief.

"Two weeks, and I already can't live without you. Christ, I hope you feel the same." I'm afraid of her answer, and instead of letting her speak, I crush my lips to hers. She drops her purse with a thud to the carpet and wraps her arms around my neck.

I suppose I don't have to say we were late for work.

The shoe print in Lily's room bothers me. The fact that Cyrus knew Lily's ex-husband abused her bothers me. I rub the backs of my fingers over my jaw and tap my pen against the blotter covering the surface of my desk. Those two things should be exclusive of each other, but the pit in my stomach tells me they're not.

I call Archer and ask him to retrieve copies of the Regency's security tapes. I'm not angry with the men who are supposed to be watching Lily. If it happened while she was here at SharperImage, there would have been no reason to watch her hotel room. That needs to change, and I tell Archer to add another man to her detail.

With that out of the way, I email my attorney and ask that his IT guy let his spiders loose on the web and search for anything about Lily that shouldn't be online. Kessler's a cop—he shouldn't want evidence on the internet, either—but he might just be slimy enough no one would believe he's capable of that. Friendly detective during the day, solving homicides to keep the citizens of Honeywell and the greater New York area safe, but in the evening, takes his anger out on the one person he should cherish most.

Samantha peeks her head around the door we share. She's shining, high off the weekend. She misses Tabby as much as I do, but until I started seeing Lily, I hadn't realized how much she worried about me. "Staff meeting after lunch. I want Lily in on that, okay?"

"Yeah," I say absently, still mulling over where Cyrus found his information.

"Oh, and I've got HR back on the hunt for a PA for you. Lily's been doing some of it, but I also have her working with Blaine. Is that okay?"

"Why wouldn't it be? He's a good exec." He's also attractive and charming, and all the women in the office swoon when he walks by, grinning, happy with the road he's chosen.

"Okay, just checking." She ducks back into her office.

"Hey, Sammie?"

"Yeah?" She leans against the doorjamb.

"If something happened between you and Clint, you'd still stay in touch with his family, wouldn't you?"

"Depends on why we weren't together anymore, but I'd have to keep in mind that my choices would affect Cole and Carter. They love Clint's family. Over time, I don't think I'd be as close to his mother as I am now. We're close because we're a family. If Clint and I weren't together anymore, it would be difficult to feel as if his family was still mine. Do you get what I'm saying?"

"Yeah, I do." That's what happened when Tabby passed away. Her family didn't feel like my family anymore.

"Is this about Tabby's parents?"

I shrug.

"Things would be completely different if you and Tabby would have had children. You can't keep kids from their grandparents. I don't think it's right and it's not something you would have done. Now? Honestly, Sam, I don't see any reason for you to stay in touch with them. Lily has her own family, and you'll get to know them, at some point. No one is a replacement for anyone else, but things change."

"What if Lily didn't have a family?"

Samantha tilts her head and narrows her eyes. "I'm not sure what you're getting at, but you've seen the size of our family, right? I'm not even talking about Clint and the kids. *Our* family. Your mom and dad, mine. My brothers and their families. Is this about Thanksgiving? Are you scared to invite her to Thanksgiving?" She laughs.

I scowl. "I wasn't, but thanks for that."

"She stared down Gary and Allessandra's father. I think she'll be just fine."

"Lily said she had a falling out with her parents over her ex-husband, that's all. She thinks a reconciliation isn't possible."

Samantha stomps into my office, yanks one of my business cards off their little easel and shoves it under my nose. "Are you a PR guy or not?"

I wave her away. "Lily's parents aren't clients."

"No, they're more important than any client we've ever had. But even with our toughest cases, we've always managed to get the job done. I don't think her mom and dad will be an exception. If they miss her, your job is half done."

"You're right."

"I usually am. Meeting, after lunch, but right now, I think you have a phone call to make."

"Yeah. Thanks. For all of it."

"You're welcome."

If I didn't have the information Archer searched out on Lily's parents, there would have been a lot of digging I'd have needed to do to find them. There are thousands of Fowlers in the United States, hundreds in New York, and more than one listed number in Honeywell. Lily didn't mention other family, but it could be she also has uncles, aunts, and cousins who live in the same city.

At every turn, I discover Kessler stole more from her than I thought.

I find their home telephone number in the file Archer gave me, and I call using the landline sitting on my desk. If they're the type who don't answer phone numbers they aren't familiar with, I'll need to leave a message. I'm thinking of what information I want to share in the best possible way that would encourage them to return my call when a faint, thin female voice answers, "Hello?"

My mouth is suddenly dry. I should have prepared what I want to say. "Mrs. Fowler?"

"Yes? Who is this?"

"My name is Samuel Sharpe. I'm a public relations executive for SharperImage—"

"I'm sorry. We don't accept solicitations."

"No, please wait. I'm not a telemarketer. Don't hang up. I'm calling about your daughter, Lily."

Mrs. Fowler pauses. "Lily? It's been several years since we've spoken. I'm afraid I don't have any information about her."

"That's why I'm calling, Mrs. Fowler. I do. I own a public relations firm in Carthage, Minnesota, and she works for me."

She sucks in a breath, the gasp audible over the line. "Lily's in Carthage?"

"You didn't know." This surprises me. I would have thought someone had told them their daughter finally left Kessler, even if it hadn't been that long ago.

"No. I couldn't . . . We didn't . . ." She tries again. "I couldn't watch what that horrible man was doing to her. She wouldn't leave him. She let him hit— We couldn't—" Her voice cracks, and a muted sob comes over the line, like she put her hand to her mouth.

"I know, and I understand," I say, though I don't, not really. Maybe they felt powerless because Kessler's a cop. Maybe they didn't know what they could do to help her, especially if she did feel some spousal loyalty at the beginning and wouldn't listen, but it would be a cold day in hell before I cut off anyone in my family simply because they were doing something I didn't agree with.

"You know? She told you?"

"She told me some of it. She's divorced now, and I met her during an interview when I was hiring a new assistant."

"She left him."

There is so much awe in her voice I would have laughed if we weren't talking about something so serious. And it is. Lily demonstrated tremendous courage leaving Kessler, and she pays for it every day, having to look over her shoulder.

"Yes, she did. She's very brave."

"She's in Carthage, working for you. How did she end up there?"

"Lily told me she moved here to feel closer to you. I brought her to The Carthage Institute of Art. I discovered you had gone there on a class field trip, and I walked through the museum with her."

"It's still there."

"Yes."

There's a pause.

"Why did you call me . . . Mr. Sharpe, was it?"

"Yes. Sam Sharpe. I called you because I'm in love with your daughter, and one day, when she's strong enough, I want to marry her. She's still raw, being married to that asshole damaged her self-esteem—excuse my language—but when she's ready, I want her to be my wife. I called you because I want to give her everything I can, and she misses you. If I can somehow help fix what happened between you and her . . . I want to give her that."

I hadn't admitted to myself that's where I wanted Lily and I to go, but once I say the words, I can't take them back because they're true. I want to marry her when she's ready to belong to someone else. I don't want her to belong to anyone but me.

"Does she . . . Do you know if she feels the same?" There's a touch of amusement in her voice and some of the tension seeps out of my body.

"I think she's beginning to, but Kessler did more than break her body, he broke her heart and spirit, too. I'll do what I can to help repair them, but I understand that once she's healed, I may not be what she wants."

"You're a very wise man, Mr. Sharpe."

"I've had my own tragedies, Mrs. Fowler. Life experience is the best teacher."

"It is, and I've had my own share of regrets cutting her out of my life, *our* lives. Her father has missed her just as much as I have, but Keaton, he threatened Ed. He told my husband if we tried to interfere, it would be worse for Lily, and we believed him. We cut her off for her sake as much as for ours, at least, that's what we go to bed believing, hoping for a good night's rest."

Someone knocks on my door, and Lily pokes her head into my office. "Oh, sorry," she whispers, seeing me on the phone.

I move the receiver away from my mouth. "No, wait. She's here," I say to Mrs. Fowler. "Would you like to talk to her?"

"She wants to speak with me?" Her voice is full of fear.

"I think she would. I'll put her on. Just a moment."

I cover the mouthpiece and hold the phone out to Lily. "There's someone who'd like to talk to you."

Lily pales, shakes her head, and steps back.

"It's not Keaton. I would *never* do that to you. Here," I say, holding the phone in her direction. "You've been waiting a long time for this."

She walks around my desk, and standing, I hand her the receiver.

"Hello?" she says, her shoulder brushing against my chest.

I wait for Mrs. Fowler's response. I hope I did the right thing. Whenever Lily spoke about her parents it was always with regret, but she never asked me if I thought trying to get in touch with them was a good idea. She didn't mention if she reached out to the man who helped her, either. It's her choice and I don't want to push, especially if she's not ready, but I want her to live like Kessler isn't in the picture anymore because one day he won't be.

Her mother must say something because Lily's gaze shoots to mine.

"Mom?" She stumbles backward and falls into my chair, tears filling her eyes. "H-how are you?"

Kissing the top of her head, I mumble into her hair, "Take all the time you need."

I indulge, and just before I step into the hallway, I look over my shoulder. Tears are streaming down Lily's face and she's laughing and weeping, answering a question, each word punctuated by a quiet cry.

I want to be there when she hangs up with her parents, and forty-five minutes later, I'm leaning against Shiloh's desk while I wait, hashing out my meeting schedule for the week. My office door flies open and Lily rushes out, staring at the floor. She hurries past me so quickly I don't get a chance to say anything before she's turning the corner toward the elevator.

Samantha watches from her office's doorway. "Are you going after her?"

What a stupid question. "I will *always* go after her."

I ignore the gleam of approval in her eyes and stride to the elevator, praying with all my heart that Lily's still downstairs when I reach the lobby.

I find her outside, near a corner of the building, leaning against the brick, hiding her face in her hands.

"Hey," I say tentatively. She could be angry I stuck my nose into her business, or a reconciliation with her parents may not have been what she wanted and our wires were crossed. Something happened to make her run out of my office the way she did, and if that's somehow my fault, I need to tread lightly.

"Why would you do that?" she whispers, moving her hands away from her face. Her eyes are bloodshot, her skin pale forcing her freckles into the spotlight. She's beautiful, tragically, sorrowfully, and my heart cracks every time I look at her. It's a wonder between Tabby's death and meeting Lily blood flows through my veins at all.

With forced nonchalance, I rest my shoulder against the building. "Tell me first if you're happy I did or if you want to kick me in the balls for interfering."

She huffs a quiet laugh. "I'm stunned. I'm happy, but I'm stunned, Sam. Why would you do that? First a cat and now my parents."

I step closer to her. "Because I want to give you everything that fucking asshole took away from you. I don't want you to ever go without, ever again. Friends, family, security, love. Because when I see you, I see my future, and when I make you happy, that makes me happy. Because I lo—"

Her eyes widen and her lips part. She's not ready to hear the word. Maybe Kessler told her he loved her after he hit her and he ruined what the word meant. It's only a word. I took care of Tabby for fifteen years and my actions meant more to her than words ever could. She depended on me, and if I wouldn't have pulled through, words would have meant little.

I need to show Lily I love her, and maybe one day she'll believe it's true.

"Fuck it," I mumble, and cover her lips with mine.

---

I text Samantha and tell her Lily and I are going to lunch. We walk to a little deli two blocks away and grab a corner table for two by the window overlooking the street. Lily holds our place while I stand in line and order our sandwiches and drinks. When I weave my way around the other tables with our lunch, she's staring out the window, a picture of sadness and loss.

"What are you thinking about?" I ask, sliding the tray in her direction and sitting in the seat across from her.

"Thanks," she says, picking up her plate that has a ham and Swiss cheese croissant, two pickle spears, and a handful of chips on it. "What you said earlier. About what Keaton took away from me. You don't notice it, you know, until someone says something and it all starts to add up. I lost my friends, but some people do when they get together and want to spend all their time with each other. It's only years later when their new love wears off they look up and realize they've pushed everyone away. My parents made it clear they wouldn't have anything to do with me if I married him, and that was my choice. But other things, like a cat, security—" she says, tipping her head at me— "little things normal people take for granted, I gave up because I married the wrong man. I didn't thank you, and that was rude. Thank you for calling her. I wouldn't have on my own."

I lift my own plate off the tray. "You're welcome. You might not think I understand what you're talking about, but I do. When Tabby died, I felt like she took my whole life with her. We never would have had children, but I still planned on us going on holidays, spending as much time with her and our families as SharperImage would allow. We got good at celebrating the little things, making each day count. I'm glad we fell into that. It made her passing more bearable, even if it didn't feel like it at the time. Kess—" I stop. I don't want her to think I've done any more snooping than I have. "The five years you spent with Keaton," I start again, "were hell for you—I can't imagine what kind of hell—but he also put you in my path. The night we met . . . sometimes I think about what would have happened to me if I wouldn't have stopped at that bar, or maybe had gone to a different one. Had maybe simply gone home for yet another night alone in the penthouse I shared with Tabby. You've changed my life so completely in these past two weeks. Everything Keaton took away from you, I hope you let me give it back. When you're ready. I never want to push."

She covers my hand with hers. "Sometimes I think about what would have happened if I wouldn't have let you sit. If I would have taken a chance with the employment agency's good graces and told Dottie I didn't want to interview for any position at SharperImage. Or, when you chased me down to the street, if I would have told you to fuck off. Imagining all those things, Sam, makes me sicker than staring down one of Keaton's fists." She sucks in a breath. "I'm ready to find an apartment."

"You don't know how relieved I am to hear that. Will you let me help you?"

She nibbles on a chip, the salt sticking to her lips. "I was hoping you would. I don't know the city very well and it would be great if you could tell me the neighborhoods that are nice that I can afford, and the ones I should stay away from."

Feeling more settled than I have in a long time, I bite into my sandwich. I swallow and say, "We'll get it sorted. Sooner, rather than later, I would imagine, since I bet you're tired of hotel living."

"For the first few days, I used the hotel and the security as a fortress. I was so sure Keaton was going to hunt me down. When my friend in Honeywell told me he was still there, that he was working a big case and couldn't leave, I let my guard down and began to enjoy it. Then we went to Samantha's and I missed having my own kitchen. I want to invite you over, cook for you, if that's something you'd like."

She's stepping right into the storybook life I've been telling myself, and it couldn't have made me happier. "I'd love that."

"Good."

We eat in companionable silence, and Lily seems more content than she did even this morning. Her shoulders are loose, and she smiles at a couple of teenagers holding hands, more than likely skipping school, stealing kisses when the sidewalk clears and they won't bump into anyone. I want her like this all the time. She might not have health issues, but I can still protect her like I did Tabby, shield her as much as I can from the harsh realities of life.

"Oh," she says, her cheeks pink, "another reason I want to find an apartment is because my mother mentioned possibly visiting in November for my birthday. Would you mind?"

"Of course not. I would love to meet them. Tell me when they want to fly in, and I'll make the arrangements. They can either stay with you, or I'll put them up at the Regency. Don't ever be afraid to ask me for something, Lily. Whatever I can give you, I will."

Crumpling a plain white napkin in her hand, she asks, "What can I give you?"

I risk telling her the truth. "One day, I'm going to ask you to marry me. I won't ask until I feel you're ready to hear the question, but that doesn't mean you'll say yes. I would appreciate it, if you say no, you say it gently and break my heart only a little."

She sighs. "You're not asking now?"

"No." I begin to gather our trash.

"Why not?" She sounds indignant and it gives me hope.

"Because I have a funny feeling our pasts aren't done fucking with us, and I think you have a better chance of saying yes if I can ask when we have a clean slate."

She grimaces and throws her napkin onto the tray. "I think you could be right."

I grab her wrist. "I will do whatever I have to do to keep you safe. You understand that, right?"

Nodding slightly, she says, "Yeah. I do."

She couldn't possibly understand what I mean. There's only one way Kessler will go down, and go down for good.

My cell rings, and I pull it out of my pocket. Archer's number glows on the screen. "I have to answer this."

"Okay."

"What did you find out?" I ask, turning away from Lily and mumbling into my phone.

"I pulled the tapes and identified the guy who let himself into Miss Fowler's room. I sent you the clip. Take a look at it and tell me what you want me to do."

"Stay on the line." I navigate away from the phone app to my texts and play the video Archer sent over of the Regency's security tapes. He must have sat through hours of footage to find the man who was able to manipulate the front desk agent into giving him access to Lily's room.

He's easily recognizable as I just saw him yesterday at church. What was he digging for, and why? Well, I know why, but what does he have to gain from gathering information about Lily? She should be of little consequence to him.

I close out of my texts and ask Archer, "Are you still there?"

"Yes."

"Don't do anything for now. I don't know what their endgame is, and I'd prefer to let it play out rather than interfere. If I stop something in progress, I'll never know how far they were willing to go, and I don't want her to live like this anymore. Dammit. We have eyes on her. Keep it that way." Archer oversees my security, and everything Lily needs goes through him. "Keep the extra guy on her room so this doesn't happen again."

"Yes, sir."

"I'll help her move to a different floor and I'm going to get her out of the hotel as quickly as I can. Good work. Thanks."

I disconnect and turn back to Lily who has dumped our trash and returned the tray. "Is everything okay?" she asks.

"I heard from the hotel. There was a little mix up and the front desk sent a new guest to your room by mistake. Once he realized the room was occupied, he left. No harm done, but I would feel better if we changed your room and the floor you're on. You've been in that room for what, three weeks? Maybe more. Let's mix it up. A suite, huh, until you can find a place to live?"

She searches my face, looking for some kind of sign that things aren't as well as I said they are. Finding none—I can lie like the best of them, as Samantha says, I am a PR guy after all —she nods in agreement. "Okay. That sounds fine. When?"

"I think Samantha will have my head if we're not at that meeting she scheduled at one. She's been walking on sunshine since you accepted the promotion. After the meeting, we'll cut out—"

She opens her mouth to protest.

"—I know you don't want to miss work, but moving your things and checking on Tabby are priorities today that won't always pop up. If you'll feel better, after we move you, we'll go back to the office and work through dinner. I'll walk you through some of our client files myself."

"I want to pull my weight, and I want to earn my paycheck," she says, letting me lead her out of the deli and onto the sidewalk. "I'm more than capable of the work or Dottie wouldn't have sent me to interview with you in the first place."

"I have no doubts, but it's only the start of your second week. We'll give you time to settle in. You're not expected to know everything on the first day, no matter where you would have ended up."

I never minded Tabby didn't work for SharperImage. Even part time, the days would have taken their toll, and she kept herself occupied with activities and fundraisers the church hosted instead. I realize as I walk back to the office with Lily, working with her adds a dimension to our relationship I didn't have with Tabby. Sharing my family's passion with the woman I love will complete me in a way I couldn't experience with my wife. It won't make my marriage any less, and it doesn't make my relationship with Lily any more than what I had, just different.

I tamp down the guilt. If I can't push it back, I'll never believe I deserve to be happy with someone else.

Samantha and Blaine are on Lily the moment we step onto the executive floor, and I slip into my office and secure a suite for Lily at the Regency.

Now that I'm alone, I watch the clip Archer sent me in its entirety. I lose the asshole when he enters Lily's room, but the time ticking at the bottom of the screen indicates he poked around for a good fifteen minutes before he reappears in the hallway's camera view.

What was he looking for? And more importantly, what did he think he found? Lily owns a personal laptop. I've seen it in her room, but I don't know if it's password protected. What else could he find? She would have her papers with her—social security card, birth certificate. A copy of her divorce decree, possibly a passport. I don't understand why he would need any of it, or what use he would have for that kind of information.

The only way to find out is to ask, but I'd rather give him rope and let him hang himself.

After fifteen years, I'd think he'd know me better than this.

I'm not going to let him get away with anything, not even for Tabby's sake.

# CHAPTER NINE

*Lily*

My first staff meeting with Sam, Samantha, and the rest of the
PR executives gave me goosebumps. I didn't have anything to
formally contribute, though Sam and Samantha once again
thanked me for the headway made on Allessandra's case.

Since she met us that morning in the office, she's appeared
on several more talk shows, has hosted a handful of smaller
benefits like the ones she told me she wished she could have,
and, with supervision, started dating, being photographed in
LA with a social media star who shot his way to fame singing a
Bon Jovi cover in his basement.

Though I gave her my number, I haven't heard from her,
but by the looks of the news segments, she's doing just fine. The
court assigned her two thousand hours of community service
and fined her for driving while intoxicated. The family she
crashed into wasn't happy with the outcome, but her founda-
tion donated a million dollars to their charity of choice, and
after that, they would have looked bad for complaining further.

After the meeting, just like Sam promised, we went to the hotel and moved all my things up two floors. Tabby was excited to see us, and the moment we opened the door to my new room, she bolted inside to explore. Sam must have called ahead—a suite was already available—and after I put my clothes and jewelry where I wanted them to go, we made love on the bed, the cat curled up on the loveseat in the sitting area. He didn't undress me, simply laid me down on the bedspread, took off my heels and slid my panties down my legs. He tossed his suit jacket onto a chair, lowered his pants and briefs just enough to free his cock, and covered my body with his.

He didn't say one word the entire time.

Slowly, inch by excruciating inch, he pushed inside me, and I sighed his name, loving every second of him claiming me.

He fluttered kisses all over my face as he came.

He wants to marry me.

Such a gift, and he didn't know he was giving it to me. I thought myself damaged goods, too broken to be loved by any man, yet he does. He almost said it outside the building after I spoke to Mom, and I wish he would have. I want to hear him say it, but he'll wait.

Maybe until I say it first, but I can't yet. Not until I know Keaton won't bother me ever again, but that day may never be a reality.

"You didn't come," he murmured, rolling off me and cuddling me to his side.

"I don't have to come every time," I said, his cum warming me. I love it when he leaves a piece of himself behind.

"Maybe not, but I like it when you do."

He reached between my legs and wet his fingers with his own semen, swirling it around my clit, massaging it into my tender skin.

"Sam," I said, my nerves sparking.

"Shh. Let me do this." Pushing his fingers inside me as far as they could go, he pressed the heel of his hand to my clit and just as he did, he crashed his lips to mine, our teeth gnashing together. I tilted my hips, increasing the pressure, and moaned into his mouth as I came, my muscles clenching around him, our cum trickling out of me.

When my heartbeat had slowed and sweat was drying on my skin, I opened my eyes. He was staring at me, his fingers still inside me, a lock of hair falling over his forehead.

"You are so beautiful when you come," he whispered, rubbing his nose with mine. "You think I did that for you, but I really did it for me."

I laughed, my lips touching his in a semi-kiss. "I have no complaints."

Reluctantly, we cleaned up and headed back to the office, and it's where I sit, in a conference room with Sam, his laptop on the table in front of us. A tall pile of files is stacked next to him—a stack I helped Shiloh put together last Friday.

"You're thinking about it," he mumbles, a pencil clenched between his teeth, typing on his laptop.

"What?"

"You're thinking about this afternoon. It's making you wet. I can smell it."

"I'm sor—"

He grins around the pencil and I swat at his arm.

"You can not. Liar."

"You're right, I can't, but that doesn't mean you're not thinking about it."

"That part is correct, Mr. Sharpe," I say primly, crossing my legs.

He takes the pencil out of his mouth and kisses me, a hand to the back of my head. "I could get used to working with you. It's pleasant."

"I'm glad. I like it too. Coffee?"

"Sure. If you don't mind."

"No, it's fine. I'll be right back."

I roll my chair away from the conference table and move toward the door. There aren't many lights on in the office, but it's not time for the janitorial crew to clean yet. We're here during the sweet spot of the day—no one is here but us.

"Hey," he says, and I turn around.

Tension pulls at his eyes and mouth and a glimmer of the man I met at the bar takes over his features and stature. I always know when he's thinking about her.

I respect her for the woman she was . . . and the man she left behind.

There's not one word I can speak against her.

Lowering my head, I give her a moment of silence. "I know, Sam."

He nods once, and I step into the hallway, the door bumping shut behind me.

We work late, and after we're done with as much as we can do without Samantha or the others, he drops me off in front of the Regency. "Goodnight, Lily."

"Goodnight. Thank you for everything you've done for me." I rest my hand against his cheek.

A sad look flutters across his face, but I don't know what he could be thinking about besides Tabby. "Anything. Anytime."

I unbuckle my seatbelt and grab my purse that's by my feet. Sam opens the truck's door for me and waits until I'm inside the lobby before pulling away from the curb.

It's too late for a bubble bath, but at the front desk, I order a glass of wine and a piece of cheesecake from room service. In my suite, I greet Tabby, change into pajamas, and while I'm feeding her and giving her fresh water, my dessert is delivered.

Sitting with my laptop at a small table near the window, I

search for the case Keaton's working on in Honeywell. A news clip of him speaking at a press conference indicates he's still in the city, his frown telling everyone how unhappy he is with the progress. My stomach slithers when he scowls and my hand trembles as I reach for my wineglass. No one should get in his way whenever he looks like that, and though it didn't work every time, I was an expert at avoiding him, or trying to, at least.

*He's still there*, I think and help myself to another bite of the rich chocolate cheesecake. He's still there, in the middle of a case that's garnering national coverage. It's fine. I'm fine.

But there will come a day when he solves that case or it will grow cold, and Sam and I will still be in the news. The social media attention will rake at Keaton's skin, fueling the rage that has only been banked by the murder investigation and his new girlfriend.

I'm fine, here, right now, but there will be a day when I'm not.

I had no idea how quickly that day would come.

---

I could get used to working late with Sam and bringing him coffee. I could get used to the goodbye kisses at my door.

I find the same contentment in my routine the next morning. I could get used to dressing for Sam, wondering which color dress he likes best. Hailing a cab and riding to work—at a company I enjoy working for, people I enjoy working with. Lunches with Shiloh, dinner with Sam, weekends with Samantha and Clint and their children. Living in an apartment, an apartment Sam helped me find, with a cat he gave me.

I could get used to this life.

I could get used to it, and that was my mistake.

Everything I ever wanted that I found with Sam, Sharper-

Image, and the friendships I've made are jerked away from me the second he approaches me on the sidewalk. A man I don't know, but a man capable of destroying my whole life and has no qualms doing it.

"Miss Fowler," he says, stepping away from the wall of the hotel and into my path.

I want to get to the office before Sam. I'm proud and happy to have a hot cup of coffee sitting on his desk when he steps into his office and he smiles, thinking about me. No matter how early I leave for the work, Samantha always seems to get there first, a mischievous glint in her eyes. Over the past few days she's turned into a good friend and I don't want to let her down.

"Yes?" I ask, distracted, searching the street for a taxi. I could ask Sam for a car, but the request for private transportation didn't seem that important knowing Keaton is still in Honeywell. Sam would never press me to use the car service. He knows how much my independence means to me after having such a domineering husband track my every move.

"You don't know me, but my name is Pastor Greenwood."

"How can I help you? I'm not interested in joining a congregation at this time." I raise my arm to get the attention of a taxi half a block away, but a businessman carrying a briefcase and a folded newspaper snatches it first, an apologetic smile on his face that doesn't excuse his bad manners.

"I'm not here in that capacity. I'm the pastor at Tabitha and Sam Sharpe's church."

I stop on the sidewalk then, the urgency to arrive at the office before Sam and Samantha falling away. Hearing Sam's name linked with Tabitha's jolts me, and I pause mid-stride, frozen in place. When he says her name, she seems real somehow, not just one of Sam's painful memories. Mentioned in present tense, she's *alive*, and my heart screeches to a halt in my chest.

Without Sam, I have no one.

I'm alone as the day I moved to Carthage, a bruise on my cheek, not a friend to my name.

"Tabitha and Sam," I say, my voice faint, my lips barely moving.

"Yes. You see, Tabitha's father spoke with me and explained the situation."

"The situation?" I echo, meeting his eyes that are shielded behind a pair of frameless glasses. He's grey everywhere: grey hair, grey skin, grey suit. There's no color but a gold wedding band on his left hand that glints in the sun when he gestures.

"Sam has been distraught since Tabitha's death, and it's only natural for him to seek comfort. I've counseled him in these two years since she passed away, urging him to find solace in the arms of God, not between a hussy's legs who only wants him for his money."

I lift my chin. "I'm not a hussy, and I think it should be Sam's choice where he wants to find peace."

Pastor Greenwood chuckles. "My dear, do you think you're the first woman he's been with since his wife's death? The first woman he's talked into bed in hopes of washing his wife's touch off his skin? The first woman he's led upstairs to his room at the Regency? He's lost and hurting. He'll throw you away as he has the others, and once again I'll have to try to convince him fucking a woman he doesn't love only makes his pain worse."

My skin turns cold.

How could I be so stupid?

Of course he wouldn't want me, wouldn't want the woman Keaton turned me into. Afraid to be touched, afraid to fall in love, afraid to belong to someone because the one time I did, it almost killed me and I don't want to do that again.

"You believe me. Good. I want you to believe this as well: I do what I must to protect members of my congregation. I'll do whatever I have to do to protect Tabitha's memory. I called your husband, Miss Fowler, or should I say, Mrs. Kessler. I wondered if it was the right thing to do, but Tabitha's father convinced me that I had no choice. A wife is her husband's property and it's his responsibility to punish you for the things you've done."

My mind latches on to bits and pieces. *A wife is her husband's property. Mrs. Kessler. I called your husband.* "Keaton? Y-you called Keaton."

I reach out to grasp something, anything, that will keep me on my feet, but my hand clutches at nothing but air. Pastor Greenwood grabs my arm, his fingertips digging into my skin.

"I did. I explained everything, and he'll be landing in Carthage in half an hour. Don't try to run, Mrs. Kessler. He'll find you, and when he does, he'll give you what you deserve for trying to hide and spreading your legs like the whore you are. I'll see to it myself, and once he's finished with you, not even God will be able to help you."

He pushes me away and I stumble, but miraculously, I don't fall, my ankle twisting slightly in my heels.

I leave him standing on the sidewalk, watching me, and calmly, I walk back to the hotel, wanting to tear the skin off my bones in agitation as the slow elevator carries me to my floor. Once I'm in my suite, I pack my carry-on with a change of clothes, fresh panties, and my toothbrush and toothpaste. Cash, my identification. I won't take my burner phone—I'll buy a new one somewhere. I'll leave my laptop, my clothes, and my jewelry behind. Tabby. She winds her lithe body around my ankles and my eyes fill with tears, but there's no way I can bring her with me.

I change quickly into a pair of jeans and the shirt and vest I wore to Samantha and Clint's. The scent of woodsmoke still lingers in the material.

Sam used me for sex. He never loved me, only wanted me for what he could get. My heart rejects it even as my mind adds up all the evidence. He latched on to me quickly, screwed me the night we met.

I can't waste any more time, but I use precious moments hailing a taxi and going to SharperImage. Sam won't be in yet, but Samantha will be.

The taxi lets me out in front of the building, but I don't have the money to ask him wait. Riding the elevator—and stopping at every floor between the lobby and the executive offices —will waste more than ten minutes, and with my heart sinking, pay him and watch the car meld into traffic.

Samantha's talking with Blaine when I step off the elevator, and I almost run across the floor in my haste. Pastor Greenwood said Keaton would land in Carthage in half an hour. That was twenty minutes ago. He can't know where I am or where I'm going, and I'm hoping in a city this large I can disappear before he even knows I'm gone.

In his arrogance, Pastor Greenwood made a grave mistake in warning me. I've gotten away from Keaton once. I'll do it again.

"I have to go," I say urgently, tugging on her arm and leading her away from Blaine.

"Why? Where? What's going on?" Samantha asks, alarmed, her eyes wide.

"I can't tell you. I just wanted you to know that you were a good friend and I'll never forget that. Sam—" I don't want to believe what Pastor Greenwood said, but our relationship, how we met, was too smooth, too quick to be real. "Tell Sam that even if he was only looking for sex to forget about Tabitha, I still fell in love with him. Tell him that I know he used me, and it's okay. He made me believe I was worth something to someone, and I'll never forget that either."

"Lily, what in the hell are you talking about? Sam would never—"

"I have to go. Please." I glance at Blaine who's watching us, his eyes filled with worry. I try to smile at him, but I fail. How can I smile at anyone when my life is crashing down around me?

Samantha doesn't try to stop me and I love and hate her for it. If she would tell me I was safe, if she would promise that Sam could protect me . . . but there is no protection from Keaton. Something else Sam said that I foolishly believed.

The elevator carries me down to the lobby, and when I step out, I pause. I don't want to run into Sam and I don't want to be seen on the sidewalk. I don't know how much Pastor Greenwood told Keaton about me, about my routine, but he'll have told him where I work and where I've been staying. I grew too comfortable in Carthage, and I need to remember I can't trust anyone and to expect Keaton around any corner.

I go out the back of the building and hurry down a sidewalk away from SharperImage. I still have a pass from my first week in the city, and before it pulls away, I hop onto a bus at a stop on the corner.

Pastor Greenwood said Keaton's flying, that means I can't be anywhere near the airport. It's too easy for him with his police clearance to check passenger lists, never mind he could still be there if his flight was delayed. No, I need to go to the bus station and pay for a ticket with cash. That's the only way I can hope to leave Carthage undetected.

With the constant stops, the bus doesn't reach the depot located in north Carthage for over an hour. I'm tired, hungry, and I have to go to the bathroom, but I don't dare slow down to do anything until I've purchased a ticket and I'm safely on the bus.

I get off at the stop along with a few other people, and the scent of diesel fuel plugs my nose. Lowering my head, I try to blend in with the crowd, knowing my red hair is like a lighthouse's beam in a storm. I wish I would have thought to wear a hoodie instead of my vest, but I'd chosen the outfit to keep Sam near me. In these clothes I feel his arms around me, his warm hand under my shirt near my ribs, his lips pressed to my cheek as he chuckles at something Clint said.

That day was bittersweet. Sweet for me, bitter for Sam who saw me as nothing more than a poor replacement for his dead wife.

The lines are long, and anxiously, I shift back and forth in my tennis shoes, my gaze darting around the depot searching for Keaton's familiar and stiff pose full of nothing but anger and violence.

When it's finally my turn, I'm lightheaded, and I sag against the counter.

"Where to?" an elderly lady asks. She's too old to be working anywhere, but that's how life is, work until you die because there's nothing else you can do.

"Anywhere. The first bus going anywhere west." I choke back a sob. It doesn't matter where I'm going just as long as I can get out of Carthage and hide.

"We have a bus to Denver leaving in five minutes. Two seats left."

It's not far enough, but the timing is right. I can buy another ticket in Denver, and I nod viciously, accepting, my hands trembling as I pull my wallet out of my carry-on.

She counts the twenties with palsied hands and shoves the stack of bills into the register. She presses a few keys on the keyboard and a printer spits out a boarding pass. "Don't lose this or you can't ride the bus. There are no exceptions."

Again, I nod, desperately grabbing the only thing I have that can save me.

Between Janelle and Pastor Greenwood, there is one thing I believe. If Keaton finds me, revenge will be swift and sharp, and I won't survive.

"You on the run, doll?" she asks as I hug my bag closer to my body.

"My ex," I whisper, trusting the kindness in her weary eyes.

"I've seen it before. Wish I haven't. Go to your right, and in the back by the lockers, there's a hallway. Go left. The exit opens to the parking lot. Bus number nine. It will be parked out there, waiting for the all-clear to go. Hurry. You have three minutes."

"Thank you."

I do what she says, turning to my right and bumping through the crowd, and I find the hallway she referred to, the mouth of it near a bank of lockers and a set of restrooms I don't have time to use. I'll have to wait until I'm on the bus.

The hallway turns into a T, and I remember through a haze of nerves the lady told me to go left. I step in that direction and stop when his voice drips over my skin like ice water.

"Where do you think you're going?"

All the fight seeps out of me, and slowly I turn around. Keaton, Pastor Greenwood, and a man I've never seen before stand in the hallway near an office door, Keaton dressed in the jeans and flannel shirt he wears when he's working the streets on a case. His eyes are hard and he clenches his service weapon in his hand, his finger on the trigger, the muzzle pointing toward the tile floor. He'll have his badge attached to his belt, and if someone asks what he's doing, he'll say there's a warrant out for my arrest.

I drop my bag and the boarding pass flutters to my feet. "Nowhere." I don't recognize my own voice, the beaten-down rasp that is so hopeless, so filled with dread, accepting my life sentence.

"Damn straight. You think I'd let you leave me, huh? That simple. Move out to Carthage, start a new life without me. No fucking way."

He wraps his arm around my shoulders and kisses my cheek. My skin crawls but I don't pull away. He'll feel the slightest movement.

"I missed you, honey," he whispers, rubbing the muzzle of his gun up and down my ribs, a clear threat that if I run, he'll use it to stop me. I want to yank away, see what would happen, but I catch movement out of the corners of my eyes.

Sam and Samantha are standing near the lockers, Samantha dressed how I saw her at the office and Sam, oh, Sam, wearing an elegant charcoal grey suit, his expression flat.

"Lily."

There's no love in his voice, my name on his lips like a stranger's.

He made a deal with Pastor Greenwood.

He's not here to save me.

He's here to watch Keaton take me away.

# CHAPTER TEN



*Sam*

Samantha's blowing up my phone and a sense of loss rushes through me. She'll never forgive me for what's going to happen, but it has to because there's no other way. Text after text, phone call after phone call, a sobbing voicemail: "Lily left. She said something about you using her for sex. She wouldn't tell me where she's going. What happened?"

I don't answer and instead go to the office. She's standing at Shiloh's desk, both of them crying into tissues.

"Come on, we have to go." I need her there to see it.

"Where are we going?"

"There isn't time to explain."

We, in fact, have plenty of time. I know exactly where Lily's going and how she's getting there. Her detail texted me the second Pastor Greenwood approached her outside the Regency, and he recorded what that bastard told her. He kept track of how long it took her to go back to her room to pack and followed her taxi to SharperImage—not a simple task in the early morning rush-hour traffic—but he was able to keep her in his sights while she used precious minutes to go up and tell Samantha goodbye. Then she slipped out the back of the building and boarded a city bus that was heading to north Carthage.

There's only one way out of a city while remaining completely anonymous.

You don't need ID to buy a bus ticket.

There isn't any parking space at the bus terminal, and I park two blocks down in a public lot.

One of Lily's bodyguards texts me. *They're here but haven't made contact.*

I went over this with Archer and his team. He was the only one who agreed with my plan, though no one could think of a better way. I'll lose Lily, but I've already made peace with that. Her safety, her ability to live her life without having to look over her shoulder every goddamned minute, that means more to me than keeping her.

If she tried to have a life with Kessler out there, she could never truly be happy. With me or anyone. I can free her. This time the loss won't hurt quite so much. Tabby was good practice.

Another bar, another beer. It doesn't matter. I've had my two shots at love and I won't get a third.

"Sam, you have to stop her," Samantha says, struggling to keep up, her heels scraping against the sidewalk. "You can't let her leave. You love her."

I don't say anything. The truth will break her heart.

The terminal is full of people, but only one of my men is inside. It's imperative that after they leave the station we don't lose them. I know what Kessler will do to her once he thinks they're alone.

*They've made contact. North wall. Between the bank of lockers and the restrooms. Hallway.*

"Why do you keep checking your phone? You're supposed to be looking for Lily." Samantha's voice is sharp, and she swats at my cell, nearly knocking it out of my hand.

"I'm working." I stop in the middle of the station and glare at her. "A client is having a crisis for fuck's sake. What do you want me to do?"

"Forget about that. Isn't Lily more important?"

I look her dead in the eye. "No."

She pales.

I keep going in the direction Lily's detail told me to go, and it's easy to find the small group in the back hallway.

Cyrus is there, practically salivating, rubbing his hands together in glee.

Kessler's weapon glints in the fluorescent lights as he slides it along Lily's side, his other hand encircling her throat.

Greenwood smirks, his gaze focused on the erratic rise and fall of Lily's breasts as she pants in fear.

Everyone in this fucking hallway is going down for what they're doing to her.

Lily's eyes meet mine, and a spark, just a tiny spark, flames bright then fizzles and dies. Samantha said Lily mentioned something about me using her for sex. There's no doubt Greenwood lied when he spoke to her outside the hotel, but I won't know what he said until I listen to the recording. Undoubtedly, he knows intimate details about me and my wife. It's between God and Greenwood now what Tabby confided in him about our marriage during their counseling sessions.

Christ only knows what he said to Lily and what she believed.

What she believed because of the way we met.

Our one night stand fueled by misery and booze, despair and attraction.

"Lily," I say, my voice not my own. I can't be the man in love with her or I'll never pull this off.

"What are you doing here?" Cyrus asks, hate bright in his eyes. Not for me, no, he's still staring at Lily, wishing, I bet, that Kessler would squeeze his hand around her throat just a little tighter.

"The question is, what are *you* doing here?" I ask, shoving my hands into my pockets.

Samantha stands next to me, her breaths coming out in little puffs that match Lily's frantic rhythm. She saw the gun in Kessler's hand.

"Did you think, even for a second, that I would let you marry, this, this *trollop*? She's nothing compared to the woman my daughter was. Nothing. Tabitha was pure, I made sure of it. Nothing touched her, nothing marred her perfection. Now you think you're going to drag what's left of my daughter's memory through the filth between this woman's legs? I'll see her dead before that happens."

*He's mad. Stark-raving mad.*

Tabby's death turned him. Turned him into a religious monster, and Greenwood encouraged it. This has nothing to do with Lily. They would have had this reaction to any woman I would have started dating, and Lily's past played right into what they needed to make her go away. A jealous, crazy ex-husband who has nothing but revenge on his mind.

"You're right," I say, stepping forward until I'm standing in front of Lily, close enough I can see the terror dilating her pupils, the beads of sweat gathering on her skin. I can smell it on her, not the desire I teased her about last night in the office, but horror, the kind that only comes from knowing what comes next.

If Kessler has more than five minutes alone with her, he's going to kill her.

"She isn't Tabby." I lift a hand to Lily's face, and with Kessler's grip around her throat, she whines in a way that I will never be able to get out of my head for the rest of my life. She thinks I'm going to hit her, that I'm capable of it, and that hurts worse than watching them lower Tabby into the ground.

"Sam!" Samantha cries, and I hold up a hand to shut her up.

I'm in control. I have to show I have as much power as Kessler or he won't buy this.

Samantha quiets, and I thank God she's not pulling her listen-to-me-and-listen-to-me-good routine that could fuck this up.

"You ruined her for other men, Kessler," I say softly, brushing the backs of my fingers over Lily's cheek. "I couldn't touch her without her thinking I was going to beat the shit out of her. She just spread her legs and laid there."

Kessler laughs. "You gotta train 'em. This one, she's a quick learner. It'll take me ten seconds to teach her never to leave me again. I guess she can't run if her legs are broken, huh, sweetheart." He moves the muzzle to her back, and my heart feels like it's going to explode. A trigger-happy cop could kill all of us. "Or a bullet to the spine. Can't get very far in a wheelchair."

A single tear runs down Lily's cheek.

"Cyrus is right, you know," I say to Lily. Her chocolatey brown eyes I love looking into, they're dead. She's shutting down, and I hope it's enough to protect her through these next few minutes. "You'll never be Tabby, but I think you always knew that, didn't you?" I straighten and step back. "Take her. You're doing me a favor."

"My pleasure." Kessler grins and begins walking her backward, Cyrus and Greenwood tagging along. "I have friends on the CPD. They'll get me to the airport. But first—" He kisses

Lily's cheek, a sloppy, crude kiss that leaves a smear of saliva on her skin. "*Hasta la vista,* baby."

Samantha rounds on me just as he pushes his back against the exit door, letting in a blinding beam of sunlight, and she slaps me so hard the blow knocks me into the wall, the skin-on-skin *whap* echoing over the tiles.

"You fucking son of a bitch," she snarls, tears in her eyes.

Kessler chuckles, his laughter growing more and more vile every time I hear it.

"I'm gonna do so much worse to you," I hear him say to Lily over the growl of bus engines before the door thumps shut and it's just me and Samantha in the hallway, my cheek burning like fire.

"I'm calling the police. You can't let them take her," she says, sobbing, scrambling for her phone in her purse.

I grab her wrists and shake her. "Listen to me. Archer's outside with his team and they're going to follow them. Kessler won't wait long to put his hands on her, and he'll drive her somewhere close where they can be alone, like an empty warehouse near the river, or the gravel pits in the industrial park. We're going after them, Sammie. I swear to God."

She blinks. "You planned this."

I nod. "Archer and I needed something like this. We didn't think it would happen so soon, but Tabby's death is eating Cyrus alive. He's gone crazy, and from what I can tell, he recruited Greenwood to help him get Lily out of the picture once and for all. Come on, the worst is yet to come."

Samantha follows me, and when we're outside, a man from Archer's team ushers us into the backseat of a basic four-door beige sedan. "They're on Route 45."

"Not to the industrial park?" I ask, surprised. I was sure that's where Kessler would take her.

"No, sir. There's a motel along the highway, pay by the hour. We think that's where they're headed."

"What about Buchanan and Greenwood?"

"They aren't with them."

"Okay."

Samantha and I buckle our seatbelts, and we merge into traffic. They aren't more than a couple minutes ahead of us.

"What did you mean, 'The worst is yet to come?'" she asks, twisting her fingers in her lap.

"We need something to charge him with, Sammie."

She bites her bottom lip. My cousin is intelligent, and she knows exactly what I mean. "What just happened wasn't enough."

"I want him put away for a long time. I never want her to be scared of him again."

"She'll never forgive you, Sam. She'll never forgive you for making her go through this."

I hold her hand, my empty ring finger a silent testament to what I'm giving up. I hoped, one day, to wear a ring again, a band of gold chosen by Lily, words spoken aloud, a promise she would never break.

That won't happen now, and it's okay.

Kessler will never see the light of day again, and that will be enough.

"I know."

She jerks her hand away.

The motel is set off the highway near a ramshackle diner and a sparse copse of trees which makes it easy for us to hang back out of sight as a white rental car turns into the parking lot ridden with potholes, Kessler's arrogance and thirst for revenge dooming his fate.

All we need is a few seconds on camera.

A few seconds that will destroy the rest of my life.

We stand on the shoulder of the highway as two cars slowly enter the diner's parking lot behind Archer. He argued he could handle Kessler alone, but even the most skilled ex-military would never go into a situation without backup if it was available.

"Sir." The bodyguard who drove us passes me an earpiece, and I fit it into my ear.

"He's pulling her out of the car," Archer says, his voice clear, narrating what we can see. "He already has a key. He planned this."

Or he had help. He wouldn't know the area, didn't have time to secure a room, but I know who did.

Sammie crunches over the rock, her suit and heels out of place on the country road. She stands next to me, not touching, waiting. Anger shimmers off her body, and our relationship will be another casualty of what I had to do to keep Lily safe.

"He's heading for the room. I'm going in."

Kessler drags her the couple hundred feet from his car to the motel door. She's gripping his arm that's locked around her neck and digging her feet into the ground, trying to find traction against his strength. My baby's fighting, but all it will do is agitate him, piss him off, and spur him on.

"Let's go," I tell the bodyguard who gave me the earpiece. "I need to be there."

Gravel spitting, we race the short distance to the motel and join the others. I bolt out of the car before it stops and charge into the threadbare room, the door hanging open, dangling from its hinges. Archer has Kessler in custody, his hands secured behind his back, his service weapon at his feet.

"You fucker," he shouts, spotting me, his skin turning a hideous shade of red. "*You fucker.* You'll pay for this."

I want to get in his face, tell him he has no idea who the fuck he's dealing with, but for now, that piece of shit is no longer my concern. Only later, when he's standing trial, will I show him who exactly is going to pay for what.

Lily's lying on her side on the floor, her face turned away from me. One of my men is crouching next to her, his hand resting on her arm, and I push him aside. I kneel on the dirty carpet and gently turn her onto her back revealing a cut above her eye and a trickle of blood running from a gash at the corner of her mouth.

"It's over, Lily," I say, bracing myself. "I'm so sorry."

She focuses on my face.

Without a word, she rolls away from me, curling into a ball, her body quaking, but I don't leave her side until the ambulance carries her away.

"They're going to say it's inadmissible."

I lean back in my chair and prop my ankle onto my knee. It's been three days since the ambulance brought Lily to a clinical spa, a rest and relaxation facility located in south Carthage. Extremely private and offering more services than a hospital, Lily will have her healthcare needs met and will also have access to a therapist, mental and physical, spa treatments, and beautiful grounds to walk through if she wants to spend time outside.

I haven't heard from her, only a nurse calling to tell me generic updates. I'm not listed as an emergency contact and HIPAA laws prohibit them from sharing anything of value. That she's okay should be enough, and up to a point, it is. I can guess the gash near her mouth needed stitches and hitting her head on the edge of the dresser could have given her a concussion.

"We both know that's bullshit," I say to Archer, and I turn

to my computer screen. I can't stop watching the twenty second clip he filmed through the dirty window of Lily breaking free of Kessler's grip and spitting in his face, a gob of white saliva landing on his cheek. In retaliation, Kessler backhands her while holding his service weapon, and her entire body shakes with the impact. I can't move my gaze from the way she stumbles and falls, slamming her face against the TV stand on the way down. And for a second, just a second before Archer stopped filming to intervene, the deranged joy on Kessler's face.

"And they're going to accuse us of framing him," Archer adds.

It might look that way, but anticipating Kessler's movements is a far cry from framing him. His defense can say whatever they damn well please, but any jury that watches that footage will have no qualms about locking that asshole up for a long time.

"I'm not worried about it. What about Greenwood and my ex-father-in-law?"

"There's nothing we can nail Buchanan with, accessory perhaps, but to what? Greenwood, with the security tapes from the Regency, will be charged with trespassing. A possible accessory himself, with kidnapping, but I'm afraid you'll have to take what you can get."

I press my lips into a line. "I'm just sorry they were involved."

Archer leans against my desk, easy now that he's not on a job. Lily's detail is still watching her, but the spa is equipped with its own security and no one can see her without her permission. I need to call her parents and tell them what happened.

They'll hate me too, for setting this up.

After Samantha watched the clip, she stopped talking to me. She said I fed Lily to a lion and hasn't been to work since.

"A man like that wouldn't have given up. I know the type, just like Kessler. He wouldn't have stopped until she was dead. Buchanan and Greenwood might have sped things up, but pictures of you and Miss Fowler in the press made him insane. I looked through Kessler's phone and the CPD went through the rest of his things. He was obsessed with you having her. You did what you could."

"I keep telling myself that."

"Anything else?"

"Her physician in Honeywell. He signed off on a lot of bogus explanations for her injuries."

"I'm on it. They're going to transport Kessler to Honeywell. After the trial, he'll likely end up in the New York state pen."

"He won't last long in there."

"Not locked up with half the populace he put away."

A small comfort, but without Lily, it's all I have.

Archer leaves, presumably to dig up dirt on Lily's doctor in Honeywell. He shouldn't be allowed to practice medicine, and he'll do his own time in prison for malpractice and accepting bribes. There's no way he would have signed off on such blatant domestic violence injuries without someone paying him to do it. I turn back to my computer screen, Kessler's expression frozen as he grins in sheer delight at Lily lying on the dirty floor, a look in his eyes I can't describe. It's so much more than joy, so much more than hate.

Samantha didn't tell me when she'd be back. Maybe she won't be. Maybe she won't be able to work with me again. That would be her prerogative, but I won't be sorry for what I've done.

I won't feel sorry for using Lily as bait to keep her safe.

Because of it, I lost her, but I can't say I've gone through worse. Death is final. I will know where Tabby is every single second until my last breath. Lily, though, she'll go on to meet someone else, live somewhere else, and I will never know who or where. At any given moment she could be on holiday, on a honeymoon, in bed with her husband. She could be walking on the beach, sitting on a porch writing in a journal, sipping a cup of coffee, and I will never know.

Kessler . . . there's no excuse for what he did, but a sliver of me sympathizes, empathizes, with his possession that turned into a dangerous obsession.

I love her so much, and I'll never see her again.

# CHAPTER ELEVEN

*Lily*

The sound of a lawnmower cuts through the silence and I squeeze my eyes shut to block out the sunlight prickling against my eyelids.

Is the mower part of my dream? It's been so long since I've heard the growl of a motor, the scent of freshly cut grass as it wafts through the warm summer air. I smile, but my jaw hurts and something pulls at the skin around my mouth. I don't want to leave the place between sleep and wakefulness, and I hang on to the wisps of the dream I remember: Sam, mowing grass in a backyard while I weed flowers in a garden.

Where did that come from? I've never weeded a flower garden. I wouldn't know where to begin.

I crack my eyes open, the lawnmower growing louder as the machine nears the building. A cool breeze blows through an open window, the sheer white curtains billowing like ghosts. Grass isn't the only thing I can smell. There's also a hint of woodsmoke, of crunchy autumn leaves. Cold, if you can smell cold. No? Crisp then, like apples bobbing in nearly frozen water waiting for children at a fall carnival.

Autumn in New—

No, I'm not in New York.

I always have been, before, when Keaton's taught me one of his lessons.

*It's over, Lily. I'm so sorry.*

I hear his voice, low and full of sorrow, as if he knows something I don't, and it breaks my heart. The pain mixes with the dull ache in my head, the burning skin around my mouth, and the throb of my ribs where I landed hard on the floor.

I blanked out until Sam rolled me over and looked into my face.

Why was he there?

The lawnmower is underneath my window now.

He let Keaton drag me out of the bus depot.

I'm too tired to puzzle it out, and I grab onto the tendrils of my dream, where Sam is mowing our lawn and I'm weeding flowers, and everything is okay because he loves me.

---

The next time I wake, the room is dark, the window's shut, and the sky has changed from blue to black. I don't know how much time has passed or where I am. In New York, when I would wake up like this, I'd have a panic attack. Keaton would be sitting near the hospital bed, his eyes hard, threatening. I couldn't tell. I could never tell, and through the pain and the shock, I would have to make something up. A fall down the stairs, a slip in the bathtub. Something that would explain away the cuts on my face, the bruises on my body.

And after I was released, I would go home with him.

This room lacks the pungent odor of disinfectant, and

instead, I detect the delicate scent of roses. Maybe that's where the flower garden in my dream came from.

Gingerly, I sit up, expecting bedrails and an IV to give me trouble, but there's nothing attached to either of my wrists, and though the head of the mattress is in an upright position, I'm lying on a normal king-sized bed, not unlike what I slept on at the Regency. The white down comforter is also similar and I skim my hand over the smooth material.

Sam made love to me on a comforter like this.

Tears fill my eyes.

He saw me.

He saw what Keaton did to me. Battered, broken, and humiliated, I couldn't process. I couldn't do anything but turn away.

The second Keaton backhanded me, I pissed myself, my bladder too full to handle the shock. I pissed myself, and Sam was there. He saw the blood, smelled the urine that saturated my jeans, and I have never been so embarrassed and ashamed.

Curiously, I look around. There's a desk near the bathroom —the sink is visible from where I'm sitting on the bed—and the lamp casts a warm orange glow over everything. The flowers I could smell in my dream take up every available surface and small white envelopes peek from between the buds.

I twist, place my feet on the floor, and cool tile meets my skin. So, not a hotel, though somehow I didn't think I was in one. Someone dressed me in a pair of lounging pants and a tank top I had at the Regency with the rest of my clothes. Automatically, I reach for my phone to check messages and voicemails, but the side table near the bed is covered with flowers, my burner phone where I left it at the hotel.

There's a brisk knock on the door, and slowly, someone pushes it open. An older woman who has short brown hair pokes her head into the room and asks, "Is it okay if I come in?"

I nod, but I don't know if she can see it in the dim light. "Yes, it's fine."

She steps into the room, and God bless her, she doesn't turn the overhead light on. She's wearing scrubs, but they look fancier than any kind I've ever seen.

"My name is Val, and I'm working the night shift. You've been out for quite a few days, young lady."

I want to correct her, say that I'm not young, but I don't know her age, and to her, maybe I am. "I have?"

"Hmmm. Three. We let you sleep. You needed it. How are you feeling?"

I lost three days, sleeping. I must have felt safe here. There's no way I can sleep if I don't feel safe. When I was married to Keaton, if I had the day off, I would nap while he was at work. I didn't realize until years later that it was the only time my body could relax—when I knew he was too busy to come home.

"Sore, and I have to go to the bathroom."

"Do you need help?" Val asks, reaching out but not touching me.

"No. This isn't my first rodeo," I try to joke, but the nurse, or whatever she is, nods solemnly.

"But it's your last."

"Keaton . . ."

"Won't be bothering anyone for a long time. I'll wait for you."

Relief rushes through me, and if I didn't need the bathroom so badly, I would have sank back onto the mattress, the knowledge that Keaton is finally in jail turning my bones to jelly. But I'm in danger of doing the same thing I did in that shitty motel room, and I force myself to get off the bed. Val is there in case I need her, but I walk to the bathroom alone.

A weak light shines over a large mirror, but I don't look at my face until I relieve myself.

When I do, I can't stop the tears from dripping down my cheeks. Keaton hit me with his gun, and the grip tore the skin near the corner of my mouth. No wonder it hurt to smile while I was dreaming. The stitches burn. Vaguely, I remember stumbling and bashing my face against the edge of a dresser. Now there's a gash through my eyebrow and my skin is dark purple under a couple of butterfly bandages. I'm surprised it didn't need stitches too.

My hair is greasy and dirty, and dried blood is crusted along the side of my face. I need a shower or a bath, but I don't know what time it is and I already feel too tired to walk back to the bed much less find a bathtub and run water to soak in.

The most dreadful thing isn't what I look like, but that Sam saw me like this. What he must have thought, seeing Keaton's hate all over my face.

Val knocks on the door. "Are you okay? Do you need help?"

"No, I'm fine." I quickly wash my hands and dry them on a soft towel hanging from a bar near the sink.

I shuffle into the bedroom, and Val assists me, her hand hovering near my shoulder.

"Room service is available twenty-four hours a day, seven days a week. Would you like me to order you anything? Coffee and toast, maybe? The sky's the limit."

Sitting on the edge of the bed, I ask, "What kind of place is this? I'm not in a hospital."

"No, you're not in a hospital. This is a medical . . . rehabilitation clinic, I suppose you can say. I'm a nurse, and we have doctors on staff. The cut near your mouth was stitched here. We have a complete medical team and a fully equipped salon and spa. Tomorrow, we'll help you bathe and we can wash your hair. A massage, perhaps, might help you feel a little better too."

"This must cost a fortune," I murmur, guessing how much a place like this must cost. Even with Sam comping my room at the Regency, I can't afford to stay here.

"You're not to worry about a thing. It's been taken care of."

"Oh. By Sam."

"Mr. Sharpe said anything you need, anytime."

I rub at my wet cheeks, the words having a familiar ring. "Has . . . has he come to see me?"

"He's been here every day. Who do you think gave you all these flowers? The morning the ambulance brought you here, he didn't leave until midnight."

"I don't remember him visiting me."

"We couldn't allow it, not while you were sleeping. The front desk won't let anyone by unless you say so. Now, no more talk. Eat, or rest. Or, eat and rest. The choice is up to you."

"Can I leave?" I ask curiously.

Val smiles. "Anytime you like."

"Then I'm not Sam's prisoner."

"Lily," she says, reaching out, but not touching, never touching, because Sam must have told them about my history, "you don't know trapped until you've looked into Samuel Sharpe's eyes. I was here when the ambulance brought you in and I was here while he waited, and I have never seen a man look so tragic, like nothing in this life mattered anymore."

I know the look she's talking about. I've seen it on his face whenever he thought about Tabby.

"I've seen that look."

"Then you know it's the most heartbreaking thing you'll ever see. Besides your pretty face, such as it is. We'll fix you up so it will look like nothing happened."

The physical scars mean nothing to me.

"Can I have some coffee? With cream? And, is there soup?"

"We have a wonderful chicken noodle. Our clients find it very soothing. With bread?"

"That sounds good. Thank you, Val."

"You're welcome. I'll call down to the kitchen. In the morning, my replacement will show you how to order your own food service, or, if you feel like socializing, the dining room is open from six in the morning until ten at night. The meals are charged against your room, no need to pay. You're not the first one we've seen whose husband decided to get his point across with his fists. You take all the time you need to heal. Mr. Sharpe's orders."

Twenty minutes later, another staff member wheels in a cart, the comforting scent of soup meeting my nose, and my stomach growls. I eat slowly, relishing the quiet. No television, no phone. A silent clock that has Roman numerals hangs above the desk. It's past midnight, but I don't feel tired. I don't think I'm going to be able to fall asleep, but after I finish my meal, drink my fill of coffee, and wheel the cart into the hallway, surprisingly, when I lie down, I begin to drift. To my delight, my dream picks up where it left off, and I'm weeding my garden, Sam mowing the lawn behind me, and everything is as it should be.

---

The next morning, a nurse named Christy knocks on my door as I'm stepping out of the bathroom. They must have cameras in the rooms, as the nurses seem to know when I'm up and about, but the idea doesn't disturb me as much as it could have. No one can sneak up on me without a staff member knowing, and instead of feeling like my privacy is violated, I'm oddly reassured.

I didn't notice the night before, but my room is larger than the bedroom where I sleep and the half-bath. Christy leads me into another part of the suite, and here I find a large garden tub, vanity, and closet.

She asks if I want her to wash my hair and I can't say yes fast enough. I sit in a chair that's similar to those in beauty salons and it feels good to have the grit and blood washed out of my curls. When she's finished, she leaves me to bathe alone, pointing out a string I can pull if I need help. I can't submerge my face, but a washcloth works just as well.

Someone, probably Sam, arranged for my things to be brought from the Regency, and I want to call him and ask what he did with Tabby. He could have left her at the hotel and asked the staff to take care of her, but I hope not. She'll get lonely while I'm here. I'm already feeling better and can leave soon, but I don't want him to see me until the marks Keaton put on my face are gone.

After my bath, I stand in front of the closet where some of my clothes hang neatly pressed. I check the armoire and my bras and panties are in the top drawer. Not all of them, though, and I don't want to think about what that means. Half my clothes here, half at the hotel.

I'm not sure what to wear. I don't need to dress for the day, yet it feels strange to put pajamas on. I'm not at the office, and I'm not at the Regency. Finally, after dripping on the floor for a full ten minutes, I choose a pair of leggings and a tunic-like shirt that has a wide neckline that slips over my shoulder. Casual and comfortable, but not pajamas.

I'm starving, and while my hair dries, I order lunch. I skipped breakfast in favor of a bath, and the soup and sandwich room service delivers tastes divine. There's nothing clinical or drably healthy about the menu.

I eat on my bed and stare out the window. Today is overcast

and feels much more of a fall day than yesterday. In fact, it looks like it's going to rain, and I slide the window open and take a deep breath. My room overlooks a wooded area, and a trail disappears between two large evergreen trees.

A different staff member than the one who brought my lunch meets me at the door when I'm wheeling the cart into the hallway. She's holding a huge bouquet of flowers. At this rate, I won't have any room for them, but I accept the vase and thank her.

Now that I know the second room exists, I place this vase on the vanity. A tiny white envelope is tucked between two roses and I open it with trembling fingers.

The card stock is white, and I recognize Sam's dramatic script.

*Lily, I'm sorry. Sam.*

My heart's pounding, and I don't know why. He's sorry. He's sorry for the things he said at the bus station? He's sorry he let Keaton drag me away, though there wasn't anything he could have done because Keaton was armed? He's sorry Keaton hit me? He's sorry, but after what he saw, he can't be with me? A woman with her face bashed in and her pants soaked with piss. I swallow back a sob and search the other bouquets for their envelopes. They all say the same:

*Lily, I'm sorry. Sam.*

I press a hand over my mouth to hold back the scream that's threatening to tear its way out of my throat.

He was here. Val said he delivers the flowers himself. He was here at the clinic and didn't ask to see me.

A tear drops onto the card I'm holding, blurring the black ink.

The phone I used to order lunch rings, startling me, and tentatively, I answer. "H-hello?"

"Miss Fowler, this is Philip at the front desk.

A . . . Samantha Sharpe is here to see you. Are you accepting visitors?"

Samantha's here. A lungful of air rushes out of me in relief. She can tell me what's going on. "Yes, yes." I pause. "If I don't want her in my room, where can I talk to her?"

"There's a lounge at the end of your hallway. I'll send her there if that's okay?"

"Thank you."

I don't know where the visitor's lounge is. I haven't stepped foot outside my room, but I didn't have to worry. I poke my head out the door and there's a discreet grey sign on the wall directing people to the elevator, a visitors' lounge, and a coffee bar neither of the nurses I've met so far have mentioned.

I find the lounge easily, and it's as comforting as the rest of the clinic. Bookshelves and potted plants subtly divide the large room into smaller, cozy sitting areas, and a long counter against one wall is stocked with snacks, drinks, and an industrial-sized coffeemaker. The other wall is made of glass, showcasing a different view of the woods than the one my room gives me. If I get tired of being alone, I can come here and read. I sink onto a loveseat near the door, tuck my hands between my knees, and wait. I'm the only one in the room, and I'm both glad to have Samantha to myself and nervous to be alone with her.

What is she going to think of my face?

I don't have to wonder for long. I hear her before I see her, the sharp staccato of her heels clicking against the tile announcing her better than any emcee.

Hesitantly, she steps into the room, and I bounce to my feet.

She sucks in a breath, her eyes raking over my face. "I hate him for this."

"Me too," I say, rubbing my hands on my leggings. She can't hate Keaton any more than I do.

"What he did," Samantha says, unbuttoning a beige trench coat and slipping it off her shoulders, "was despicable. I'll never forgive him for letting that monster hurt you. Come, sit. Tell me how you feel."

She isn't dressed for the office, isn't here on her lunch break. I blink in confusion at her jeans and navy blue, V-neck sweater. "You didn't come from work," I say, sitting next to her on the loveseat I just vacated.

"I haven't been to work since the morning this happened," she says, reaching out to touch my face. I let her skim her fingertips over my cheek and down to the corner of my mouth. "Fucking bastard."

I grab her hand. "I don't understand. I thought you were talking about Keaton. You mean Sam? What did he do?"

Her eyes widen. "You don't know. Has an officer come by to talk to you? Take your statement?"

I shake my head.

"Of course not. Sam would never let a cop talk to you so soon after what your ex-husband did." She sighs.

"I better make coffee, and then you need to tell me what happened." The request sounds strange. I was there. I know what happened.

I use the Keurig and brew us large mugs of coffee and add a generous amount of fresh cream that's in a stainless steel mini fridge under the counter. Once we're settled in a corner of the room, I say, "Tell me what you think Sam did."

Saying his name hurts. He was here and didn't ask to see me. All the flowers in my room must have cost a fortune, and he's apologizing for what, I have no clue.

"We followed you to the bus depot, Lily."

When Sam and Samantha showed up, Keaton had already found me, but them being there made perfect sense. Since the night we met at the bar, Sam has always been there for me, and when Keaton grabbed me in the hallway, it didn't seem unnatural that Sam would be there to rescue me.

"How did you know I would be there? I didn't tell you when I said goodbye."

Samantha stares at the hardwood floor. "Sam didn't want your ex-husband to have a chance to hurt you, and he hired bodyguards to protect you when he wasn't around."

"But . . . he didn't stop Keaton from taking me. He said—" His nasty words come back to me now, and the way I flinched as he spoke, waiting for him to hit me. A different kind of shame fills my heart and I want to cry. Sam would never hurt anyone, yet I let Keaton and my fear taint my perception of him.

"He said those things because he *wanted* Keaton to take you." Tears drip slowly down Samantha's cheeks. "He said they needed something concrete, something to charge Keaton with. Evidence. I slapped him so hard. He let that asshole hurt you, and I'm never going to forgive him for the rest of my life."

"Sam filmed it?" I barely recognize my own voice.

"His security team did. The second they had enough, Archer busted into the room. I told Sam there had to be a better way. There had to have been. He'd done it to you for years, there was already proof."

I skim over that. I've learned that "proof" was subjective depending on who was looking at it. "Where's Keaton now?"

"Jail. That's all I know because I refuse to talk to Sam to find out anything else."

Keaton's in jail, just like Val said. With the video Sam has, I can press charges and he'll be put away for a long time. Kidnapping, assault. None of his precious buddies will be able to get him off. There's not a judge in the world who could deny Keaton hitting me, and with his service weapon at that.

I sip my coffee and wet my mouth. I need to ask the question, and I need to hear Samantha's answer, then I can decide what I'm going to do. If Sam's disgusted, if he can't look at me, I'll have a lot to figure out because somehow, he became the most important piece of my future.

Somehow?

Oh, right. I fell in love with him.

"Samantha, why hasn't he come to see me?"

She laughs in disbelief.

It's worse than I thought, then.

"You have to ask? Christ, Lily. He knows you hate him as much as I do. What you went through to get his fucking evidence . . . now you're here on his dime like that will make up for letting that fucker do that to you. There was a better way. We just didn't have the time we needed to think of it."

Do I hate Sam? I never thought to. Didn't have a reason to. What Samantha says has merit, yet, her reasoning is flawed. Sam did it to protect me, and it worked. Keaton's in jail, and he will be for the rest of his life, if I know Sam.

"And of course I don't expect you to want to come back to work." Samantha scoffs, but the sound is uglier than that. "Why in the hell would you want to work with him? Look at him every day knowing he so easily gave you up."

"Was it?"

She meets my eyes. "What?"

"Was it easy for him? You would know. Out of anyone in your family, you know him best. Was it easy for him to say what he said to me in that hallway? Was it easy for him to compare me to Tabby and declare her the winner, knowing that if I believed him, it would ruin me? Was it easy? I haven't seen him since the ambulance came for me. He didn't leave my side until the medic pushed him back. I remember that part of it, him leaning over the gurney. He wouldn't let me go."

The shock is fading, and the more I poke and the more I prod, the minutes after Keaton hit me, they're coming back.

Lying on the floor, the carpet rough under my cheek, waiting for him to come at me again, only . . . he didn't. Archer stopped him, and then suddenly Sam was there. The nasty things he said didn't matter because he was there when I needed him most.

"I . . ." Her voice fades.

"I don't want to get between the two of you and the relationship you have. You respect him, Samantha, and he's earned it or you wouldn't. Please believe he was doing what he thought was best. It's not your place to hate him on my behalf." I reach out and touch her arm. "You two are closer than brother and sister. He doesn't deserve this."

She doesn't say anything, and I'm afraid I made her mad. I don't want her to think I don't appreciate her in my corner, but my corner is Sam's too.

"There was no time. I spoke with a friend in Honeywell not long ago and she said his friends were passing around paparazzi photos of us and making fun of him for losing me to a rich guy. It fueled his rage. That man who was in the hallway with us, Pastor something, he told me he called Keaton because he and Tabby's father didn't want Sam and me to be together. There was no time. Sam did what he had to do."

"I may not ever believe that." She sips her coffee. "What are *you* going to do, Lily?"

I wrap my cold hands around my half-empty mug. "I don't know. He saw me like this." I can't keep the tears out of my voice. "He saw me like this, and I can't—"

"Do you think he cares?" she demands, the fire coming back. "Do you think he cares what he saw Keaton do to you?"

"He might not, but I do. *I do.* He saw me, my face smashed up, bleeding. I had to pee and I was going to go on the bus, but Keaton grabbed me. When he hit me at the motel, I went all over myself, and Sam found me that way. Do you know how humiliated I felt? Has Clint ever seen you so beaten down you didn't know if you could look him in the eyes ever again? Sometimes I just want to run, start over in a place where no one knows who I am. Start fresh with a man who won't see bruises and stitches whenever he looks at me, whether they're there or not. Put all this behind me the best I can."

What she says next hurts me more than Keaton ever could.

"He wants you to. He wants you to live your life without being afraid Keaton's around every corner. He freed you. He wanted that for you."

I stare into my mug. "Then maybe I will."

I stay at the clinic until I can hide most of the damage with makeup. My stitches are gone, but bruises and faint pink lines linger beneath my concealer. It's selfish, to use the time for such vanity, but I started seeing a therapist too, and we go on long walks through the woods. We talk about the past and the things Keaton stole from me, but also the things he gave me: courage to go after what I want, like moving to Carthage, the bravery to stand up for myself and others, like confronting Allessandra's father, and best of all, Sam. Meeting Sam has given me more than I thought possible. He gave me a job I love, a safe place to stay, the relationship with my parents back. Tabby. He could have easily dropped her off at a shelter, but he gave her to me.

"Do you feel you owe him for any of that?" she asks smoothly, the beads in her dreadlocks clicking together as we cross a wooden bridge built over a wide, but shallow, creek.

I think for a moment before I answer. I appreciated him comping my room at the Regency, but I didn't need him to. I could have found a different job without his help. One day I would have adopted a cat, but I may never have had a relationship with my parents again.

"I don't feel like I owe him in the way that you mean. Not like I need to pay him back. But there's gratitude there. Appreciation he took the time, cared enough, to do those things for me."

A twig snaps under her boot. "That's healthy, I think," she agrees. "It's when couples start tallying and keeping score. That can lead to resentment because there will always be someone needier than the other. That's life."

"I feel better knowing I helped him, too. I was the first woman he was with after his wife passed away." I know he hadn't been with anyone since Tabby died. That horrid man wanted me to think I didn't mean anything to Sam, but I won't believe his lies. "I'd like to think I opened him up to love again."

"But not with you?"

"He saw me." We've been over this.

"Yes, he did. Does he still bring you flowers every day?"

"Yeah." He drops off a bouquet every day during his lunch hour, never delivered by a florist, always him. One day I stood near the lobby around the time the receptionist said he usually stopped by. I didn't have to wait long before he walked in, carrying a huge bouquet of blood-red roses, the same small envelope tucked among the flowers, the white stark against the red. He looked sad, his shoulders hunched, so much like he had at the bar, and I almost stepped out of the shadows and asked him to wait, but I couldn't call attention to my face. I let him leave only to do it again the next day. And the next. "He's given me so many I have to put them in other areas of the clinic." The lobby, the coffee kiosk. The lounge. I give them to other patients who don't have visitors. They're all beautiful and all with the same message. *Lily, I'm sorry. Sam.*

"You still haven't spoken with him." There's disapproval in her tone, an accusation I'm not facing my fears.

"No. He hasn't asked to see me, and I haven't called him. I know I should."

"But you're scared."

"Yeah."

"He is too, you know."

We walk down the path—we're about a mile away from the clinic now—nothing but squirrels jumping from tree to tree and the birds chirping.

"Why do you think that?" I settle on a hollowed-out log.

When she sits close to me, her knee bumping into mine, I'm not nervous like I would have been in the past. "Wouldn't it scare you, if you gave someone important to you an apology and they didn't accept it? He apologizes every day, yet every day you tell me he has nothing to apologize for. Shouldn't you be telling *him* that, instead of me?"

"I—" I laugh. "You're right."

"Do you blame him for what happened, Lily? Samantha seemed to think it was a given, but you don't mention it."

I pause, thinking it over. It's one of my favorite things about her. She lets me process, come to my own conclusions. She tips her head back and closes her dark brown eyes to wait me out.

"It would be easy to, but Keaton would have gotten me, somehow, some way. Walking out of a movie theatre with a friend or at a signing at a bookstore. A crowded mall. He would have gotten me, and there wouldn't have been anything Sam, or anyone, could do. This time, he controlled it. He controlled it, and Keaton barely touched me." I tap the corner of my mouth. "This is nothing compared to when Keaton was angry. The dresser I fell into hurt me worse than he did."

"I'm sorry. You're not the first domestic abuse survivor I've counseled, and unfortunately, you won't be the last."

I stand from the log, and we keep walking down the trail. She hasn't suggested we turn back, and I'm content and don't mention it either. "What's funny is that I can count on two hands the number of times he hit me. Over five years, that's not many. After he would smack me around, I would lie on the floor and think, 'It could be worse. Someone always has it worse.'"

"Once is too many." Her voice is mild.

"I know, and now, thanks to Sam, there won't be anymore."

We head back, and she asks me what's next.

"I'm not sure. He saw me, and I don't know what to do with that."

"We're seldom always at our best. We give birth, we're in car accidents. We get cancer, something Sam knows quite a bit about. If something happened to him, you would still love him. Accusing you of loving him for his looks is just as insulting as saying you want him for his money. Neither are true. You love him for who he is. Why do you think it would be different if the tables were turned?"

"It's not that." I piece together what's been lurking in the dark corners of my heart. "I wanted to be better than his wife. He put her on a pedestal, and I can't compete."

She raises an eyebrow. "Did anyone say you have to?"

I shrug. "Not really, but sometimes I feel like it's there. They were married for fifteen years. They would still be married if she hadn't passed away."

"And you would still be married if Keaton wasn't an abusing asshole. You married him because you loved him. Made a promise in front of your family and friends, stayed with him after the first time he hit you, and the second, and the third, and the fourth. Maybe, late at night, Sam thinks about that."

"You think Sam believes I'm still in love with my ex-husband?"

"No, but you both lost the futures you thought you would have with the people you loved. It doesn't matter how. His wife is gone, and he brings you flowers every day. Your ex-husband is in jail, and his mark is still on your face. It's up to you what you do with that." She takes a deep breath as the clinic comes into view. "I think we're done. It's time you tell him what he wants to hear or make the choice to leave and let him know that, too. Put him out of his misery, Lily. Don't hide behind your scars."

We part ways at the door. "Thank you, for everything," I say, clasping her hand, her skin warm and soft.

"You're welcome. Good luck to you."

I start a list on the way to my room. I need to check out, if that's what one does in a place like this, and go to the Regency and pack the rest of my things. Find Sam and tell him . . . tell him what? I don't know what he's going to say when he sees me.

Near the door to my room Christy approaches me. "Miss Fowler, a courier delivered an envelope while you were in therapy. It's at the front desk."

"Thank you. I'll go down and pick it up right now."

The receptionist is quick to find it and give it to me, and my name in care of the clinic's address is written in Sam's elegant script. My heart catches, but I manage to keep it together until I'm sitting on the bed in my room. With trembling fingers, I open the brown manila envelope and slide out a thin stack of paper.

There's a letter from Sam, but it's not in his handwriting. He typed it, printed it on SharperImage stationery, and signed it at the bottom.

*Dear Lily,*

*Not quite what we had planned, huh? Well, things happen. Things we can predict, things we can't. I knew what this partic-*

*ular outcome would be, but I didn't think it would hurt this much. I did what I thought was best, and I would do it again. It cost me you, but I will never regret what I did, what I let Kessler do to you, in exchange for your freedom.*

*I told you I would take care of you, and I will. The bank card will help you get back on your feet. The checks are for whatever you need. Rent an apartment, buy a house. Find a life and make it yours. The plane ticket is for New York, first class. Your parents have been calling and asking me where you are, but I haven't told them everything. That's your story to tell, and you'll want to do that in person, so they can see you're okay.*

*If anything, I want to thank you.*

*You saved my life.*

*Always yours,*

*Sam*

Christy looks in on me and finds me sitting on my bed, sobbing. I took too long, and he's telling me goodbye. He's giving up.

"Lily," she says, dropping formality in concern, "what's wrong? Did you get bad news?"

"Yes. I need to pack. I need to leave, today. As soon as I can. Will you help me?"

"Of course."

Sam used one of my suitcases, and Christy and I quickly throw my things into it. I'm downstairs in less than half an hour, signing my discharge papers while I wait for the taxi the receptionist called for me. It's late, my therapy session going over my allotted time because I understand now she hadn't planned on seeing me again. I missed dinner, and my stomach growls queasily as I sit in the back of the taxi on the way into the city.

I gave the driver Sam's penthouse address, hoping he's home and not working late. I could have called Samantha, but I haven't spoken with her since she visited me at the clinic. I don't know if she and Sam made amends. I don't know if they're on speaking terms again.

I'm on my own, and I'm just as scared as I used to be.

The driver helps me with my suitcase, pulling it out of the trunk and setting it on the sidewalk. Grimacing at the irony, I use the debit card Sam gave me to pay the fare. Sam must not have thought I'd need my purse at the clinic, and I don't have a penny on me besides the card and the book of blank checks.

The concierge calls up to his penthouse, and he's on the phone long enough that I grow uncomfortable. Sam doesn't have to let me up. Maybe he doesn't want to see me. Maybe he doesn't want me in Carthage anymore—he gave me a plane ticket to get me out of his city as fast as possible. Maybe he thinks he made a mistake getting involved with me—

"He's available and said you can go up."

"Thank you. Will you keep this for me?" I ask, steadying my voice against the panic. With my toe, I push the suitcase toward him.

"Absolutely, Miss Fowler."

The elevator ride lasts forever but not long enough. I don't know what to say or how to say it. There's no time to figure out the best way to say thank you. He thinks I hate him for what he did, when I'm grateful.

Sweat is dripping down my side when elevator bumps to a stop and the doors slide open. Sam's waiting, dressed in jeans and a University of Minnesota, Carthage sweatshirt. He holds out his arms and blocks the elevator doors like he did the day of Allessandra's concert at the children's hospital.

We stare at each other, and as the seconds tick by, I know my worst fears have come true.

I waited too long, and he's not going to let me in.

# CHAPTER TWELVE

*Sam*

"Hey, can I talk to you for a second?"

Samantha pokes her head around the door that connects our offices minutes after I send a courier with an envelope for Lily. I bring her flowers every day, and every day, the words are on the tip of my tongue: "Will you call her room and ask if she'll see me?"

But I never do.

I can't face her after what I did.

Samantha was right all along. There must have been a better way, never mind the prosecuting attorney says that with the video, it's an open-and-shut case. Risking Lily's safety had been too reckless. Kessler could have done something much worse than just hit her. He could have shot her, and it wouldn't have mattered how fast Archer was, he wouldn't have been able to save her.

I'd counted on Kessler wanting to draw it out, to make her suffer.

It had been a gamble. I won, but I bet with Lily's life.

Turning from the window, I tip my head, acknowledging her request. We haven't spoken during the three weeks Lily's been at the clinical spa. She's rarely come to the office, but I picked up the slack without complaint. She carried me after Tabby passed away, and it was the least I could do. I even reached out to my father and asked him what would happen if Samantha and I couldn't work together anymore. Dissolving the company isn't an option but being business partners won't last much longer.

Quietly, she steps into the room and twists her fingers in front of her. Tears glimmer in her eyes. "I'm sorry for the way I treated you."

I shrug. Things have come too far to go back now. "I deserved it. You were right. I put Lily in a position that could have gotten her killed. It's why she doesn't want to see me. She hasn't called, hasn't emailed or left a voicemail. She's done with me, and I sent her a letter saying goodbye and a little money. I made a mistake, and I can't undo it."

"That's not why she hasn't gotten in touch with you. She's waiting until she heals."

I shove my hands in my pockets and speak to the window. "You don't heal from something like that. I'll never get over Tabby's death. She'll never forget Kessler's hands on her. I thought maybe we could move past it, but we haven't known each other long enough, haven't spent enough time together. There was too much against us. I sent her a plane ticket to New York. If she happens to call, tell her I wish her well. I need to go ho—" I stop. The penthouse is no longer my home.

"Will you come stay with us?" she asks, stepping closer and resting her hand on my arm.

Shaking her off, I say, "I'll be okay, but thanks. Maybe I'll see you tomorrow."

"Sam." Her voice is low and sad, and she knows as well as I do nothing will be the same between us. I did the damage, but she added to it. It was her right block me out these past three weeks, but I've been alone, scared and missing Lily, and I needed her support.

She supported Lily instead, and there's nothing I can do but agree with the side she'd chosen.

"It's okay, Sammie. There's no reason to feel bad. I talked to Dad about what will happen since we can't work together anymore. He said we'll figure something out. I don't expect you to want to run this company with me, and I won't try to force you. We'll have a family meeting this weekend. I have to go."

She stands in the middle of my office, her face pale, her eyes wet.

I leave her there, biting her lip, wanting to say something that will fix this, but there's nothing. Lily could be on a plane, right now, and I didn't tell her goodbye.

Archer picks me up, and I slump in the backseat and rest my head against the cushion. I'm bone tired and there isn't enough sleep in the world that would help me feel rested. Archer's clip plays in a horrifying loop behind my eyes. Lily spitting on Kessler and him hitting her, his gun in his hand. The soundless crack as she hits the dresser, the way she lies on the floor, tucked into herself, waiting for an assault that doesn't come.

There wasn't a better way.

I thought I heard it in my head, but it was Archer's voice. "There wasn't a better way."

"I really want to believe that."

"You weren't dealing with only Kessler. Buchanan and Greenwood were watching her, too," he reminds me, pulling up to the curb. "Buchanan wanted her dead almost as much as

Kessler. We haven't been able to make anything stick there, so we'll have to be careful, for the next little while."

"Yeah. Thanks."

He lets me out, and the doorman greets me with solemn eyes. Everyone knows what happened. An enterprising young journalist for the *Carthage Chronicle* uncovered the story, and a cop who was probably sleeping with her leaked the clip. The video inspired public outrage against our police forces and brought to light others who have been mistreated by the officers sworn to protect us.

Lily's a celebrity now, a brave woman who stood up to a man she had no chance of defeating. I should have warned her the video leaked and that the case was generating a lot of interest in her personally, but I figured since she was going to New York, she would take up the mantle in Honeywell with her parents' support.

The penthouse is full of moving boxes. I'm not on good enough terms to share Tabby's things with her parents and out of spite, I'm tempted not to, but I will. She left so much behind, and I haven't done anything with any of it. Slowly, I'll start packing away the life I had with her.

I change into jeans and an old sweatshirt, and I'm going through the bookshelves in the living room with Tabby "helping," jumping in and out of the empty boxes, when the house phone rings. I want to ignore it, but it could be Sammie wanting to speak with me, asking for permission to come up rather than assuming she's still welcome here. It could be a delivery, a package I don't remember ordering a long time ago. It could be anything, really, fragments left over from the life I had before I met Lily.

The weariness hasn't left me, and I struggle to my feet and stagger into the kitchen. "Yeah?" I say into the phone.

"Miss Fowler is here to see you. May I say she can

come up?"

Dumbfounded, I lean against the counter, the concierge's request the last thing I expected. Lily's downstairs. What does that mean? She received my letter, the money. Is she here to say goodbye? Tell me she hates me before she goes home? Her real home. Not the one I was hoping we'd create together.

"Yes, she can come up. Thank you."

The wait is excruciating. It's a two minute ride from the lobby to the penthouse, and every second that goes by is like someone jabbing me with a million needles. My skin is hot, prickly, and painful by the time the lift bumps to a stop, and my vision swims with nerves and agony.

I want so much for her to tell me she doesn't hate me and we still have a chance, that when the doors open to reveal her face, I'm frozen, unable to do or say anything but drink her in.

Her eyes are bloodshot, wet, like Sammie's when I left the office. She's been crying.

The gash through her eyebrow is almost healed, and there's only a faint scar near the corner of her mouth she tried to cover with makeup.

Her clothing is rumpled, jeans and a wrinkled blouse under a leather jacket.

She's beautiful, the same tragic beauty that struck me in the bar the night we met.

And for the first time since I sat at her table, Tabby is far from my thoughts.

She clears her throat. "Can I come in?"

When she stopped by after I abandoned Allessandra's hospital benefit, I couldn't let her in. There still had been so much of Tabby in my relationship with Lily that I hadn't felt it was right to allow her to intrude. So many things have changed in so little time, and Lily seeing the place I shared with Tabby for most of our marriage doesn't seem wrong anymore.

"Sure."

I drop my arms and let her step out of the elevator. She doesn't have a purse, not any luggage. It could be she's already stopped by the Regency and cleaned out her room, and everything is sitting in a taxi downstairs waiting to go to the airport.

She drops to her knees and scratches Tabby under the chin. The cat heard her voice and didn't waste any time running into the foyer. "You kept her. I wasn't sure you would."

"She belongs to you. I didn't know what else to do with her. Have you come from the Regency?"

"No. I came right from the clinic. I read your letter. I waited too long."

*Too long for what*, I want to ask, but I quirk my lips, feigning nonchalance. "No harm done."

Stepping around me, she gives me a quick glance out of the corners of her eyes and walks into the living room. "You're moving?"

"Planning on it. There's no point in staying here. I won't be able to let Tabby go if all I do is wallow in the life we used to have."

She stops in front of the couch, a large oil painting of Tabby and me on our wedding day hanging in an intricate gold frame. The picture is like anything else in anyone's home. I can look at it, but not see it. It's hung on our wall since the first day we moved in.

"Tabby's parents had that commissioned for our first anniversary."

"It's beautiful. She was like a fairy, wasn't she?"

I stand next to Lily and look at the painting through her eyes. Tabby was shorter than I am by over a foot, blonde hair, translucent skin. I suppose in her wedding dress she does look like a fairy, or maybe an angel, too weak to withstand the harsh realities of living life on earth.

The differences between Tabby and Lily had been a shock: Lily, healthy, her skin glowing, and only a couple of inches shorter than me, her red hair a beacon, drawing me to her presence. She's solid, and I mean that in every positive way possible. I was always Tabby's rock, the person she needed most in the world, and while we were married, I wanted to be there for her, give her anything, everything, she needed. After I met Lily and found I could lean on her, it was a miracle. She had needed me to keep her safe from Kessler, yes, but late at night when my world fell apart, she was there, strong in her own way, her ex-husband's fists toughening her, teaching her to withstand anything.

"Yeah, she was." I pause. I don't know how long she'll stay. I don't know how long I have to explain. "I'm sorry her father was involved in what happened."

She stiffens.

Breaking the contact of our arms brushing, I kneel in front of the box I was packing when the phone rang. Tabby's taste in books was different from mine, and I stack them carefully, conscious not to over pack. I could hire someone to do this, but I can't let a stranger touch her things, even after all this time. I'll do it myself, say goodbye on my terms.

"It wasn't your fault," she says, watching me. "He didn't want you with me and thought he found a way to make that happen."

"He did." She opens her mouth to say something, but I speak over her. "I keep thinking about what he said. That Tabby was a virgin, that he made sure of it. She was, but I assumed it had to do with her personal beliefs, her conviction in the teachings of her church, or maybe because of her health. She told me her body was a gift just as much as her heart, and I was nervous, humbled, that I was her first lover. All this time I thought about it, thought about the relationship she had with her parents. We didn't live together before we got married, obviously didn't have sex until our wedding night. Her first night away from them was the first night of our honeymoon. I think, when it came right down to it, she married me to get away from them."

Lily sinks next to me on the floor, but I'm caught up in the day I met Tabby at the university.

"She latched on to me, and I thought it was because we clicked." I lightly brush Lily's hand with my fingertips. "I've always believed in love at first sight. I thought I had that with her, but now I think she took any out she could find because her father was an overbearing asshole who didn't let her live her own life. We spent a lot of time with her parents, but I didn't get to know Cyrus while I was married to Tabby. I didn't want to. Now I know everything Tabby and I had was because of him."

"Don't do that," she says, resting her hand on my arm. Her skin is warm, seeping through the material of my sweatshirt.

I scoff. "Don't do what? Tell the truth?"

"Don't let her father destroy what you and Tabby had. You loved her, Sam, and she loved you or you would have felt it. Over time, you would have felt it. You loved each other, and I'm sorry you lost her."

I lift a shoulder in what I hope is a careless shrug. "I lost you too. And Samantha. I guess I'm getting good at it."

"She's still not speaking to you?"

I add another book to the box. "No. Well, she tried some half-assed attempt at an apology today, but I know she didn't mean it. She blames me for what happened." I rub my thumb over the corner of Lily's mouth, and if she wouldn't have been so close, if I wouldn't have been so in tune to her, I would have missed it.

When I raised my hand to her face, she didn't flinch.

"I told her not to. I don't."

I don't believe that for a second. "Of course you do. Where have you been all this time?"

She gives me one of her half-smiles. "Talking to a therapist, mainly. Trying to wrap my head around you and me, what we have compared to what you had with Tabby. What you and I have compared to what I had with Keaton. I loved him or I wouldn't have married him. People I loved and who loved me, told me not to trust him, but I did anyway. He did more than ruin my self-esteem, he destroyed my judgment. You and me, how we met, what we have . . . you said you believe in love at first sight, and I always have, too. Keaton ruined that for me, while Tabby solidified that concept for you. I gave my heart time to tell me that I love you, and the longer I stayed at the clinic, the louder my heart spoke. I love you, Sam, and I have since you sat with me at the bar."

I want to believe what she's saying. I want to pull her into my arms, tell her I love her, too, and ask her to marry me. But she's been in the penthouse for barely fifteen minutes, and I need more, my heart needs more, before I can. "What about this?" I ask, once again grazing the line near the corner of her mouth. "He could have killed you, and it would have been my fault. I took a chance, and it could have blown up in our faces."

Solemnly, she nods. "It could have, but it didn't. You thought of everything, and now there's proof, irrefutable proof, that Keaton is an abuser. It won't be my word against his. His buddies on the force can't get him off, lose paperwork, hide photos of my face. The video is out there, and there's no way he can run from this. All that is because of you, Sam. Because of you, and I don't hate you. I'm *thankful* that you gambled to protect me."

I shake my head. "He could have shot you. Like he threatened at the bus depot." Kessler's gun in his hand, pressed against Lily's back, Cyrus's glee, Greenwood's satisfaction that her husband would make her pay for running, that dreadful moment, locked in time, keeps me awake at night.

"I lived with it for five years. I know how bad it could have been." She pauses, then stands, using the cardboard box for support. Instinctively, I want to reach out and help her, but as she's demonstrated well, she's fine on her own. "I'm sorry Samantha's angry. I'll talk to her again. And I'm sorry I stayed so long at the clinic. I needed it, but I took too much time."

I stand, too, deliberately avoiding the box. Soon Tabby's life will be whittled down to storage containers and keepsakes and it can't hold me up anymore.

Lily stops in front of the half-empty bookshelf. Tabby's unicorns are still displayed, and she skims her finger along one's back. "These are beautiful."

"I think she liked the hope they represented. The magic. Her life wasn't easy, even with me in it. They gave her faith that there was something better to look forward to."

She smiles, this one pulling the corners of her mouth just a little higher. "She didn't need those when she had you. I better go."

I grab her arm, the leather soft and buttery under my fingers. This is my last chance. If I let her leave, I'll never see her again. I can decide to spend the rest of my life with Tabby and our memories, or I can trust that Lily knows her own mind, her own heart, and she's chosen to forgive me. "Tell me one thing."

"Okay."

"What were you looking for when you came here?"

"When I moved to Carthage all I could think about was getting away from Keaton. My mother talked about the city a lot, and though I never visited, I felt like I knew this place. I was running, had nowhere to go, really, and her memories made coming here feel comfortable. I wanted to make friends, find a job I liked. Maybe eventually date again, though meeting someone wasn't a top priority when I could still feel Keaton's parting gift on my cheek." She taps the area under her eye where her bruise had been when we first met. "I don't think that's what you were asking, though. What was I looking for when I came here, to your penthouse?"

I nod.

She holds her hand up, and I press my palm to hers and link our fingers. In that one small gesture, I know things will work out between us. She remembered what I said, what I offered, and she's here because she wants the same.

"I want a partner, someone who thinks of me as an equal. I want to go to work with the man I love, at a company I respect. I want to marry him, let him make love to me whenever he wants. I want Sunday morning brunches and long walks through the park. I want family holidays and romantic vacations. Mostly, I want a man to treasure me because I'm his wife and he loves me. I've never had that before. I thought I found it, but he's not sure. Because of something I did?"

I stare into her eyes, marveling that this beautiful creature chose me, is choosing me, after all that happened. I grip her hand. I'm never letting her go.

"No, nothing you did. Tabby's father made me doubt that what I had with her was real. What I had to do to keep Kessler out of your life once and for all made me doubt I was the right man for you. You took time at the spa to heal, and I'm glad you did, but it also gave time for things to fester under my skin when I should have been brave and asked you to see me. I was afraid, Lily, that if I asked, you would have turned me away. I love you so much, if you hated me for what I did, I wouldn't have survived it. I wouldn't have."

She smiles, and it lights up her face. She's blooming, and I will always give her the light and love she needs to grow. "Tell me again."

"I love you, and I have from the moment I sat down next to you at the bar."

She launches herself into my arms, and I hug her so tightly her spine cracks.

We stand like that for a long time while Tabby winds around our ankles.

Pulling away, she looks around my living room. "Now what?"

"I don't want to stay here. Are your things still at the Regency?"

"Yes. The suitcase you packed for me is with the concierge downstairs."

"Do you mind if we stay there until we figure out what we're going to do next?"

"Can we bring Tabby with us?" she asks, picking up the purring cat and cuddling her to her chest.

"She's part of our family. We'll never leave her behind."

Lily waits while I pack a bag and stepping into her room at the Regency is like coming home. To celebrate, we have a drink downstairs at the bar where we met. We talk late into the night, planning our future.

I'll never believe what Cyrus said. Tabby wouldn't want me to live the rest of my life alone. She was kind and generous, and clichéd or not, she would have wanted me to move on.

That night, with Lily lying in my arms, I say goodbye to Tabby. I'll miss her, and I'll always be grateful for the time I had with her.

I have a second chance at love, and I know, without a doubt, this was the way it was meant to be.

# CHAPTER THIRTEEN

*Sam*

Lily and I moved into a penthouse near SharperImage until that next fall. We wanted a house, but we also wanted time to look at land and talk to Clint about building. We settled on a large plot not that far from Sammie, Clint, and their kids, and we moved just in time to decorate for Christmas.

I didn't ask her to marry me until one cold winter's night when we were sitting in the living room as a violent blizzard beat against the house. We were snuggled on the couch, a fire crackling in the hearth, Tabby curled up in her lap.

It took her so long to say yes, I thought she was going to say no, but it turned out she was trying not to cry.

A few weeks after that, we were cooking dinner and the six o'clock news came on the small TV we have sitting on the counter. Kessler ended up with a twenty-year sentence. Not only was the video clip instrumental in his conviction, other women with whom he'd had aggressive physical relationships and altercations came forward, including Amanda, the woman he started seeing after Lily divorced him and moved to Carthage. He was ordered to serve his time at the New York State Penitentiary, but that isn't where his story ended. As Archer predicted, Kessler wasn't a welcome inmate, and the quick news blip we watched stated a man convicted on murder charges thanks to one of Kessler's investigations sought his revenge in the cafeteria and found it, ramming a fork into Kessler's throat.

Lily froze, a spatula in her hand, and stared at the screen, her face white. When the news segment cut to a commercial, calmly, she went back to sautéing garlic in butter, and we never spoke of him again.

Her parents, after a little persuading, moved to Carthage to be closer to her, and we spend the holidays together. I'm growing fond of Fran and Ed, and it's rare a week goes by without her telling me how thankful she is I gave them their daughter back.

Needless to say, we don't go to church.

Lily talked to Samantha like she said she would, and Sammie and I moved past the things she said and the things I've done. I compare our relationship now to a broken mug that's been glued back together. Maybe you can't see the cracks, maybe the mug is just as strong as it used to be, but it will never be the same. I'm sad we lost the closeness we used to have, but maybe one day we'll be that close again. Time heals all wounds, and that's something I whole-heartedly believe.

Though Archer and I tried, we never could pin Tabby's father with any wrongdoing—it's not against the law to stand in a bus depot's hallway—but Lily pressed charges against Greenwood for snooping in her room. The trespassing charge didn't amount to much, but he's no longer the pastor at the Buchanan's church. He retired, and he and his wife left the city.

Ardith saw our engagement announcement in the paper and sent us a crystal punch bowl with eight crystal glasses and a matching ladle. Lily laughed and said she wasn't quite sure what we would do with it, and we put it in a storage closet where it still sits covered in a thin layer of dust.

We talk about Tabby sometimes, and her collection of unicorns has made their home on one of our bookshelves. Lily understood how difficult it would have been for me to pack them away, and for my birthday, she bought another I added to the collection.

Lily taught me I wasn't replacing Tabby in my heart with her, I was adding her, and there's more than enough room.

I'm thinking all this while mowing our yard. It's massive, but I like pushing the lawnmower over the grass while Lily weeds a garden she planted along the edge of the house.

During a break while we drink lemonade, she says she had a dream exactly like this.

After Tabby passed away, I never dared dream I'd be this happy, but Lily turned my dreams into reality.

Oh, and the plot next to Tabby's? I donated it to a family who couldn't afford to bury their daughter, who, coincidentally, passed away from cancer.

Lily and I don't have chosen plots. I've had enough thinking about death. I want to think about life. I want to think about the rest of my life with Lily, and it began with the night she let me sit.

# BLOG SIGNUP

I hope you enjoyed *Rescue Me!* If you'd like to stay connected, sign up for my blog! You'll have front row seats to all my new releases, sales, and extra content. As a thank you, you'll also be able to download a free book—*My Biggest Mistake*, a billionaire, ugly duckling standalone novel. https://vmrheault.com/subscribe/

ACKNOWLEDGMENTS

Thank you to my writing groups who are a continual source of support, and also, thanks to S. J. Cairns for lending me her writing expertise and helping me with the blurb for this book.

## ALSO BY VM RHEAULT

Captivated by Her (Cedar Hill Duet Book One)

Addicted to Her (Cedar Hill Duet Book Two)

---

Rescue Me

---

Give & Take (The Lost & Found Trilogy Book One)

Lost & Found (The Lost & Found Trilogy Book Two)

Safe & Sound (The Lost & Found Trilogy Book Three)

---

Faking Forever

---

Twisted Alibis (Ghost Town Trilogy Book One)

Twisted Lullabies (Ghost Town Trilogy Book Two)

Twisted Lies (Ghost Town Trilogy Book Three)

---

A Heartache for Christmas

Cruel Fate (King's Crossing Book One)

Cruel Hearts (King's Crossing Book Two)

Cruel Dreams (King's Crossing Book Three)

Shattered Fate (King's Crossing Book Four)

Shattered Hearts (King's Crossing Book Five)

Shattered Dreams (King's Crossing Book Six)


Loss and Damages

# ABOUT THE AUTHOR

VM Rheault writes billionaire romance and contemporary romance under Vania Rheault.

She lives in Minnesota with her two children and a newly adopted tuxedo cat named Pim. When she's not writing, she's working her day job, sleeping, or enjoying the four seasons with a hot cup of coffee in hand.

Find her at vmrheault.com.